Beyond the Swearing Stone

Rebecca McKinnon

Copyright © 2019 Rebecca McKinnon

All rights reserved.

ISBN: 9781094670577

for the people of Castledermot

*your town, your history, and your heritage
will forever be a part of me*

BRIANNA

Bri darted a worried glance at her grandmother. "I think we're nearly there."

Gran's smile was faint, but her voice strong. "It's not far. These old bones can feel it — they've come home."

Old bones. Bri wanted to laugh but couldn't manage it. It would be easier to cry. The long years were finally catching up to Gran.

"You feel it, yes? That pull deep inside your belly is magic. True magic runs all through this land." Gran held up her hand in dismissal. "I know you haven't my trust in it, but we were called here, the both of us."

"Gran —"

"Wheesht. I'll not hear it. We were meant to come."

Bri pressed her tongue to the roof of her mouth and focused on safely maneuvering their rented Volkswagen off the M9. Over an hour outside of Dublin and she still wasn't used to driving on the left side of the road.

Bri dared another glance at Gran. Traveling had taken a toll. The older woman's face was worn and weary. "We'll go straight to the

B&B. We can explore the churchyard tomorrow, after you've gotten some rest."

"The day's not yet come when I'm unable to handle jet lag, lass. We'll go to St. James' now."

"Be reasonable. It's been a long day and we're both worn out." Bri stifled a yawn. She hadn't slept on the plane.

"Aye, but if we go now the lighting will be right — you can take pictures with that wee camera of yours." Gran's eyes glinted. "Sure and your magazine wants a variety of pictures. You can't take them all at midday."

Bri caught her breath. The sun was sinking toward the horizon. If they made it to the church as the sun set, the lighting would be perfect. She should insist Gran rest, but a short wander through the churchyard might do them both good. "I suppose we can stop at the church on our way."

As she drove through Castledermot, Bri tried to ignore the way everything about the old town felt perfect. Her grandmother was a superstitious woman who'd left Ireland when she was young, but Bri was smart enough to recognize the idea of a magical land for the load of malarkey it was — even if the setting sun cast the town in a magical glow. Buildings sat close up to the road, but even without the large front gardens Bri had always imagined, the town wasn't lacking in greenery or nature. Trees offered patches of shade while planters boasted gorgeous displays, adding to the charm of the older buildings.

Navigating through the light traffic, Bri noticed a couple of signs proclaiming the buildings were *To Let*. She hoped Gran wouldn't notice. She was likely to decide she wanted to open some kind of shop.

A month in Ireland wasn't enough time to start a new business.

Gran was focused and seemed not to notice much about the town as she directed Bri to turn. Following her instructions, they drove to the old church on the east edge of town. There were no other cars around as Bri pulled to a stop at the side of the road.

beyond the swearing stone

Bri stepped out of the car and stretched her travel-weary muscles. The sweet scent of blossoms and cut grass filled her lungs. Across the street a house boasted a lush front garden similar to what Bri had anticipated seeing. She smiled and moved to help Gran step into the fresh Irish air she always talked about.

Before Bri could even get around the car, Gran was climbing out. She swayed, steadying herself against the car door. Bri moved faster. If Gran fell and broke something Bri would never forgive herself. "Gran, take my arm."

Gran ignored her wobble, waving Bri away with a glare. "Don't coddle me. It doesn't matter I've not been here in years, these old bones know the lay of the land."

Bri stifled a groan. Gran's Irish lilt was getting stronger. Gran always called it "getting her Irish up" but Bri could have sworn it was just an excuse to let her stubborn streak run free. "Fine. Fine, then, I'll just get my camera."

Once the beloved Nikon hung around her neck, Bri started snapping pictures. The beautiful tunnel of trees across the street would photograph better with more light — she could imagine how the walkway would look lit with dappled sunlight — but she took a few shots now anyway. She'd come back another day to take pictures from the other end, coming toward St. James'.

She turned to face the church and caught her breath. Past the gate an impressive arch spanned the walkway. It was ancient. The upper half of it was beautifully carved, and long, narrow stones set on the outside made it look rather like rays coming from a half-sun. "Gran? What did this used to be?"

Gran paused by the entry of the churchyard and looked back over her shoulder. "You've heard the stories since you were a wee lass. Give it time, you'll place it."

Couldn't Gran just answer the question? Bri closed her eyes a moment, wondering how she'd let Gran weasel her way into coming on this trip. As much as she loved the woman who'd raised her, she needed to focus on her photography. She'd been trying to land a big break for years. Now she finally had it she couldn't afford to throw it away.

Grumbling under her breath, Bri followed Gran through the pedestrian access to the left of the gate and entered the churchyard.

She'd never been spooked in graveyards before, even in full dark on Halloween night, but as soon as both her feet touched the ground inside her heart felt like it was being squeezed. Could it be something about the church? The age, or something in its history?

Bri looked at the round tower directly in front of her and tipped her head back, her gaze following its length. The conical top had long since been replaced with crenels, but it was the oldest thing around — Gran's stories claimed it was a thousand years old. Perhaps the feeling in her chest came from the energy of the stars some claimed Ireland's round towers were built to harness.

It was just as possible she felt nothing more than the awe of being near something that had seen so many centuries.

Bri shook her head and turned her attention to the task at hand. Snapping as many pictures as she could, Bri forgot her awe and focused on framing each shot. On capturing the beauty and allure of the place. When her light was too far gone for the pictures she was after, Bri turned to look for her grandmother.

Gran stood a little apart from the church with her back to Bri. Her head tilted down and her hand rested on an upright stone. Stepping carefully through the grass, Bri went to her.

The air felt thicker over here, as if a storm threatened. Bri glanced at the sky, expecting to see roiling clouds. Instead, a few wisps of cloud just blurred the edges of the moon. Unable to stop herself, she raised her camera. She took half a dozen pictures before deciding she'd caught the image she wanted.

Stretching her sore feet inside her sandals, she turned to Gran. "I

beyond the swearing stone

really think we should be going now. We could both use some rest."

Gran's only answer was to run her hand across the top of the stone.

"Gran?" Bri reached out and touched Gran's shoulder. "It's nearly dark. We should go."

"Not yet." Gran turned to smile at Bri. The old woman's tiredness had sloughed off and playfulness filled her face. "I've a job for you. Get those flowers out of the car for me."

Bri wrinkled her brow. "I thought we were taking those to the B&B."

"Good plans are flexible. There's a more pressing need for them here. I've some nice chocolates in my bag we can gift to our hosts in place of the flowers."

Mumbling her frustrations, Bri returned to the rental car. The windows in the home across the street glowed cheerily, illuminating a small portion of the front garden.

Bri hoped her grandmother would finish whatever crazy scheme she was planning quickly. Somewhere in town, a cheery glow would be waiting to welcome them to a comfortable place to sit — and hopefully the kind of mattress that would guarantee Gran a quick recovery from the long flight.

Once Bri got Gran settled she'd find a pub and meet some of the locals. She didn't want to spend the next month visiting with no one but Gran. She loved the old woman dearly, and hoped the trip would be a good thing for them to share, but Bri would go crazy if she didn't have other people to hang out with.

Bri grabbed the bouquet of wildflowers and headed back toward Gran. The deeper into the churchyard she got, the more something itched the back of her mind. The place had such an odd feeling. Like she was walking into the past.

Gran had always placed great import on the churchyard in the stories of their ancestors, and so many of those stories had taken place here in Castledermot. That might be why Bri felt such oddness here, but it certainly didn't explain why Gran was treating the place with such reverence. Gran was the most irreverent person Bri had ever met.

Except when it came to her precious Irish heritage.

"Where did you want the flowers?"

"I'll take them." Gran stepped away from the stone she'd been focused on as she reached for them.

The stone rose from a slab base. A worn Celtic cross decorated the ancient relic and a hole was carved through the stone where the lines of the cross intersected.

Bri gasped. "The swearing stone."

How could she have forgotten the swearing stone was in this churchyard? No wonder Gran wouldn't leave.

"For generations our family has come to this stone for weddings." Gran paused. "Of course, as times changed we've had to hold other ceremonies as well, but vows spoken here at the stone are the ones that matter."

So many stories flooded into Bri's mind. So many memories she'd all but forgotten. "The two couples who chose to be married somewhere else had marriages that didn't last. You always said that was the reason my parents didn't stay together."

"Aye. It was sorry, to be sure. If your mother had listened to me — but that's over and done with." She pinned Bri with a stare that felt sharp even in the near-darkness. "You'll not be making that mistake."

Bri rolled her eyes. "I'm not getting married any time soon, if I ever do."

"My ears work just fine, dear one. You've been saying the same for years."

She'd be saying it for a lot longer, from the sound of things. "I have plenty of time."

"You're twenty-six years old, dear one. You'd have done well to marry five years ago. You'd have a family and I'd not need to worry over you being alone when I'm gone." As she spoke, Gran began sprinkling the flowers on the ground around them. Her silver hair caught the pale moonlight as she moved to leave the blooms where she wanted them.

"Things are different now. The world's changed since you were my age. Women don't have to get married in order to have a decent life. Besides, I finally have my big break as a photographer. I'm not giving that up."

Gran grumbled under her breath. When she'd dropped the last flower, she struggled to free her travel-swollen feet from her shoes.

"What are you doing? Put your shoes back on. We need to go." If Bri didn't force the issue, Gran would likely spend the entire night dancing barefoot around the nearby headstones — to soak in the magic, or some such nonsense — while their perfectly good beds stood empty.

"Wheesht. We'll go soon. Humor me, there's a good lass. Slip off your shoes, just for a wee moment. I want you to feel it."

Bri shook her head and bit back her retort. She could argue until her breath ran out, but Gran was more stubborn even than Bri. She kicked off her shoes and stood next to Gran, her toes sinking into the cool grass and earth. "What am I supposed to be feeling?"

"You're always in such a rush. Slow your breathing and close your eyes."

When did Gran become a yoga instructor? Bri tried to calm her mind and listen. The sooner she did, the sooner she'd be able to get a drink at the pub. After putting up with Gran's craziness she deserved an extra round. Maybe two.

They stood silently, letting the air still around them. As Bri pressed her feet more firmly into the earth she began to feel subtle shifts in the world around her. The air thickened, slowly at first, then in a rush it filled with the waiting energy she'd noticed earlier. After a few more minutes, an almost imperceptible thrumming began to travel from the earth, through the soles of her feet, and deep inside her.

Bri's eyes popped open. "What is it?" She whispered the words, sure if she spoke louder she'd lose the feeling.

"I told you," Gran said, her face splitting into a wider grin. "There's magic in this land."

What a ridiculous answer. Bri opened her mouth to say so, but it was pointless. Gran would never listen.

"Now you need to practice," Gran said, giving her a gentle shove. "I'll likely not make it to your wedding. These old bones won't cross the ocean again, I'm thinking. You need to know the words."

"Excuse me?" Gran couldn't have meant what Bri thought she did. It was too crazy, even for Gran.

Gran just laughed.

No, it was an evil cackle. She pointed to the swearing stone. "Go on, now. Put your hand in the hole. You have to know the way of it. You'll not want your marriage to end like your mother's, will you?"

Bri flinched.

"Come now. It's a small thing to please your old Gran. Let me remember our history tonight. I've the need to pretend I'll be there when it's your turn."

"It's dark. Let's come back tomorrow and you can talk me into it then." That would give her the whole night to come up with another excuse. She didn't want to pretend she was getting married. It was an absurd idea. "I can hardly see you anymore. We should wait for it to be light."

"You've no need to see me, and I see you just fine."

Bri glanced down. Her periwinkle blue dress seemed to glow in the moonlight, making her stand out against the night. She sighed.

"Listen to the magic," Gran said. She cocked her head to the side as if she could actually hear something. "It's supposed to be tonight."

Bri sighed. When Gran got like this there was no point in pretending anyone else's opinion mattered.

Determined to act out the ceremony correctly so she wasn't made to repeat the embarrassment, Bri dug through her mind for details from the family tales she'd learned by heart as a child – back when she still believed the world held magic. She closed her eyes for a last deep breath.

Letting her eyelids flutter open, Bri stepped up to the stone and reached out her right hand.

She paused. Despite living for the stories when she was young, Bri had no idea if she was supposed to stand or kneel. Gah. If she was going to do this, she wanted to see what she was doing. She dropped to her knees in the grass and peeked through the hole as she slid her fingers, then her entire hand, inside. Blades of grass tickled her bare calves, but she pushed that to the back of her mind.

"I, Brianna Meghan Hughes, do willingly pledge my heart and body to thee. I am yours, as you are mine, throughout all time. I so swear."

Bri froze. Another voice hung in the air. A whisper of an echo, soft enough Bri wasn't sure she'd heard anything at all. She was quite sure, however, that she wasn't imagining the warm, callused hand enveloping hers, or the bright blue, startled eyes staring into hers. She couldn't be imagining the man with windblown hair who loomed over her from the other side of the stone.

"Brianna," he said. His voice was deep and rough. The timbre shot through her like a jolt of electricity.

Some part of Bri must have heard him say his name during the vow, because it came unbidden to her lips. "Duncan."

Her voice was hardly even a whisper, but he heard. His short, rumpled beard twitched and his brows pulled together as a crease appeared between them.

Bri's heart pounded and she pulled her hand back, knowing only that she had to separate herself from the anger in the man's face.

The second the touch of his skin was gone, he disappeared. Bri's breath caught in her throat.

Her hand hovered by the stone, her fingertips just at the opening of the hole. She stared at the empty space across from her. What in all that was —

Duncan's warm fingers brushed hers again, and he materialized in front of her as he folded her hand securely in his. He still glowered, but more than that, his gaze was curious.

Bri rose to her feet, needing to be closer, drawn to his eyes as she tried to place the other emotions she could see in them.

He drew her hand through the hole. With his other hand, he brushed her fingers open and traced them before pressing something cool and hard into it. He closed her fist around it and murmured, "Come back later tonight, when I'm alone. Please."

His warmth left her hand as his image faded from view. Bri stared at the place where he'd been. She was relieved he was gone, and more concerned than she'd like to admit that part of her was upset the apparition had vanished.

Bri turned on her beaming grandmother. Her legs trembled, making it difficult to stand. "Did you see — What was that?" she whispered. "What just happened?"

DUNCAN

uncan stared past the swearing stone. The church, the high crosses, the trees — they all remained. Why then had the woman faded into nothingness? And how?

If he reached through the swearing stone he'd find her hand in his. He knew it as surely as he breathed.

The memory of the woman's accusing stare hovered before him.

Would she be any less fierce if she expected his touch? He forced his hand to his side. He'd return to face her later, as he'd promised. When he was alone.

"You've made your point," Ciaran said, coming up beside Duncan and nudging his arm. "You needn't have made vows to the air to convince me you'll not marry again."

Duncan glanced at Ciaran. His foster brother hadn't had so much ale as to be drunk. He must have seen the woman appear.

Ciaran's voice changed, becoming serious. "I know you loved my sister, but Neve did tell you to move on and find happiness. If you were any other man you'd have married again and fathered three or four children by now."

Duncan shook himself and pushed the woman's face from his mind. It was more difficult than it should have been.

Unable to face the same tired conversation again, Duncan stepped past Ciaran and made his way toward the church. Pausing at the portal, he leaned against the side of the arch. He'd looked forward to seeing Ciaran for weeks. They could have spent the evening drinking and sharing stories, but Ciaran had insisted on suggesting Duncan remarry.

He'd not break his vow to remain a widower. To put another woman at risk of dying because of a babe he'd put in her belly — Duncan refused to do so. Avoiding that agony was worth every lonely moment.

His vow had brought them to the churchyard. An oath made at the swearing stone was more binding than mere words.

It hit him in the gut, like a horse's hoof trying to avoid a shoeing. The woman's hand appeared in his own as he spoke his oath.

As she'd spoken an oath.

And without taking time to consider his actions, he'd given her a gold coin in the old tradition of marriage.

Duncan closed his eyes. The woman's face sprang to life in the darkness only he could see. He could all but feel her small hand trembling against his palm.

He cursed and looked up to see Ciaran standing in front of him. Duncan grabbed the front of Ciaran's *leine* in his fists. "Did you see her?"

Ciaran's brows pulled together.

"*Did you see her?*" Duncan repeated. "At the swearing stone. Did you see the woman who was there?"

"How far into your cups were you when we left the tavern?" Ciaran asked. "There was no one there. Surprising, really, to find any empty space in this town."

Duncan released Ciaran's *leine*, his hands dropping. How had Ciaran not seen her? "She was there, I swear it. It was — her hand met mine through the stone. She said a vow."

In concern, Ciaran took Duncan's elbow and began to walk, leading him through the town. "Let's get you home. You can sleep off that mead."

Duncan's thoughts returned to the woman. Brianna, she'd said in her vow. She'd worn a blue dress — it was an odd sort of dress, to be sure, but definitely blue. Her feet had been bare — and on her side of the stone there had been flowers circling them.

He cursed again. The woman couldn't have been more prepared for a wedding in the old way. Somehow she'd known. But her face had clearly shown surprise. Being honest with himself, she'd looked shocked, and not entirely happy.

Mayhap they'd both been tricked.

Tricked into marriage, after seven years avoiding it. Seven years turning down offers brought to him by dutiful fathers whose daughters had mistakenly decided they could be happy with Duncan.

"I have a wife." His voice was hoarse to his ears, and filled with disbelief. "Again. How did I allow this to happen?"

They strode past the tavern where music and ribald voices spilled into the street. They were nearly to the smithy before Ciaran replied. "Is she not only in your mind, then?"

They reached the smithy and Duncan led the way up the narrow staircase on the side of the next building over, and through the door into his home. Embers glowed on the hearth. Duncan went to stir the embers to life as Ciaran lit a candle.

"She's as real as I am. I know nothing of her but her name." Duncan straightened and met Ciaran's gaze in the glow of the flames. "On my word, she lives."

Ciaran pulled out a chair and sat, resting his arms on the smooth, oiled wood of the table. "How do you plan to find this woman, then, with no more than a name? A woman who can turn to wind will not be easy to find should she choose to hide."

Duncan scrubbed his face with his palm. "I've not yet thought on that." He'd not managed to think at all. He shook his head. "Brianna looked no happier than I am to find ourselves wed."

Ciaran leaned back, his copper-tinted mustache and beard not coming close to hiding the grin behind them. "What does your Brianna look like?"

Duncan leaned over the pot he'd left to keep warm in the embers and spooned soup into clay bowls. Straightening, he joined Ciaran at the table and cast his mind back to the woman. "She's small. Her hand was nearly lost in mine — and it was smooth, without calluses."

"That doesn't tell me what she looks like," Ciaran said, tapping his spoon against the side of his dish. "It only says she's not one to work with her hands. She likely has servants to do everything for her."

Duncan considered that for a moment. It mightn't be bad if she was used to servants. If the woman really did come from wealth, she'd not want to leave a large, comfortable home to live in a single room. She'd not want a mere blacksmith.

"Duncan."

He sighed. Ciaran wasn't wont to give up when he got something in mind. "It was dark. I couldn't see well."

His eyes had seen Brianna perfectly in the moonlight. Her dark hair, floating loose around a freckled face. The surprise in her large, dark eyes as she'd seen Duncan across from her. "I'll have to find her kin. It's possible they'll not want her wed to a blacksmith and we can go our separate ways."

If she were native to Ireland, that would work. Divorce was common among his father's people. And if she belonged with his mother's people, who refused to accept a marriage could end?

In truth, only the Irish would consider the vows binding at all. There'd been no priest, and no witnesses who actually saw what happened.

Which didn't change the fact that Duncan knew what he'd done and was obligated to uphold his vow.

"You saw nothing of her?" Ciaran asked, an eyebrow raised in doubt. "Nothing at all?"

Duncan grunted.

Ciaran sat back, folding his arms across his chest. "You only make that sound when you don't want to admit to a thing, yet don't wish to lie."

Of all the friends who could have been with him, it had to be the one man who knew Duncan as well as he knew himself. He pushed his soup away, no longer hungry. "I saw her."

Ciaran gestured impatiently.

"What would you hear, Ciaran? That she's beautiful? Or that she has a hooked nose and is uglier than you are?"

"I want to hear you noticed her."

Duncan released a slow breath. "She's nice-looking. Unusual. Her hair was dark and her eyes were large."

Ciaran gave him a calculating look. "So you did notice her."

"I notice many things. For instance, you're trying to keep me talking of Brianna, yet you've not shared the news you clearly wished to tell me when you arrived at midday." Duncan grinned at Ciaran's annoyance. "Tell me."

Ciaran cleared his throat. "I don't know anything certain, mind. I've heard whispers is all."

"Nothing is ever certain with you," Duncan said.

Ciaran spooned the last of his soup into his mouth before continuing. "MacMurrough is itching for a fight again."

"Running King Richard out of Ireland wasn't victory enough for him?" The King of Leinster had butted heads more than once with England's former king, and made a fool of the man in the process.

"He may have run Richard out of the country, but he didn't regain his lands. Tristledermot and the other towns still stand, and your neighbors are still comfortable within these walls."

Duncan shook his head. "This town hasn't belonged to the Irish for more generations than I can count, and the MacMurroughs are the ones who invited the invaders to Ireland in the first place."

"All I can tell you is the whispers say MacMurrough is unhappy with the way things stand. He wants the land his wife was to receive as a dowry."

The Leinster king had tried to get those lands since his marriage. Duncan frowned. If those in a position to send more soldiers to the local garrison refused to do so, the town could take up a collection. Paying Art MacMurrough to leave them be had worked in the past.

Duncan pushed his thoughts aside and turned the conversation to other topics. The night settled in more deeply, and Duncan relaxed as the ale poured freely.

Eventually, talk subsided and Ciaran sprawled on the bed in the corner. His snores soon filled the room.

Duncan waited a handful of breaths, then went over and nudged his friend. Ciaran rolled over, wrapping himself more firmly in the woven wool blanket. The snoring stopped, but Ciaran was deep in his slumber.

With a stretch to ease his tired back, Duncan crossed to the pegs hammered into the wall near the door. He lifted his cloak from the peg on the far right, threw it over his shoulders, and let himself out.

The streets were empty but for the unfortunates with no homes of their own. Even they slept, some wrapped in cloaks, others in blankets.

Duncan walked quietly, not wanting to draw the attention of anyone still awake.

The waxing quarter moon hung over the church as Duncan made his way to the swearing stone. He crouched beside the stone, preparing to put his hand in the hole.

He knew it was necessary, yet wished he could walk away.

Wished he could turn his back on his honor.

He'd made a vow. While he hadn't expected any more to come of it than Ciaran's silence on potential wives, Duncan always kept his word.

Surely he and this Brianna could find a way to sever their unexpected tie.

He eyed the stone a moment longer. Unsure what to expect, he plunged his hand through the hole. He felt . . . nothing.

Reaching farther, he grasped in vain. No small hand found his, no woman appeared.

He stayed there as the moon crawled its way across the sky.

When the sky to the east showed the first lightening of morning over the town wall, Duncan pulled his hand from stone.

The woman hadn't come.

Duncan tried to be pleased, to believe it was a sign they were meant to be apart. His hand and arm were sore and slightly numb from lack of movement. He shook the offending limb to waken it. The town would be stirring to life soon. With luck, he'd make it home before Ciaran awoke.

As he left the churchyard, Duncan ignored the small ache of disappointment in his heart.

The smell of baking bread poured through the baker's open windows, causing Duncan's stomach to rumble with hunger. He stopped and called through the window. "Have you any loaves ready?"

Michael lifted his head with a smile. "Aye, I'll get one for you. You're out early today."

Duncan smiled. "Just stretching my legs before building up the fire."

"My wife wants to buy a dirk for young Dorothy." Michael reached his thickly muscled arm through the window to hand Duncan his loaf. "I suppose she's of an age now to use one. When they come see you, will you sell them a dull blade so she'll not hurt herself as she learns to use it?"

"So long as your wife doesn't see what I'm about," Duncan said. "If she insists it be sharp, we'll both have a hard time changing her mind."

Michael shook his head in regret. "I never realized how stubborn Elizabeth was before it was too late."

As Duncan walked away chuckling he wondered where Brianna was and why she hadn't come to him. Was she just being as stubborn as Elizabeth? Or perhaps she didn't realize they were wed.

He took the stairs two at a time. After adding a log to the fire, Duncan set about readying for the day, not bothering to be quiet about it. Ciaran would need to be up before long.

As Duncan tore a chunk of bread off the loaf, his mind turned to the way Brianna had faded into nothingness. It was possible she'd been there and faded into the gloaming as she stepped away. The in-between light was known to play tricks on the eyes. Ciaran hadn't seen her, but he'd been half drunk.

Or perhaps Brianna was all in his head and she'd not truly been there at all. His chest tightened at the thought.

BRIANNA

here are your pictures taking you today?" Gran asked as she poured herself another cup of the excellent breakfast tea.

"I haven't decided." Bri reached for the little pot of port and plum jam, and unscrewed the checkered lid. "I have a list of ruins to visit, but I need to sort through and find which are medieval. Since that's what the magazine's spread is focusing on, that should be my priority."

Ryan looked up from the rack of fresh toast he was setting on the white linen tablecloth. Bri had been expecting the B&B to be run by the middle-aged couple on their website. Instead, their unmarried son had taken over the place. Gran had started pushing Bri and Ryan together within minutes of arriving.

Ryan raised an eyebrow at Bri and spoke quickly. "If you're looking for medieval you should try Rindoon."

"Where's that?" Bri asked.

"Not two hours away, to the northwest." Ryan returned to his chair across from Bri. He ran his hand over a crease in the tablecloth, as if trying to iron it smooth. "It was a medieval walled town, like Castledermot, but it was abandoned back in the fourteenth century."

"Ah, I remember poking about Rindoon when I was a lass," Gran said. "The castle was a marvelous place to roam, and the church as well."

Bri grinned. An abandoned town — with a castle! — would be full of things to photograph.

Ryan leaned forward. A lock of dark blond hair fell into his eyes. He impatiently brushed it aside as he pointed to the bookcase behind Bri. "There should be a book on it somewhere over there. My father's a bit of a historian. He's always kept that shelf full of old books. Feel free to read anything you like."

Bri ran her gaze over the worn spines of the books and stifled a groan. If the titles were anything to go by, they promised to be dry and boring.

"Of course," Ryan added, "you should explore the town here as well. The abbey and St. James' Church would both be interesting places to include."

The excitement Bri was feeling about visiting Rindoon popped like a soap bubble. She'd gotten her fill of the churchyard the night before. She was afraid if she went back, her imagination would get the better of her again.

She hoped it was just her imagination. Gran certainly hadn't seen the handsome, if grumpy, man.

Bri shivered. Even her wild imagination wasn't good enough to create a coin out of thin air. She slipped her fingers into the pocket of her jeans and sighed.

It was still there.

She looked up to find Ryan's pale blue eyes roaming over her. Bri flushed. Ogling was expected in bars and clubs, but not at the breakfast table. She shifted in her seat, wishing she'd worn a sweatshirt, or an old T-shirt, or a potato sack. Anything less revealing than the clingy tank top she'd grabbed out of her still-packed suitcase.

He met her gaze and lifted one corner of his lips in a half-smile.

Before he could say anything, Bri jumped in. "The abbey sounds wonderful. I'll add it to my list. It's in town, you said?"

Ryan settled back in his seat. He dropped his eyes to his toast and slathered it with jam. "I can show you where, if you like."

Like a date? She hoped not. Yes, he was cute, in a boy next door kind of way. But as Bri kept telling Gran, she had more important things than men on her mind.

"Thank you for the offer, but not today," Bri said. "I think I'll head out to the abandoned town. Rindoon sounds perfect."

She'd have a chance to pull herself together. And it would give her an escape — Gran had wanted Bri to go back to the churchyard with her, but there was no way she was doing that. One trip there had messed with her head plenty.

"Gran, you'll be okay while I'm gone?"

"You go take your pictures," Gran said. "A quiet morning here with my knitting will suit me fine, and I've a cousin in Galway I'll be needing to telephone."

Bri squashed down the guilt of abandoning Gran their first full day in Ireland.

"I'll be around," Ryan said. "If your grandmother wants to go anywhere, I'm happy to help."

"Thanks," Bri said. She offered a tiny, polite smile before pushing her chair back and getting to her feet.

Bri went into the hallway and climbed the staircase. It was a narrow passage, and Bri had to focus to avoid bumping the pictures hung against the striped wallpaper.

The small bedroom she'd been given was halfway down the hall. A window overlooked the back garden and let in the morning sun. Bri crossed the braided rug to where her suitcase sat open on the worn wood floor. She dug through the pile of clothes for a light sweater, then turned to pick up her purse from the straight-backed chair in the corner.

Back downstairs she headed for the dining room. As she passed Gran's room, guilt hit again. Gran wouldn't be around for too many more years, and Bri wanted to make that time the best Gran had known.

Bri sighed. If she let guilt take over all the time, she'd never find time for the job she came here to do. The job that was the only reason they'd come.

She slipped into the airy bedroom. Bri smiled. The room was decorated in cream, but all the textures kept it from feeling boring. She picked up Gran's knitting bag from beside the nightstand. Taking it out was the least she could do. Maybe somewhere on the way to Rindoon she could find Gran a couple balls of good, Irish wool to ease her conscience.

Gran smiled as Bri hung the knitting on the back of a chair. "You'll need to hurry back if you don't want me to get ahead of you," Gran said.

"If you finish your shawl before I'm halfway through mine, I suppose I can live with it." She smiled and kissed Gran on the cheek. "I'm not here to knit. I'm working."

Gran nodded toward the kitchen with an evil glint in her eye, then turned her head to whisper in Bri's ear. "If you can spare the time, I'm thinking that young man would give you as much attention as you'd be willing to take. Unless you've someone else on your mind?"

Bri froze. Had Gran seen something at the swearing stone, even though she said she didn't? Bri narrowed her eyes. She opened her mouth to ask, but decided she didn't want to know.

Gran's wrinkles deepened as she smiled and laughed.

Footsteps neared, and Bri steeled herself to face their host. Ryan walked out of the kitchen, coming to stand a fraction too close for comfort. He gave Bri a warm smile and handed her a paper. "Directions to Rindoon," he explained.

Bri thanked him again and left as quickly as she could. If they hadn't paid such a hefty deposit to spend a month at the B&B, she'd move to a hotel. She had her own life to live, and it didn't include having a summer fling. Meaningless relationships weren't her style, even if she wanted to take the time away from her photography project.

She shook her head. She was tired. Maybe she'd misread Ryan. It was possible he was just a guy doing his job. Weren't small towns supposed to be friendlier than cities?

She maneuvered the Volkswagen onto the road and found herself driving toward St. James' Church. She wouldn't stop, of course. She just wanted to drive past. To prove she could be near it without anything strange happening.

She passed slowly, peeking in through the gate. Nothing looked out of place. Even the group of tourists snapping selfies with the high crosses looked perfectly normal.

Bri smiled and pulled away. Nothing to it. If Gran forced her to return, she'd be fine. She'd just blend in with the rest of the tourists.

Bri stared at a sign that read *Beware of the Bull.*

Laughter bubbled up her throat. She'd never seen a sign anything like that in the states. Of course, that might be because she lived in the city and didn't often travel to rural areas.

She hadn't noticed the sign on her way in. A group of teenagers had been gathering in the area and Bri had just gone around them. Probably a good thing. If she'd known about the bull beforehand she may have chickened out about going, and she'd gotten some great shots of the ivy-covered castle ruins. She'd come back another day and spend more time watching the light patterns and deciding what time of day and which angles would make for the best pictures, but she had some great shots from poking around today. Some distance shots, as well as close-ups of timeworn details.

Bri snapped a picture of the sign to show Gran and made a mental note to transfer all of her photographs to her laptop when she got back to the B&B. Both her memory cards were almost full.

On her way back to the car she fingered the coin in her pocket. Again. She'd rubbed it so much she worried she'd start to wear it smooth.

Bri laughed. She was starting to sound like Gran. Next she'd start blaming it on magic.

There was no doubt Ireland was special, but there was nothing actually magical about it. Magic wasn't real, even if the part of herself she'd tucked away after her mother died wished otherwise.

Leaving the coin on the dashboard where she could keep an eye on it, Bri headed back to Castledermot.

Every so often, the coin caught the sunlight streaming through the window and bounced it back at Bri. The nearer to Castledermot she got, the more it happened.

With a strangled sigh, Bri grabbed the coin and held it up where she could look at it with half an eye while still watching the road in front of her. "What do you want from me?"

The coin glinted merrily at her.

"I know you're real, okay? Let it go already." Bri set the coin back on the dashboard.

Huh. She should probably take her own advice to let things go.

Sure, Duncan had seemed real at the time. When jet lag was setting in and she was frustrated with Gran.

That didn't mean he actually existed.

"You're my good luck charm, right? To bring me the luck of the Irish." Bri laughed. At herself for talking to the coin, yes, but also at the Americanized idea of the Irish being lucky. Anyone who knew the bloody history of Ireland knew the country wasn't overflowing with luck.

Bri pulled the car into the driveway at the B&B and could just make out Gran sitting in a comfortable chair under the large ash tree. The white house with cheerful green shutters and a slate roof made a picturesque backdrop. A riot of colored wool spilled from Gran's lap.

Gran had been serious about trying to finish the shawl before Bri could get through the first pattern repeat.

As she took in the view, Ryan came through the front door, letting the screen door swing shut behind him.

With a quiet groan, Bri closed her eyes and took several deep breaths. She was basically stuck with Ryan for the month they were staying in his home. She may as well be polite.

Gran would skewer her on a knitting needle if she wasn't.

With a plastered on smile, Bri stepped from the car. She grabbed her camera case and a large bag from the trunk and walked through the tiny front garden to the shady spot where Gran waited.

"How was your day?" Ryan asked, setting an extra chair next to Gran. "Were you able to get the pictures you wanted at Rindoon?"

Bri bristled. Why did he have to sound like he was welcoming home someone he cared about? "I was, thanks."

Turning away from his smile, Bri pulled out her camera and brought up the picture of the caution sign. She held it out to Gran. "I took this one for you."

Gran furrowed her brow in confusion, but looked. She started to chuckle. "Were you careful, then? You must've been, I can see you've not been gored."

Bri could feel Ryan's eyes on her. Fighting for the politeness she knew she needed to show, she turned to face him. "Thanks for the suggestion. Rindoon's a beautiful place."

"I'm glad it worked for you," Ryan said. He gave her a half smile. "I thought we'd all go to the pub for dinner, if that sounds good?"

Bri paused. She was hungry. The candy bars she'd snacked on hadn't done much to curb the appetite she'd worked up wandering around Rindoon. But going out with Ryan, even with Gran along, felt strange.

Bri took in Ryan's expectant gaze — and Gran's shrewd look — and agreed. Maybe if she gave the guy a chance, he'd prove she'd misread him earlier. It was possible he was just being friendly. "Why not? I'd like to get a feel for the town."

"I'll leave you and your grandmother to yourselves for a while before we go." With a small wave, he went back inside the house.

"What's in the bag there, then?" Gran asked. "Did you do some shopping while you were out?"

"Just a bit." Bri sat in the chair Ryan had so kindly provided and pulled out a long, gorgeous strip of fluffy wool dyed to match all the greens of an Irish hillside. From the bottom of the bag she pulled two boxes, eight or nine inches long and about three inches wide and deep.

Gran reached over to burrow her fingers in the wool. "What's this, now?"

Bri opened one of the boxes and held out a tapered stick with a round disk and hook on one end. The flamed wood had a deep sheen to it. "Would you like to try spinning your own yarn?"

"Oh." Gran's voice was breathy and her lips trembled. She blinked back tears and cleared her throat. "My own Gran had a drop spindle. She always said the best yarn was a good, sturdy homespun."

Bri took out her own spindle, a length of yard already on it from when the shop owner showed her how to use it. She reached for the wool. "This roving has some silk mixed in with the wool. The woman at the shop said it would make the yarn stronger."

Gran rested her hand on Bri's cheek. "Thank you, lass. You've brought back some dear memories for me."

Bri swallowed the lump in her throat. "Should we see if we can do this? Did your grandmother ever teach you?"

They set to work with their drop spindles, laughing at their mishaps. By the time Ryan came out to go to dinner they each had a good length of spun wool — Gran's yarn was smooth and even, while Bri's was full of lumps and bumps. She pulled a face at it as she bundled it into the house.

The pub wasn't far, but they decided to drive to make it easier on Gran. Ryan helped Gran into Bri's rental car, then walked around to hold the door open for Bri. She tried not to bristle at the attention. He was treating her with the same courteous respect he'd shown Gran. There was no reason for it to put her on edge.

As she slid into the driver's seat, Ryan's eyes zeroed in on Bri's coin, still on the dashboard.

"Where did you get that?"

Bri grimaced and settled the coin into her palm. If she'd been thinking, the coin would have been tucked back into her pocket where it belonged. "It was given to me."

"May I see it?" Ryan asked.

Her fingers tightened around the coin. The gold was warm from sitting in the sun. She forced her fingers to loosen and held it out. As Ryan took the coin, Bri's fingers started to tingle. It was the oddest feeling, as if the piece of metal resented leaving her hand.

"Someone gave this to you, with no reason?" Ryan held it closer to his face. "This is very old. My father studies old coins. Would it be all right if I sent him a picture of it?"

Bri hesitated.

"I'm sure he could tell you more about the history of it," Ryan explained.

Bri wanted to say no, and she couldn't put her finger on why. Without a good reason, she pushed her hesitance aside and gave a tiny nod. "Okay."

Ryan took pictures of both sides of the coin and sent them in a text. "It shouldn't be too long. He knows a lot about these things."

Bri took the piece of gold and slid it back into her pocket.

They'd barely gotten settled at a corner table in Doyle's Pub when Ryan's father replied. As Ryan looked at the screen, the color drained from his face.

"Your coin," he said, his voice hard to hear over the din of voices and music. "If it's not a fake — and my father doesn't think it is, even though it looks brand new — it's worth a fortune. It's over six hundred years old."

The coin seemed to get heavier in Bri's pocket. She knew it hadn't really changed, that she was imagining it, but hearing it was valuable left her wondering why it wanted to live in her pocket.

"It's the type of coin that was a family heirloom," Ryan continued. "Back before wedding rings were common, a man would give his bride a coin like this. It could be new, or it could have been given to him by his mother, who'd received it at her wedding."

Bri balked.

The coin was a token of marriage? A token that had been given to her after she'd said vows at the swearing stone, a traditional place for weddings. Duncan's grumpy face filled her mind. Bri's stomach dropped and she found she was no longer hungry.

She turned to glare at Gran.

Gran returned the look with a twinkle in her eye and a smile. The lights of the pub caught the silver of Gran's hair and made her laugh lines stand out even more than usual.

She looked awfully pleased with herself.

Bri's anger flared. She wanted to blame this mess on Gran. And oh, how Gran deserved it, sitting there all smug.

But Bri deserved it as well. She hadn't really been forced into saying that vow. Yes, she'd done it to get Gran off her back, but she could have walked away.

She could have, but she hadn't.

She dropped her gaze to the wooden floor so no one would see the confusion in her eyes. What on earth had she gotten herself into?

DUNCAN

Duncan pumped the bellows, sending air into the bowl furnace. The charcoal flared bright in the darkness of the smithy. He pulled the iron from the furnace to check the color of the metal. Satisfied with the bright yellow, he moved to the anvil and began to hammer the iron into shape, working quickly while the heat was right. Once the iron cooled too much to work, he returned it to the furnace and reached for the bellows pump.

"Why did you not wake me?" Ciaran's voice cut through the darkness.

"You sleep like the dead," Duncan said, continuing to work the bellows. "Did you find the bread and cheese?"

Ciaran moved closer and pushed another bar of iron into the charcoal. "It was left in the middle of the table," he said. "It was hardly hidden, was it?"

Duncan grunted as he pulled the iron from the fire and returned to his hammering. Ciaran took over pumping the bellows to heat the bar he'd added, but turned to watch Duncan.

"You're thinking of the woman again?" Ciaran asked, although it was hard to hear him over the metallic sound of hammering and the whooshing of air through the bellows.

"I returned to the stone last night." Duncan set his work aside. It held no appeal. "I didn't find her there. Perhaps you were right and she was only in my mind."

The iron Ciaran had left in the furnace began to spark. Duncan removed the too-hot metal and set that aside as well.

"Last night you were certain she exists." Ciaran spoke slowly, his brow creased in thought. "We could ask your neighbors if they know where she's staying."

Duncan rubbed a hand over his face. "She's not from town. Her manner of dress was unlike anything I've seen. She'd not go unnoticed for a moment. The gossip would have reached even me."

"Should I stay, then, and help you find her?"

"Tara will be waiting for you," Duncan said, shaking his head. Ciaran's wife wasn't known for her patience, particularly when she'd been left to care for five children on her own. He didn't want Ciaran's help, in any case. He didn't trust his best friend to keep things quiet. If word spread Duncan was asking about a woman, he'd receive no peace.

Ciaran laughed. "If you need me, Tara can wait another day."

Duncan shoved Ciaran's shoulder — gently, as the smithy wasn't the safest place for roughhousing. "Go home. Your wife and children need you. I'll be fine."

"Until next time, then," Ciaran said. At the door he turned. "If your wife appears, send word to me."

Duncan tossed the end of an iron bar at him, and Ciaran laughed.

When the church bell rang for Vespers, Duncan began to put the smithy in order. He cleared away the debris, refilled his charcoal buckets, and replaced his tools on the nails buried deep in the stone walls.

All the while, his mind was going over the encounter in the

churchyard. If he'd not accidentally married the woman, Duncan wouldn't have given Brianna a second thought.

But he had.

In the yard outside the smithy, Duncan stopped at a barrel of water to wash. He trudged up the stairs, exhausted. He'd pushed himself hard, determined to wear himself out. Determined to push the dark eyed woman from his mind.

He'd failed at the second task. An unintended marriage was no easy thing to forget.

Duncan stood near the window, eating the heel of bread left on the table. The day was still bright, and the noises of town life filled the air. The bell wouldn't ring for Compline for some time, but he didn't care. He was tired enough to sleep.

Brushing the crumbs from his fingers, Duncan readied himself for bed. He stretched out and, despite the light and noise, slept.

Duncan awoke to the cool stillness of night. His brain foggy, he lay there, listening for something. What that something was, he'd no idea. With a stretch, Duncan stumbled to his feet.

Had there been some noise in the night? At midsummer Duncan had discovered one of the homeless men sleeping in the smithy. He trusted his neighbors to know the dangers of the forge, but travelers were another story. Knowing he'd not rest until he'd checked, Duncan dressed and pulled on a cloak.

Lantern in hand, he entered the forge. The light filled the smithy, making it brighter than when Duncan worked there during the day. Everything remained untouched.

First he'd imagined a woman, then he began hearing things. It was good Ciaran had returned to his family. Duncan had no need of the comments on madness his friend would have spoken.

He turned to go back upstairs. Instead, he found himself gazing down the road toward the church.

No. He couldn't go back. He'd made a big enough fool of himself staying there, alone, the previous night. But a glimmer of hope had sprung to life. Perhaps she was there, waiting for him.

He'd like to see her again. Against his better judgement, he'd like the feel of her small, soft hand in his. Heaven help him, Duncan wanted to know more about the woman.

He glanced at the sky. The night had clouded over, but by Duncan's best guess it wasn't long past Matins. With a sigh, he blew out his lantern and set off. If nothing else, the visit to the church would give him some sort of confirmation.

Confirmation of his madness if he was alone.

Madness could be the better option. If Brianna was there, it would open a host of other problems.

Duncan kept his steps silent. The relative stillness of the night seeped into his bones as he made his way along the narrow road.

As he neared the church, the air filled with power. Duncan glanced again at the clouds. The storm held off, yet the air felt charged with lightning.

The way things were going, he'd likely be caught in a downpour.

Duncan paused at the church's portal as he always did. He couldn't shake the thought that this night would shape his future, one way or the other. It was, as his mother would have said, a moment of portent.

Enough. If this was Duncan's moment of portent, he refused to cower in the darkness. He'd meet it with his face forward and his eyes open.

Duncan drew in a deep breath and let it out slowly. He turned and, taking long, sure strides, walked to the swearing stone. He went around to the far side of it, where he'd been when he'd first seen Brianna.

He knelt on the ground and, before he could change his mind, placed his right hand in the hole.

All he felt was empty air.

Duncan went to withdraw his hand, but a heaviness in the air, that weight of import, convinced him to leave it there.

He felt a fool, kneeling alone in the churchyard in the dead of night.

Surely he'd feel yet more foolish were he caught talking to a woman only he could see.

Unwilling to stay through the night again, import or no, he sighed and moved to stand.

As he shifted, a small, warm hand slipped into his own.

Across from him, Brianna came into view. She was standing, watching him over the top of the stone.

"You're real," Duncan said. He pushed to his feet as he silently berated himself. It was a stupid thing to say.

Brianna's eyes narrowed. "Of course I'm real. I'm just not sure if you are."

Duncan tried to hold back his laughter but failed. "I've spent the day wondering if I'd gone mad. I came back last night to see if you were real — and you didn't come."

Brianna huffed. "I'm not at your beck and call. I don't know anything about you, not even who you are."

"I could say the same thing, Brianna."

The thin line of Brianna's mouth warned Duncan too late.

"I — I don't know what to say to you. I don't really even know why I'm here." As Brianna spoke the words, her eyes cut to the side.

"Truly?" Duncan asked. The woman had no reason to lie to him, yet she clearly had.

Large, dark eyes narrowed at him. "Who are you to question my word?"

Duncan tried to look as unthreatening as possible. "It would seem, after what happened when I first saw you, I'm your husband."

Brianna's wrath flew. Duncan almost expected sparks to burst from her eyes, sizzling like overheated steel.

"You are not my husband. You're — you're — you're just not. I would never have married someone I'd just met. In fact, I plan to never get married at all. It's up to me to break this stupid family tradition." She snorted. "It's more of a curse, anyway."

Surely the woman had the need to stop for air. As she continued to yell at him, Duncan tried to patiently wait out the storm of words.

Finally her fury sputtered to an end. "So, you see, we're not married. Obviously."

"You spoke a vow," Duncan said, once he was finally able to get a word in. "You spoke my vow, a vow I created in that very moment. I'm no more pleased than you to find myself wed, but such a vow is binding. Saying it here at the swearing stone makes it even more so."

Brianna's mouth opened and closed, like that of a fish pulled from the water. "It wasn't your vow, it's my family's vow. Members of my family have said that exact vow, right here, for centuries."

If her family had sworn vows at the stone for centuries, they must be local. Yet if they were, he'd have met Brianna before now. "How have I not seen you before now? The town isn't so large as to let people go unnoticed."

The look Brianna gave him was strange. "I don't live here. Gran and I just came for a visit."

Ah. She'd be staying at the inn, then. "How did you keep me from seeing you without the touch of your skin?"

"I could ask you the same thing." She paused. "A trick of the light, maybe?"

Duncan's brow creased as he considered her words. They didn't ring true in his heart.

"The coin you gave me," Brianna said, drawing Duncan's attention back to her. "Where did you get it? And why would you give something so old and valuable to someone you'd never met?"

"Old?" Duncan asked. The woman was beginning to exasperate him. "It's newly minted."

"So it's a fake?" Brianna tilted her head.

Could the woman not tell true gold from sight alone? "Of course not. It was made at the mint here in Tristledermot."

Brianna's eyes widened and her lips parted in a gasp. She dropped his hand and disappeared again.

Duncan's chest tightened. He stretched his fingers wide and reached farther, grasping for her. He'd not let her go just yet. They'd things to settle. A moment later, her hand found his.

"Did you say Tristledermot?"

"Aye," Duncan said. The woman whitened, her freckles becoming more pronounced. "Where did you think you were?"

Brianna's thin neck convulsed as she swallowed hard. "This is Castledermot. It hasn't been called Tristledermot in centuries."

Duncan stared at the woman. "I've not heard of Castledermot."

"What year is it?"

Duncan scowled. Brianna had seemed in her right mind as she yelled at him, yet the woman didn't know the year. "This is the year fourteen hundred and five."

BRIANNA

No. Oh, no. It was impossible. The man in front of her couldn't be from medieval times. It just wasn't possible.

"You're pulling my leg." He had to be.

"I'm what?" Duncan asked. His dark beard twitched. Did it hide a smile, or something else? Bri wished she could see past it to his expression. The only hint she had in the darkness was the widening of his bright blue eyes.

"Pulling my leg," Bri repeated. "You know, trying to put one over on me? Make a fool of me?"

Duncan stared. A sinking pit in Bri's stomach opened wide. The man really believed he was from another century.

He rose to his feet and Bri looked past Duncan's face for the first time. His clothes were hidden under a cloak. An actual medieval cloak. He looked like he was practicing for the local Heritage Week celebrations.

"This isn't happening," Bri said, shaking her head. "Just not happening."

Duncan's fingers tightened around her own. "What are you saying?"

beyond the swearing stone

Bri stared into the man's face. He wasn't the most handsome man she'd ever met — his features were almost too big to fit in his face. But something about the confusion those features showed was endearing. "It's been over six centuries since 1405."

The only word to describe the look on Duncan's face was panic. "It cannot be." He lifted his face to the sky and muttered something Bri couldn't hear.

"What?"

As he lowered his head, Duncan paused, staring over her head.

"What's the matter?" Bri asked. She shivered, half expecting a giant spider to land in her hair.

"There are stars."

Maybe the man was crazy after all. "Of course there are stars."

Duncan shook his head. "There are stars over your head, but over mine there are clouds. It's beginning to rain."

Bri looked up. He was right — there were nasty storm clouds gathering over Duncan's head. They stopped abruptly, like someone had taken an eraser and drawn a line through them.

Curious, Bri reached out a hand to touch the raindrops Duncan claimed were there. Just above the stone, her hand stopped. It felt like her fingers had run into a wall, but there was nothing there.

Bri pressed her palm to the invisible barrier. She had an idea, an impossible idea. "I want to try something," she said. "I'm going to let go of your hand. Don't go anywhere, though, it'll just be for a minute."

Duncan looked ready to argue, but Bri didn't give him a chance. She pulled her hand free. Her left hand, pressed against the invisible wall, immediately fell through. Keeping her hand on the other side of the stone, she reached for Duncan's hand again.

As she felt the already familiar warmth of his hand, her other hand was pushed back to her side of the stone.

"Try to put your hand across," Bri said.

Duncan reached out a hand, poking at the air. His eyes widened. "What is it?" he asked. "It wasn't there before. I walked around the stone before your arrival."

Bri grinned. "It's like a force field."

"A what?"

She shook her head. There was no way anyone from the fifteenth century would believe her even if she knew how to explain it. "Never mind, it doesn't matter. What does matter is what this means."

Bri looked at Duncan, amazed she was even considering speaking the words. "We may be actually having this conversation, but we live over six hundred years apart."

Duncan was quiet for so long Bri started to think something was seriously wrong.

"Duncan? Are you okay?"

Confused eyes met hers. "We live apart not in distance, but in years? How is this possible?"

Bri laughed, excitement making her babble. "We live far apart in distance, too. I don't actually live in Ireland. I only got here yesterday. Gran was born here, and lived here for years before moving, but I'm from America."

"I find myself not only married against what I'd have chosen," Duncan said, his word drawn out long, "and my wife not only lives in a different time, but in a place I've not heard of?"

"Obviously the vows don't matter," Bri said, her mind scrambling. "They can't. There are actual centuries between us."

Bri didn't like the way Duncan was looking at her.

"I'd not have chosen it," he repeated. "Never."

The words hammered into Bri, each one stinging as if she'd been slapped. She glared at the man. She might not believe they were married, but she was starting to take his rejection personally. "Why not? What's wrong with me? Am I too ugly for you?"

"Of course not."

"My career isn't good enough, then? You don't want to be married to a photographer?"

Duncan's brows pinched together. A sliver of relief slipped into Bri's stomach that she wasn't the only one upset by it all.

"I don't know what a photographer is," Duncan said, an exasperated edge to his voice. He shook his head. "It's nothing to do with your trade. It's naught to do with you at all."

It's not you, it's me. Bri rolled her eyes. Had men really been using that line for centuries? "Then what?"

"I had a wife," Duncan said quickly. "She died several years ago, but I swore to never remarry."

There was no reason for the pit that opened in her middle. None at all. "Was she pretty?"

"What?"

"Your wife. You must have really loved her to promise not to get married again." A sick feeling settled around Bri's heart. It took her longer than it should have to recognize the jealousy. "Never mind. That was stupid of me."

After a deep breath, Duncan spoke. "It's no matter now. I made a vow to you. It may have been an accident, but I did swear myself to you."

Bri looked down at their hands clasped in the stone's hole. She hoped Duncan wouldn't notice the tears clinging to her eyelashes.

"I came here tonight to give you your coin back. I wanted to release you from your vow." Bri was proud of herself for keeping her voice steady. She may have come to release him — and demand he release her — but she found she didn't want to. She looked back at Duncan, confused by the tumult of her emotions.

Duncan raised his hand toward her face, wincing as his fingers ran into the barrier. "Brianna."

Bri's heart tore a bit more, and she wondered what it would be like to hear him say her name in a voice that didn't resent her.

"Brianna, you cannot release me from the vow. Do you not

remember the words we spoke?" he asked. His voice was gentle, which confused Bri even more. "We swore ourselves to each other 'throughout all time.' It's no matter if we live centuries apart. No matter if this is something we'd have chosen for ourselves. Our vows are binding. We belong to each other."

The wind picked up, dancing Bri's hair in its fingers. She felt emotionally wiped out. She sniffled, trying to keep her nose from running because of her mostly-unshed tears. "What do we do now?"

Duncan squeezed her hand. "I think we both need to sleep. The night's half gone. Will you return tomorrow, once the darkness settles in?"

He wanted her to come back? That shouldn't be making her happy. He had no business making her happy. "I suppose I could."

"I'd like the chance to get to know my wife," Duncan said. "And for you to get to know me."

His wife. She'd never had a relationship last more than a few months, and now she was expected to be married?

Bri looked at Duncan. His short, untidy beard and mustache, his wild hair pulled back and held at the nape of his neck. Those brilliant eyes, glowing like sapphires in the starlight. His shoulders, broad enough to shield her from anything the world could place in front of her.

She couldn't deny she felt drawn to Duncan, but to be this man's wife, without even a say in the matter?

She was scared, both of the idea of marriage and of her attraction to this man she didn't know. Wouldn't know, if she didn't give him a chance.

That's all he wanted. A chance. Bri could give him that much. She took a breath and searched his eyes one last time before nodding. "I'll see you tomorrow night."

That much wouldn't break her. Please, don't let it break her.

Bri woke to the cry of birds out her window and the smell of sausages cooking. She looked at the clock. Almost seven. She rolled over and pulled the covers back over her head. She hadn't gotten to bed before three, and she'd lain awake for a long time, trying to figure out exactly how she'd gone from wanting to stay single forever, to being heartbroken when she learned her husband didn't want to be married, to excitement when he said they were stuck with each other.

That kind of a rollercoaster night deserved a day of sleeping 'til noon.

Someone knocked on her door. She decided to ignore it. If she didn't answer they wouldn't know she was awake.

The knock came again.

"Bri?" Ryan's voice came through the door. "Your grandmother sent me to ask you to come down."

She was tempted to ignore him again, but if she did, Gran would probably try to climb the stairs to kick her butt out of bed. Gran's balance wasn't the best anymore and she refused to rely on a cane, or even a bannister. Bri sighed. "I'll be down in a minute."

She closed her eyes again, and Duncan's voice echoed in her mind. He wanted to get to know her. It was a good start. Bri hugged herself. Her hair was still windblown, and her smile was dopey.

Agreeing to see Duncan again shouldn't have made her giddy, but it had. Was the excitement because it was Duncan? Or was this how it felt to decide finding love might be worth giving up so much of her independence? She couldn't decide.

Bri pushed herself off the bed, threw on a pair of jeans and the first T-shirt she found, ran a comb through her hair, and headed downstairs.

"Good morning, Gran. Morning, Ryan." Bri hurried into the dining room and slid into an upholstered chair across the table from

Gran. She even managed a real smile for Ryan. "What did I miss?"

Wrinkles appeared between Gran's eyes, and she stabbed a spoon at Bri. "You're up to some sort of trouble. I can smell it."

"I don't have any idea what you mean," Bri lied. Having her heart turned upside down and inside out could be the very definition of trouble. "What would you like to do today?"

Gran looked even more suspicious. "I thought you were taking your wee camera out somewhere."

Oh, right. She was supposed to be taking pictures. Bri shrugged. "We'll be here for a whole month. I think I can spend a day with my favorite old lady."

Gran spluttered, nearly spitting tea all over the table.

Bri laughed. It was nice to surprise Gran for a change. It had been years since the older woman had lost control like that. "We can do anything you'd like."

"Well then, I'd like to go back to St. James' Church and see things in the daylight." Gran watched Bri like a hawk.

Bri hadn't given Gran a chance to discuss what happened the night Bri and Duncan had gotten married — Bri's heart fluttered at the thought — and Bri was sure Gran wanted to go to the church to find out more about why Bri had flipped out. When it had become clear Gran hadn't seen Duncan, Bri clammed up and refused to tell her anything.

"Sure. There are some things I'd like to get pictures of in the daylight." Bri thought for a second, trying to come up with something specific. "I'd like a closer look at the round tower, too. It's hard to believe something so old is still in such good condition."

Gran gave her a look that clearly said she wasn't falling for Bri's act.

Oh, well. She'd find something to tell Gran when they were alone. Bri turned to Ryan. "What are your plans for the day? You could join us if you like."

She'd invited him on a whim, but spending time with Ryan might be a good idea. If she could open herself to his advances it might help her decide if she just wanted to feel attractive, or if she was truly interested in Duncan.

Gran kicked Bri's leg under the table.

Bri just smiled. That's what Gran got for pushing her at the man.

Ryan looked from Bri's smiling face to Gran's grumpy one. "I need to do some work in the garden," he said.

Bri couldn't blame him for wanting to escape Gran's temper, but a part of her wanted to call him a coward for it. "No worries."

After breakfast, Bri and Gran climbed into the rental car for the short drive back to the church.

"There was no need to invite the man," Gran said as Bri buckled her seatbelt. "You knew I wanted to talk to you."

Bri raised an eyebrow and pulled onto the road. "That's why I invited him."

Gran harrumphed and refused to talk until they were out of the car. "Are you going to tell me what's going on, then?" she asked.

Following Gran into the churchyard, Bri shrugged. "I haven't decided."

Gran walked away.

Bri's heart sank a bit with each of Gran's steps.

"Have you ever seen something that wasn't really there?" Bri asked, just loud enough for Gran to hear.

Gran turned and eyed Bri. Bri tried not to squirm too much.

Finally, Gran spoke. "What are you seeing?"

"You're going to think I'm crazy."

"I've known you too many years, lass." Gran laughed. "I know quite well how loosely screwed in your mind is."

That didn't make Bree feel any better. She walked to the southern high cross and looked at the engravings. They were beautiful. She wondered how much more easily seen the images had been in Duncan's time.

"When we were at the swearing stone the other night, I thought I saw someone," she finally managed to say. No need for Bri to let on she knew who it was, or when he was from. Not yet, anyway. "There was a man."

Gran glanced at the group of tourists pouring in through the gate. She snagged Bri's arm and led her to the swearing stone. Bri stared at the limp, wilted wildflowers they'd left on the ground, then at the still-trampled grass where she'd been last night.

A slow warmth filled her.

Bri tried to push it away. She wasn't some stupid girl in a stupid romance novel who fell in love with men willy-nilly. She made men work hard to even get her attention. She had no business feeling that curling warmth fill her belly.

Gran looked around, spreading her arms wide. "There's hardly anywhere for a person to hide."

"He wasn't exactly hiding," Bri said. She swallowed. This was so much harder than she'd expected. "He was holding my hand."

DUNCAN

Duncan stared at the glowing charcoal in the bowl furnace in front of him. A rod of steel sat in the charcoal, overheated and abandoned. It was hardly past Tierce, the morning not half gone. He should be working.

He kept seeing Brianna, with tears clinging to her lashes.

Duncan was having a hard time understanding the woman. She'd clearly prepared for a battle, ready to fight him to end the marriage. Yet by the end of their time together she looked so fragile, so full of hope.

His heart still ached for her pain at learning he'd been married before. It confused him. Was she jealous? Or worried about competing with Neve's memory? How could she be, when she'd wanted to pretend they'd not wed?

Brianna had asked if Neve was pretty, and how well he'd loved her.

Duncan shifted, uncomfortable with the realization that his memories had faded. Aye, he'd loved Neve in his own way. She'd been a good companion. She may not have welcomed every part of marriage, but she'd always done her part without complaint. They'd been friends for years before wedding.

Beyond that, there was little to speak of.

It saddened him. There should be more to her legacy than the memory of a mostly-pleasant, compliant wife.

Particularly now. Something about Brianna drew Duncan to her. And that tear she'd tried to hide was just the start of it.

"Duncan?" a voice called from outside.

Duncan jumped at the sound. With one last look at the sparking iron in the fire, he gave up. He'd not get any work done today. He set the iron aside, spread the charcoal, and went to see who was after him.

"What can I do for you, Brogan?" Duncan asked as he emerged from the darkness of the smithy. His eyes squinted against the light, even with the dark clouds obscuring the sun. The rain still drizzled down from the gray sky.

"Would you be able to help me at the inn? A cartload of supplies has arrived, and I need to get them unloaded quickly," Brogan said. "I wouldn't bother you, but the cart is needed elsewhere and the man is threatening to toss the load to the ground."

Duncan shook his head. It wasn't the first time the inn's delivery had gone wrong. "You could get your supplies from a different merchant," he said, trying to hide his amusement. "Go ahead, I'll just take care of things so I can leave."

He stepped inside the smithy and allowed himself to chuckle openly over his friend's predicament.

He put things to rights and left the smithy, turning toward Dublin gate. Quickly weaving his way through groups of people, he joined Brogan halfway to the inn. "Do none of your employees ever help you unload, or am I your servant of choice?"

Brogan turned his head to Duncan with a furrowed brow.

Duncan grinned.

Despite his rush, Brogan stood still in the middle of the road. "You're not serious." He paused, and his eyes narrowed. "I see your smile. You've not teased in years. What's happened?"

What's happened, indeed? The words had slipped from Duncan without a thought.

Brogan snagged Duncan's sleeve and leaned in so he could be heard over the sounds echoing around them. "If I didn't know you better, I'd think there was a woman to thank for your lightheartedness."

Duncan frowned. "You do know me, however, which means you know I allow myself a single jest in a season." He began to walk again, pulling his sleeve free of Brogan's fingers and vowing to heed his words more carefully. No one was to know he'd married.

Brogan followed, seemingly unconvinced. "Is there a woman involved?"

Duncan continued to walk. The inn was two doors farther on. Surely they could make it there before Brogan became too suspicious. "Is that barrel meant to be on the side of the road, or are you losing your order?"

Brogan's face paled and he rushed ahead. "We had an agreement," he hollered. "You were to wait while I got another set of arms to help unload."

The man shrugged and set another barrel near the inn's steps.

Eager to keep Brogan from going back to the idea of a woman in his life — and to stop himself debating if Brogan had the right of it and Brianna was the reason for his smile — Duncan began hauling the supplies around the side of the inn to the burgage behind.

Halfway to the inn's small stable was a storage shed. Duncan left his load inside and went back around front for another barrel.

Brogan haggled with the deliveryman, who was anxious to be gone.

Duncan shook his head. At this rate he'd be doing all the carrying. On a whim, he lifted a barrel from the cart and set the weight of it on the deliveryman's shoulder.

The man grabbed it before it could fall and turned his anger on Duncan.

Extending a hand to stop the tirade he could see building, Duncan said, "You'll be gone much faster if you help carry these around back. Arguing won't speed the work."

Brogan's jaw dropped.

Duncan turned away long enough to lift a bag of grain from under the oiled cloth protecting it from the drizzle before smiling at Brogan and tossing him the load. "You can help, too, as I'm no beast of burden."

"When this is done, you and I have a conversation to continue," Brogan said as he walked away. Following close behind, Duncan clearly heard him add, "He's much too cheerful."

Between the three of them, the unloading was over and the deliveryman on his way before the church bell rang for None.

"Stay and eat with us," Brogan said as Duncan tried to slip away.

Duncan glanced over his shoulder to the road. He'd no wish for his friend to return to questioning the good mood he'd felt throughout the morning. "I should be going."

"Stay," Brogan insisted. "You earned the meal."

Shoulders falling in defeat, Duncan nodded. If he left without giving Brogan a chance to show his gratitude, their friendship would become tense.

His feet dragging in the straw beneath him, Duncan trudged after Brogan.

When the meal was served in the otherwise empty tap room of the inn, Duncan found himself trapped between Brogan and his wife on one side, and their daughter on the other.

The girl was several years younger than Duncan, but of a marrying age. More and more lately, Brogan had been pushing them together.

Duncan glared at his friend. He should have known the invitation to stay was another excuse to force him to spend time with the girl. He'd have been happier if Brogan were asking about his cheerful mood.

Brogan rolled his eyes and tilted his head toward his wife.

The women in town had left Duncan alone since a disaster at midwinter when a young woman had dissolved in tears. He'd done nothing more than turn down her request that he marry her, but from her reaction he might have poisoned the lass's mead.

It would seem his reprieve from the meddlers was at an end.

Duncan took a deep breath and began a conversation with Brogan about how the inn was faring. Brogan took pity on him, and they spent the meal discussing business.

When the meal ended, Duncan nodded to the women and left, followed closely by Brogan.

"I'm sorry about that. It's not only Alana. She said the women have decided you've dragged your feet much too long. They're determined to settle you this time." Brogan narrowed his eyes. "If you'd just mention to me, somewhere Alana could hear, that you've a woman in mind . . . they'd leave you alone, then, wouldn't they?"

Duncan grunted. The women were not only meddlers, their tongues wagged at both ends. Were any one of them to hear there was the possibility of him reconsidering his life as a widower, the entire town would hear of it before nightfall.

His life would become miserable.

Although, if the women were truly convinced he'd be happy of their "help" his misery was already assured.

Grudgingly, Duncan nodded.

As he followed Brogan around the corner of the inn, near an open window where Alana was surely hiding, Duncan considered walking away. Leaving the women to plot was dangerous, but using Brianna — a woman who'd never appear to defend herself — in such a way felt cowardly.

Brogan smiled at him, gesturing to the window.

Duncan sighed. He'd play Brogan's game, then treat himself to some mead. "You know I like your family, but you need to convince Alana to stop trying to find me a wife."

"Ah, you know the women," Brogan said. "They won't listen to the likes of me."

"I know they're concerned, but I will never wed a woman they choose for me. They must have discovered that by now." Duncan paused. He couldn't use Brianna. She deserved more from him. He smiled, his mind settled. "Perhaps a woman — of my own choosing, mind — will catch my eye. Until then, the women will stay clear of me."

Brogan stood, open-mouthed at how the conversation had turned. "But—"

Duncan nodded. His way was much better than Brogan's heavy-handed plan. "Do they not believe I see what they're doing? Can they not understand the choice is mine to make? If they continue to push, the disaster at midwinter will be made to look mild the next time I'm approached."

"Their intentions are good." Brogan's voice held a quiet intensity.

"Perhaps, but their intentions are not my concern. The only opinion that counts here is my own. I see the way they push those girls to me, assuring them they're pretty enough, or charming enough to change my mind," Duncan said. "It will stop. Now."

Brogan finally managed to close his mouth, just before a fly could investigate the small cave. "How will you stop them?"

Duncan looked to the window. It was suspiciously quiet inside the inn. "I won't. You will, if you want my help with your next delivery — or if any of those meddlers want their husbands to be welcome at the smithy."

Whistling, Duncan walked away.

Laying down such an ultimatum felt much better than it should have.

When Duncan returned to the smithy, the feeling of rebellion went with him. It was an oddly freeing sensation.

He looked into the darkness where he spent his days. It was gloomy and dreary. Not the kind of place he wanted to spend the rest of this day.

Instead of going through the doorway he continued down the straw-covered road. The butcher was a short walk from the smithy, and Duncan hadn't been there in far too long.

After buying a mutton shank, he stopped at the baker's for a trencher.

"Don't send your wife for that blade today, I'll not be there," Duncan said as he walked away. He ignored the questions Michael called after him.

As Duncan walked down the road, smiling and humming to himself, he hardly noticed the stares of his neighbors.

After stopping to leave the food on his table he went into his burgage and gathered a few vegetables and a handful of herbs from his small garden before going back upstairs.

Drawing the freshly sharpened knife from his waist, he cut the mutton into large chunks and tossed them into his cooking pot. The cabbage, parsnip, and wild radishes followed, along with a splash of dark mead.

The rest of the mead would soon meet his belly.

Duncan hung the pot over the fire and sat back to rest and enjoy the remainder of the day, completely oblivious to the grin on his face and the gossip in the road below his window.

BRIANNA

ri reached out to steady Gran. She should have kept her mouth shut. It was stupid of her to have said anything. What had she been thinking?

"He had hold of your hand?" Gran asked.

"Never mind," Bri said. Maybe she could backtrack and take the comment back. "It's nothing. I probably just imagined it."

Gran reached up to touch Bri's face. "Don't doubt yourself, dear one. Magic spun free that night. Even you felt it, though you'd pretend otherwise."

Bri glanced at the tourists wandering through the churchyard. They were too close. Such a private conversation should be — well, private. "We should talk about this later. Where people won't think we're crazy witch wannabes."

Gran took Bri by the arm and led her to the back edge of the churchyard, where they had a little privacy. And a really good view of the swearing stone. Bri tried to turn her back on it, but Gran wouldn't let her. She was stronger than an old lady had any right to be.

"It calls to you yet," Gran said. "I can see it."

beyond the swearing stone

Bri shook her head. "It doesn't matter if an old stone is interesting, Gran."

Gran's voice took on the no-nonsense edge that told Bri she'd better pay attention or there'd be hell to pay. "Use your ears, Brianna Meghan Hughes. I said it calls to you, not that it's an interesting old stone. Something happened to you in this churchyard, and you'll not be pretending it didn't."

"Fine. I felt something that night. Are you happy now?"

Gran smiled, her temper blown out as quickly as it had risen. "It's a start. Now tell me about your man. Does he have a name?"

"Everyone has a name, Gran."

"That tone of voice will only bring you trouble, lass. Do you know his name?"

A part of Bri wanted to keep this to herself. But after growing up in Gran's house, she knew Gran wouldn't give up. "Duncan. His name is Duncan."

Gran's smile grew, and wisdom bloomed in her eyes. "Ah, is it now. Duncan's a fine name for your wee ghost at the stone."

"He's not a ghost, Gran." Bri bit her tongue. Those words had come on their own, and she didn't want any others joining them.

"What else could he be?" Gran cackled. "He was there for you, but I didn't see anything beyond you practicing the family wedding vows."

Bri cursed. Of course that wouldn't get past Gran. "How was I to know there was a man on the other side of that stone saying the same vow? It's not like I could see him before our hands touched."

"Ah, there's your trouble." Gran's tone was solemn but her eyes still teased Bri. "You married the man and don't want to admit it."

What? Had she said anything about marrying Duncan? Bri paused, thinking. The vows. Of all the stupid slips of the tongue. She hadn't meant to admit to that.

Bri walked away, staying far from the swearing stone on her way back to the car. She sat inside with the windows open wide, staring across the street at the beautiful front garden next to the tree-lined walk.

Gran was going to get every last detail from her, and it didn't matter that she was trying to keep them back. Her tongue was loosened, refusing to obey her will.

It wasn't long before Gran struggled into the car beside her. Bri tried to stay mad, but found she didn't have it in her. Gran was all she had left in the world. She didn't want to argue.

"I'm sorry Gran, I don't know what's gotten into me." Bri took a deep breath. "I've never wanted to get married, and now I'm supposed to have a husband who lived back at the turn of the fifteenth century? It's crazy."

Gran's glare bored into Bri. "You may not have chosen this, but it came to you. It's your fate, my dear."

Fate. It was one thing for Gran to believe in her own fate, but Bri had only ever wanted to be free to make her own decisions.

"We'll be needing to go on a wee trip," Gran said, her voice worn and tired.

"We're on a trip already."

"Tomorrow we'll go to Galway. We've distant relatives there, and we'll be needing to talk to them."

Bri would have argued, but Gran had that look on her face again. At least they'd be near some great places to take pictures.

And the little part of her brain insisting on acting like a teenager cheered that by leaving in the morning, she'd be able to keep her date with Duncan. She'd given her word that she'd be there, after all.

Who was Bri kidding? She'd never gotten those butterflies as a teenager. They were a very new experience.

Bri crept out of the house, doing an odd sort of dance to slide through the doorway without opening the door wide enough for the hinges to creak.

Not that she was sneaking around. She had every right to wander the town at night, or to skulk around the churchyard, for that matter. She'd checked. The church's hours specifically stated it was open twenty-four hours a day.

She set off down the street with a glance up at the thick clouds. They'd blown in during the afternoon and hung heavy, threatening to let loose their load. Bri tightened her grip on the handle of her collapsed umbrella. Bri hummed to herself as she hurried along the tree-lined avenue leading to St. James' Church, more excited than she wanted to think about.

The denseness overhead blocked the stars and moonlight, leaving the churchyard darker than the previous night as she crept through the old archway and angled to the right. She stepped off the gravel path and into the grass. Moving slowly, Bri made her way to the swearing stone and leaned her umbrella against it. She crouched down and ran her hands along the grass. The flowers were gone, blown away or removed by a caretaker. Hopefully the magic of the stone would work without them.

The magic. Bri's muscles slackened and she pitched toward the ground. Her shoulder stung as she landed on it. She sat up, rubbing at the ache.

Bri hadn't believed in magic for so long. Not since Gran had blamed her mother's death on fate and magic. Even as small as she'd been, Bri had known nothing could have saved her drunk mother from herself.

Magic wouldn't have been so cruel as to make her mother drive the car into a tree.

She shook her head against the fuzzy memories. Determined to keep her mind on anything else, Bri pushed her hand through the hole in the stone.

Duncan's warm hand enveloped hers, and he slowly appeared.

The butterflies in Bri's stomach went crazy. "Hi," she said.

Duncan's smiling face reflected starlight from the past. "Good evening."

Bri stared at him, unsure of what to say.

He seemed happy just to look at her. Or, more likely, try to see where she was in the dark.

"Are you hungry? I brought food." Duncan pulled his hand away until only their fingertips touched. He set something on his palm and pushed it down his fingers and into Bri's hand.

Bri took it with her other hand and raised it to her nose. Whatever it was smelled good enough to make her stomach growl. "What is it? It's too dark to see."

"There's mutton and vegetables on a trencher," Duncan said. He raised his own food and took a bite.

Bri copied him, lifting a flat piece of bread to her mouth. The chewy meat piled on it was juicy and flavorful. Her mouth too full to speak, she allowed a small moan of pleasure to escape.

Duncan's fingers twitched against hers. He faded in and out of view a few times before taking Bri's hand more firmly in his own. "I'm glad you like it."

Bri could hear the laughter in his voice. She tried to be offended that he was laughing at her, but she couldn't manage it. "I'm glad I could amuse you."

A strange feeling welled up inside Bri and she realized she *was* glad. She'd gotten him to laugh, and he looked truly happy. The stern, angry man she'd first seen in him was gone.

"Tell me of life in your time," Duncan said. "Things must be very different."

He had no idea. "What makes you say that?"

"Your clothing."

Bri looked down. She couldn't make out her clothes in the dark. How could Duncan? "A lot of things are different. Clothes are just a tiny part of it."

"Tell me?" Duncan asked. "I would know of your time. Of the things you do, and how people have changed."

"My world is boring," Bri said.

"You mentioned something you do. A trade? Pho— Pho—"

"Photography?" Bri asked. "I'm a photographer. I came to Ireland to take pictures of — well, of things that remain from your time, actually."

"Pictures? Are these paintings?"

Bri took several minutes to explain. The more she told him, the larger Duncan's eyes widened. Her heart swelled at the awe and pride shining from them.

He was proud of her. Warmth spread through her, filling her with a happiness she couldn't quite explain.

"What about you?" Bri wanted to know everything about him. Wanted a reason to be as proud of him as he was of her. "How do you make a living?"

"I'm a blacksmith." Duncan paused. "It's not as magical as copying images from life, but it's a useful trade. I earn more than is sufficient for myself."

"I don't know much about blacksmithing," Bri admitted. "Maybe someday you can show me."

They both paused as they realized what she'd said.

Bri's cheeks burned. Again, the words had escaped without permission. Where had this problem come from? She usually had such good control of herself. "I didn't—"

"It would be my honor," Duncan said.

The butterflies in Bri's stomach danced a little faster. If she was lucky, Duncan wouldn't notice the sudden clamminess of her hand in his.

"Will you tell me more of your life?" Duncan asked. "You're not from Ireland?"

"No, I'm from America." She frowned. "The country hasn't been formed yet for you. It's far across the ocean to the west."

Duncan's eyes widened.

Bri grinned at his response and went on to tell him more about America, and what life in a modern city was like.

As their conversation moved from one topic to the next, Bri became more comfortable with Duncan. She started teasing him, and laughed when he teased her back.

"What's your biggest complaint?" Bri asked. "If you could change anything in your time, what would it be?"

Duncan grunted.

"Come on, you have to tell. I've told you all sorts of things about my life."

After a minute, Duncan raised his eyebrows. They nearly touched his hairline. "I'd have the women stop trying to find me a wife."

Bri felt as though she'd been punched in the stomach. "They've been trying to find you a wife?"

"Aye."

"And what was your response?" Bri tried to push aside her anger. It was a lost cause. She'd heard it lacing her words.

Duncan stared at her, and Bri felt like he was trying to convey more than his words. "This has been going on for years. I've always refused. Today I told them if it was a woman of my own choosing I would consider marrying."

Bri choked as her jealousy rose even more. "Your choosing?"

"I could hardly tell them fate had stepped in and married me off to a woman who lived six centuries from now." Duncan sighed and laced his fingers more firmly through hers. "Do you want to be married to me?"

Did she want to be? Two days ago the answer had been a definite no.

Bri rested her free arm across the top of the stone and leaned her forehead against the invisible barrier. "I don't know."

Duncan nodded, his shoulders slightly lowered.

"I wouldn't have chosen marriage at all," Bri hurried on. "There's my career to think of. I've just gotten it started and I'd planned to focus on that for now. I always thought there'd be plenty of time for marriage later, if I wanted it."

Plenty of time, even if she'd had no plans to follow through and actually find someone to marry.

"Which doesn't explain my jealousy." Brianna barely spoke the words, but from Duncan's half-hidden smile, he'd heard them.

Duncan pulled on Bri's hand until her wrist passed through the hole as if to keep her from escaping. He leaned toward the barrier, his forehead coming to rest just opposite Bri's. If only the barrier weren't there, she'd feel his touch. "Your jealousy?"

Bri closed her eyes so she wouldn't have to see how much he was enjoying her embarrassment. "Your neighbors don't need to find you a wife," she said.

"They don't?" Duncan's voice was quiet, but so intense Bri opened her eyes again. His bright blue eyes held her own, demanding an answer.

"Of course not. You already have me." Bri held her breath as she waited for his reply.

Duncan moved slightly, and Bri felt his mouth meet hers. He was warm against her own chilled lips.

Shocked at the touch, Bri stilled.

Duncan nibbled at her lips, defying the barrier. His warmth seeped through Bri, filling her with longing. She deepened the kiss, leaning into him, reveling in the feel of him.

The wind picked up. It pulled Bri's hair from her loose ponytail and whipped it around her face.

Time became a tangible thing as the barrier between the two shifted. Thunder rolled across the sky and rain began to pelt down.

Still, Duncan kissed her. And Bri kissed him back, as if their lives depended on this moment, this small pocket of time.

When they finally separated, Bri was so dazed she couldn't see straight. She might have imagined Duncan's victorious smile.

She knew, however, that the panting as he tried to catch his breath was real.

DUNCAN

The woman would be the death of him.

As Duncan fought to get his breath under control, he stared at Brianna. He could easily believe he'd enjoy even death at her hands.

Irish hearts were strong, but not so strong as to fight their way free of an Irish will. Or so Duncan told himself as his own heart fought for freedom.

Brianna was drenched, the rain still pouring down around her. Her wind-torn hair hugged her face. It was short, hardly past her elbows. Her wet clothing formed itself to her body, and he wished for the ability to cover her with his cloak.

"Are you chilled?" he asked.

Brianna's eyes had taken on a smoky hue, and she looked as though she'd been knocked over the head. The tip of her tongue drifted over her lower lip.

Duncan's traitorous heart tugged on him, and he reached out to her — only to be stopped by the cursed barrier. "Brianna?"

Brianna turned her eyes on him, and the last of his control fled. He wanted this, wanted to be hers. Wanted to be wed to her. Duncan's hands began to tremble at the realization.

"How did that happen? I thought we couldn't get through." Brianna lifted her free hand as if to touch his.

Their hands didn't meet, but for the first time, Duncan could tell her hand was there as the barrier flexed and pushed against him.

Brianna's eyes widened. "Do you feel that?"

"A pressure?" Duncan asked. "Aye. It's as if you're pushing the barrier at me."

"That's not what I feel," Brianna said. "There's an energy, like static electricity."

With effort, Duncan kept his groan to himself. "I don't know the meaning of those words."

Brianna paused, her brow creasing in thought. "Like the air before lightning strikes."

Duncan nodded. That he knew. He pushed back against the barrier, and the energy ran up to his elbow, lifting the small hairs on his arm.

Brianna grinned. "Do you think kissing gave us some control over the barrier?"

"Perhaps," Duncan said. He didn't see how an unplanned, stolen kiss could have any control over the barrier. Not knowing even how it was possible that he saw Brianna, he had to admit he understood very little of what was happening.

"Let's test it." Brianna's face and voice were full of mirth. "Will you kiss me again?"

Duncan's heart nearly stopped. One kiss had undone his will. What would a second do?

It was something he'd no desire to learn.

No desire at all, he tried to tell the well of anticipation that filled him.

Brianna's impish laugh drove the hesitance from him. He'd already lost the battle and was halfway in love with her. Another kiss would do nothing to change that.

Slowly, they leaned over the stone toward each other. Brianna's gaze never left Duncan's.

Their lips met in a whisper of power.

Duncan began to pull away. He'd given her enough of himself for the time being. Brianna followed him with her lips, leaning into him, refusing to allow the kiss to end.

With a groan, Duncan gave in to her, as he felt he always would. He reached for her, longing to bury his fingers in her dripping hair.

The barrier kept his hand from reaching her.

He wanted nothing more than to pull Brianna to him, to press her against him as he wrapped her in his arms. Being able to touch her with nothing more than a kiss was a kind of hell he'd never before known.

When they finally parted, raindrops speckled Duncan's face. "You'll catch your death in that rain."

Brianna's laugh was interrupted by a shiver. "I should go," she said. "I have to go to Galway with Gran in the morning."

Galway?

"How long will you be gone?" As Duncan waited for his answer, he tried to figure the days of travel in his mind. He'd never been to Galway, so he could find no more than a guess.

"I'll be gone one night, I think," Brianna said.

That couldn't be right.

At Brianna's laugh, he smiled. It was a beautiful sound.

"We travel much more quickly in my time. It will take a couple hours to get there is all."

Duncan marveled at the idea of travel so fast one could travel so far in a single day. Unable to understand such speed, he chose not to try. "So I'll not see you tomorrow night."

The thought did unpleasant things to his insides.

"No. I'm sorry," Brianna said, and she looked it. "I'd stay if I could, but Gran said we need to visit some distant relatives. She's already arranged everything with them."

Duncan nodded. "My friend and foster brother asked me to celebrate Lughnasa with his family tomorrow. I'd considered staying away, but if you'll not be here I should go to the hills with them."

Brianna shivered again.

"Go now," Duncan said. "I'll not forgive myself if you fall ill from tonight."

Brianna's grasp tightened. "Will you be here when I get back?"

His chest tightened. Was she concerned she'd miss seeing him? "I will."

Nodding to herself, she pulled her hand from Duncan's and faded from view.

Duncan remained where he was, wiping the rain of a different century from his face.

Duncan trailed behind Ciaran and Tara, with a boy on his shoulders and one grasping each of his hands.

Colin, the oldest, had nearly reached the age of nine and was much too grown up to climb Uncle Duncan. Instead, he walked just before Duncan as they climbed the hill outside of town. He'd glance over his shoulder, then pull the knife from his waist, run his fingers over it, and put it back.

Duncan chuckled under his breath. Colin's pride in the knife was easy to see. Surely Duncan was meant to ask about it.

Only when Colin looked ready to explode did Duncan give in. "Your parents think you're grown enough to carry a knife now, do they?"

Colin straightened his back. "As long as I'm careful of it with the kids and don't let baby Finola get it," he said.

"Your father makes good knives," Duncan said, watching for Colin's reaction. The boy's pride wasn't just for owning it, he'd clearly made the knife himself.

"Not this one." Colin's smile grew. "This is one of mine."

Ciaran turned around, stopping their progress up the hill. "*One* of yours?"

Colin flushed. "It's the first one I've made," he said. His eyes begged Duncan to rescue him. "I'll make others, though. This was just a learning knife."

Duncan let go of the children and lowered the small boy from his back, then reached for the knife. He managed to keep a straight face as he inspected the boy's work. "A very nice job you've done. You're certain it was only practice?"

The boy swelled with pleasure and carefully put the knife away.

"Take your brothers and go on ahead," Ciaran said. He handed the boy a stack of baskets. "You can start collecting bilberries without us."

Colin nodded and herded the younger boys along.

Duncan saw the glint in Ciaran's eye and moved to follow the boys.

"You're not going," Ciaran said, grabbing Duncan's arm. "Has there been any news of your mysterious woman?"

Tara laughed and bounced the babe she held in her arms. "Duncan has a woman? When did this happen?"

"Did I not tell you?" Ciaran asked.

Duncan gazed at the white clouds on the horizon and sighed. He knew a practiced team when he saw one. "You don't fool me," he said, stepping around the pair and continuing up the hill. "You'd have been far more surprised if Ciaran hadn't already told you of her, Tara."

As Duncan continued up the hillside, he could hear his friends whispering behind him. He ignored them and found a spot where he could see down the hill where a row of horses, small from such a distance, waited for the start of a race.

Duncan smiled. The excitement he'd felt for the Lughnasa races as a boy threatened to rise up. He'd not cheered the races in years.

Ciaran came up beside him and let out a wild whoop.

"Bring out the races and the two of you turn into children," Tara said. She tucked up her *leine* to free her lower legs and began to dance, the baby nestled close to her breast. "If I don't keep you nearby, you're likely to join the games and end up wrestling each other."

Ciaran's eyes lit up and Duncan laughed in spite of himself.

They stayed where they were, watching the races below until the boys returned, baskets overflowing with the tiny bilberries.

"Can we go higher?" Colin asked. "The other kids were saying they're going to bury the sheaf soon."

Duncan glanced to the trail where groups of people made their cheerful way up the hill.

There were too many young couples, happy and in love. The day had always been one of courting and matchmaking. This year it pulled on Duncan in ways he didn't care to think on, and he'd have given much to have Brianna beside him.

"Are you coming?" Ciaran asked as he joined the children.

Duncan shook his head. "I'll stay here."

Ciaran whispered something to Tara, who took the boys and continued up the hill to the place where the first sheaf of corn would be buried.

"Tell me," Ciaran said.

Duncan muttered a curse to himself and turned back to watch the horses be led across the river.

As foster brothers, Duncan could have handled Ciaran's arguments or threats. His brother-in-law's silence was a fight he couldn't win.

"She's getting to me."

The weight of Ciaran's hand settled on his shoulder. "There's no shame in living."

"Neve died because of me." Duncan choked out the words he'd kept inside for so long.

Ciaran swung Duncan around to face him. "You've believed that all this time?"

Duncan looked away.

"Neve's death was tragic, yes, but never your fault." The words were expected, but the force behind them wasn't. "Everyone blamed themselves. My parents. The midwife. You. Some things can't be helped or changed, and if Neve had seen how you've punished yourself, she'd be ashamed. She told you to live."

Ciaran's voice pounded into Duncan. Duncan felt something inside ease and begin to heal. "I'd have taken her place."

"Of course you would have," Ciaran said. "Everyone knows you'd have saved her if you'd been able. It's time to stop holding to the guilt. Neve loved you from the time she met you."

Somehow, Duncan managed to smile. "She was half Colin's age when I came to your family."

"And she never looked at anyone else."

She'd followed him around constantly. He'd not had it in him to turn her away — siblings were a new, untried thing for him. That Neve had been besotted with him was never a secret.

"I looked away enough for the both of us." Looked, and toyed with, and then ignored. He'd have been married well before Neve was of a marrying age had he not spent all his time at the smithy with Ciaran, learning from Ciaran's father.

When Neve had grown enough, she'd approached him. Duncan had become accustomed to having the girl underfoot, and she'd grown into a beautiful woman. When Duncan agreed to marry her, half the young men in the area had been jealous. Duncan smiled at the memory. He'd been proud of his wife. He'd just not expected her infatuation to cool as he spent time in his smithy earning a way to provide for her.

Ciaran sat on a fallen log that sat rotting among the vetches. His eyes never left Duncan. "Have you learned any more of the woman at the stone? Brianna?"

Duncan sat next to Ciaran and took a deep breath. His friend had never been so nosy before marrying Tara. "I've hardly slept since I saw you last. I've only seen her at night, in the churchyard."

"Does she know the two of you are wed?"

Duncan nodded. "She does."

After a bit of silence, Ciaran elbowed him. "You're supposed to tell me if you'll stay married."

"Aye, I know what you're about, you nattering woman." Duncan's laughter died away. "We will, as there's no way to end it."

"She's one of them, then?" Ciaran asked. He'd never made a secret his disdain for Duncan's mother's people, or their refusal to accept divorce.

"No, our problem is much bigger than that." Duncan pulled his gaze from the ground and looked at Ciaran. "She lives many centuries from now."

BRIANNA

"Such dark circles under your eyes." Gran gave Bri a disapproving frown. "Did you find even a wink of sleep?"

Bri stifled a yawn and pulled off the M6. "I might have gotten more than an hour if you hadn't gotten me up so early."

Gran ignored the barb. "And what were you up to all night, if you weren't sleeping?"

What indeed? Gran wasn't likely to believe Bri had been kissing a six hundred year old man.

Bri shrugged. "If you'd care to tell me anything about these relatives before we get there, you'd better do it soon."

Gran chuckled. "You're wanting to steal the surprise?"

Bri tried to hold onto the last of her patience. She was still jet lagged, and meeting with Duncan at night hadn't done anything to help her body adjust to the new time zone. "If you don't want to tell me, don't. I don't care anymore."

Gran made a noise that could only be described as a grunt.

Bri grinned. Nothing got to Gran as much as people not caring about her little secrets.

"Where did you sneak away to last night?" Gran asked. "Imagine my surprise when I peeked out to check on the storm, only to see you creeping up the walk. At four in the morning, mind."

Bri tightened her grip on the steering wheel. She thought she'd made it inside without being seen. "I, um, had a date last night."

"And just when were you going to tell me you'd gone for drinks with a man?"

Brianna waited until she'd turned the next corner, following the instructions the GPS was giving her. "Never?"

"Brianna Meghan Hughes," Gran started.

"I didn't go for drinks with anyone, okay?" Bri said. "I just went back to the churchyard to see if I could see anything."

Gran was slightly mollified. "Did you find anything?"

"Yeah, a storm. I still don't feel dry."

"You're not too old for a good paddling young lady," Gran said. "Did you see your Duncan last night?"

"We're here," Bri said. With luck, Gran would let things drop.

Gran looked past Bri at the little brick cottage. She sighed. "Answer my question, then we'll go in."

Bri considered digging in her heels. It wasn't worth it. "I saw him." She turned her head toward Gran and waited.

Gran nodded and seemed to shrink in on herself. "We'd best be going up. We're expected."

Bri went around and helped Gran out of the car. "What's in here?" she asked as Gran handed her a bag to carry.

"My wedding Bible."

"You brought that all the way to Ireland?" Bri hadn't seen the Bible since she was small. Gran had received it on her wedding day, and it held the names of her ancestors going back hundreds of years. It wasn't the only copy, but it was a family treasure. "You didn't think it was better off in a safety deposit box or something?"

Gran walked to the door before answering. She glanced at Bri, then rang the bell. "I had a feeling there'd be need for it."

A middle-aged woman, slightly plump and nearly as short as

Brianna opened the door. Her dark hair was speckled with gray. She fidgeted for a minute before speaking. "My name's Grace. You must be Caitriona," she said to Gran.

"That I am," Gran said. "Many years ago, I knew your mother well. You look quite like her."

"Come in." Grace's hands fluttered a bit, and she gave Bri a strange look. "Would you like some tea? Or we could get right into the matter."

"Tea would be lovely, dear," Gran said.

They followed Grace to the kitchen, the sound of their footsteps on the slate floor quieter than Bri expected. Sunshine poured through a set of windows, brightening the cluttered room. Grace ushered them to the small square table and moved to lift teacups off a shelf set into the dark cabinets.

"The water's already on, so it shouldn't be long," Grace said. She brought a plate of cookies over and set it in the center of the table.

Gran sat back and smiled, seemingly at ease. She was the only one. Grace's fidgeting was starting to make Bri nervous.

The sound of arguing preceded two teenage girls into the kitchen.

"Mam, tell her she can't come with me."

Grace closed her eyes for a second, then turned to the girls. "We have company. Can you at least try to be civil? This is Caitriona and Brianna, relatives from America. Ladies, these are my daughters, Katie and Hannah."

"Nice to meet you." The older girl, Katie, tossed her long blond braid over her shoulder as she watched Bri and Gran with curious eyes. She flushed and turned away. "Mam, I'll be late."

"Both of you go. Enjoy the outing." Grace stopped her daughter's argument with a raised hand. "Either both of you go, or you both stay."

Katie sashayed across the room, her long legs moving with a dancer's grace. She stopped to dig through a pile of odds and ends in a basket for a set of keys before dashing out the kitchen door.

Hannah glanced back and caught Bri's eye. "Will you be here later? I'd love to get to know you."

"I don't know," Bri said. She still didn't know why they were there in the first place, let alone how long they planned to stay before finding a hotel. "It's not up to me."

Hannah's eyes crinkled at the corners and her delicate face lit up as she laughed. She tucked a lock of dark red hair behind an ear. It was short enough it fell right back in her face. "Then Mam will talk you into staying." Avoiding her mother's good-natured swat, she ran out the door behind her sister.

Before anyone could speak, the kettle whistled. The next few minutes were spent readying tea and settling in more comfortably around the table.

With her daughters gone, Grace seemed to have calmed. "May I see your Bible, Caitriona?" she asked.

"Aye," Gran said. "Bri, will you pull it out for me?"

Bri bit her tongue against the complaint that so far, she'd been all but ignored by their host. The Bible was old, but not ancient. It had been new when Gran was married, the ancestry copied painstakingly onto the thin, blank pages at both the front and back of the book. She held it out to Gran.

Gran raised a hand and pushed it back to Bri. "It's yours now, my dear, but Grace has need of it for a bit."

Confused, Bri handed the book across the table to Grace.

The relative she hadn't known about until yesterday took the Bible reverently, placing it in front of her and opening the cover. She followed the genealogy from the place where Gran had added in Bri's name all the way back to the first recorded name.

When she'd finished, she smiled. "It's true, then."

"What's true?" Bri asked.

"Aye," Gran said, ignoring Bri. "And the time has come."

Grace nodded. She stood and left the room. When she returned, she held another Bible, this one much older than Gran's. She set it on the table in front of Bri and opened it to a family tree.

"Here's me, and my family," Grace said, her fingers tracing over the names. "Your record follows your history, and this one follows mine. The two connect at the start."

"So when Gran said you were a distant relative, she meant so far distant that we're strangers?" Bri was getting that prickling sensation she'd come to associate with seeing Duncan.

Grace smiled. "Distant, yes, but not strangers at all. Did your grandmother ever tell you the tale of the two brothers?"

Bri almost wished Grace would go back to ignoring her. Old family tales were best left in the past - or in the imagination, as there was a good chance they'd never actually happened — even if Gran sharing her stories were some of Bri's favorite memories. "Of course."

"It was Brianna's favorite story as a child," Gran chimed in. "She begged for that story every night."

"I'd be surprised if it hadn't been a favorite." Grace was laughing. She gave Gran a significant look. "It would have called to her."

Bri looked at the woman she'd just met, unsure how rude she could get away with being. "Why does the tale matter?" she asked. "What's so important about it?"

Grace went back to her chair across the table from Gran. "The brothers lived many, many years ago. Ciaran, your many-times great-grandfather, lived in an Irish clan. His brother, my ancestor, lived in a town called Tristledermot."

The tingling grew until it covered every inch of Bri. "Castledermot, now."

"Yes. The brother I'm descended from is the reason the records were kept in these Bibles. Instructions passed from one generation to another, kept within both families. Stories that were to be told to each new generation, so that one day, when the time came, a woman would learn the truth of her destiny."

Bri glanced at Gran. The old woman she loved dearly looked back and smiled a worn, teary smile. "The time is now," Gran said. "Listen with your heart, dear one, not just your ears. Logic has no place here today."

Bri stirred her tea as she took in Gran's solemn eyes. "Tell me."

Grace raised an eyebrow. "Once you're told, you can't be untold. Your life will change, and I can't stop that."

That infernal prickle grew stronger. She wanted to ignore it, but it was too strong. "Fine."

"My ancestor, the oldest name in my Bible, was born in 1379. We don't know much about the first part of his life. That was never in the tales."

Gran nodded. "Not everything needed remembering."

"What we are quite sure of," Grace said, "is that he married in 1405, at the swearing stone at what is now called St. James' Church. The words he spoke were important enough that every member of our family has used the same vow when they're married at the stone."

"You learned the vow as a child, as have all the rest of our line," Gran said.

Bri snorted. She'd have forgotten the words long ago if Gran hadn't continually shoved them down her throat.

Grace leaned across the table and pushed her Bible closer to Bri. "Look."

Gran's hand twitched toward Bri, but at a glance from Grace, she pulled it into her lap and clasped both hands together. It didn't stop Bri from feeling the force of Gran's gaze.

"Why?" Bri didn't want to look at the Bible, suddenly afraid of what she'd find.

"I'll explain everything," Grace said, "after you look. Some things need to be done a certain way."

Hesitant, wishing she could look without an audience, Bri traced her way back to the first name recorded in the book. Heart in her throat, confused, she stared at the name. Written in bold strokes and faded ink was the name Duncan O'Leary. Beside that, the name of his wife. Brianna Hughes.

DUNCAN

"You're getting old," Duncan said, offering a hand to help Ciaran to his feet.

"Did you want to go another round?"

They were both breathing hard and dripping sweat. Tara may not have told them to join the wrestling match, but she'd certainly put the idea in their heads.

The bout had been long and the well-matched strength of blacksmith against blacksmith had drawn a crowd. Duncan stretched the knot in his back. "If neither of us won by now, I think we can abandon the field to another pair."

Ciaran nodded, then jogged over to where Tara watched. He stopped in front of her and flexed his muscles, showing off for his wife before scooping her into his arms for a kiss. Much to the crowd's delight. Duncan followed more slowly. When he was almost to the family, Colin came trotting out to him.

"It's my turn," he called to Duncan. "I bet I can beat you this year."

Duncan drew to a stop and grinned. "When you're ready, lad."

Colin ran back to his parents and ceremoniously hand over his knife. "So I don't truly hurt him."

The small boy stood before Duncan, waiting for the signal to start. The cheers from those watching were louder than they'd been even for Ciaran and Tara.

The signal came, and Colin launched himself at Duncan.

A careful dance followed on Duncan's part as he fought enough to be a challenge for Colin, yet not so hard as to overwhelm the boy.

When Colin began to tire, Duncan allowed himself to be pinned to the ground. The cheering couldn't have been louder.

"Did I hurt you, Uncle Duncan?" Colin's anxious face hovered over him.

Duncan jumped to his feet, raising Colin onto his shoulder as he did. With a whoop of victory, he ran the boy around the circle of onlookers before depositing him on his feet beside his parents. Duncan hadn't had such fun in years.

Ciaran solemnly held out Colin's knife. "Your blade, sir."

Colin collapsed in a pile of little boy giggles.

"Off to the river now, all three of you," Tara said, pushing them along. "Wash off the dirt. The feast begins soon."

They returned and started toward the gathering area.

"Stay nearby, Colin," Tara called over her shoulder as the boy slowed to watch a pair of older boys engaged in swordplay.

Duncan glanced at Colin, then at the groups of children playing and running free. "I'll stay with him. We'll join you later."

He dropped back to stand beside Colin. They watched as a sword was knocked from one opponent's hand and he ended up with the other boy's sword at his throat. Duncan joined in the applause, but his mind was on Colin. "Why aren't you running off with the other wild ones? Feast days are meant to be enjoyed."

Colin sighed, the weight of the world on his still-small shoulders. "Mother says I'm too young."

"Does she, now? And what do you think?"

"I'm not young. The other boys my age are being sent to foster with other clansmen." The boy took a deep breath and met Duncan's probing gaze. "I want to be fostered, too, but Mother won't allow it. She says I can learn to be a smith at home, there's no need to go anywhere. It's nice to hold something I've made myself, but I don't want to be a smith."

As he waited for the lad to find the courage needed to finish saying his piece, Duncan dug his toe in the ground. He sensed he'd not like what was coming.

Colin looked over where another game of swordplay was readying. "I want to be a warrior."

Duncan's chest tightened at the idea of the boy facing true battle, but he was smart enough to keep his concerns to himself. He stood his ground, waiting for Colin to continue.

"They'll not let me, and I don't know why."

"Have you asked them?"

Colin shook his head. He watched the swords flashing in the afternoon sun.

Duncan waited, but Colin didn't say anything else.

If it had been Duncan's son, what would he have done? His son would have been seven, hardly more than a year younger than Colin. Would he have allowed his worries to hold the boy back from living his dream?

He hoped not.

"Come with me." Duncan pushed his way through the people, Colin just behind him. He was about to make Ciaran and Tara very unhappy.

As they passed the pile of swords the contestants could choose from, he grabbed two of the smaller blades. He walked farther on, to an area with no audience. He turned and handed Colin a sword.

Colin's eyes widened and happy awe shone from his face.

"I can't force your parents to arrange a fostering, nor to allow you to become a warrior," Duncan said, cutting circles in the air as he tested the balance of the blade in his hand. "But every Irishman deserves the chance to know the weight of a sword in his hand."

Duncan walked Colin through the basic lessons most Irish boys learned using wooden swords when they were knee-high. Colin learned the movements quickly, pushing himself. They both knew this would be their only chance. For Colin, the chance was to dream. Duncan's chance was to teach a boy he loved as he would have loved the son he'd lost.

They practiced until Colin could hardly lift his shaking arm and the daylight began to dim. "What are you going to tell my parents?"

What indeed? The boy needed the freedom to grow, to learn and try new things. "I've no idea."

"No idea how to tell me you gave my son a sword?" Ciaran's voice cut through Duncan's thoughts.

Duncan turned to the sound and saw Ciaran's face, red with anger. "I didn't give it to him, they're borrowed."

"It makes no difference, as you well know." Ciaran turned to Colin. The boy shrank in on himself, all his joy and excitement doused. "Go find your mother, and if you value your life, tell her nothing of what you've been doing."

Colin dropped his sword and ran.

"That lad's dreams have been crushed," Duncan said, pointing after Colin's disappearing form. He refused to allow Ciaran to start their argument. "He's a half-grown lad who deserves to explore what kind of man he'll grow to be."

"Warriors don't live long lives," Ciaran yelled. "My son will not go off to battle to never return."

Duncan grabbed the front of Ciaran's *leine* in his fists and pulled him close. "That boy will run off to join them one day if you don't let him learn of the life warriors lead. If you want to keep him safe, let him try. There's a good chance he'll decide he prefers working with iron like his father, but forcing the lad will do no good."

Ciaran yanked free and started to stalk away. "Tell me that again when it's your son wanting to run off to battle."

Each word cut Duncan as deeply as the blade in his hand could have. "I'll never have that chance."

Ciaran stilled. He turned to Duncan with eyes that reflected Duncan's anguish.

Duncan picked up the sword Colin left behind and walked back to the pile he'd gotten them from. He couldn't listen to Ciaran's apology. It was naught but words.

Duncan put the crowd between himself and Ciaran. When he knew his foster brother could no longer see him, Duncan made his way to the horses. He easily found the giant beast he'd borrowed from Brogan. He mounted and, without a backward glance, buried his feet in the horse's sides and set off for Tristledermot at a gallop.

It was full night when he arrived. He was tired, and hungry, and drained. He'd known better than to interfere with Colin, and he'd done it anyway. Even Duncan knew what hurt most wasn't an argument with his friend.

He left the horse in Brogan's stable and walked through town to the graveyard, ignoring the few people staggering home from a late night at the tavern.

A simple iron cross, made by Duncan's own hands, marked the place where Neve and their tiny son, curled in her arms, rested. Wind rustled the leaves overhead. Duncan fell to his knees before the cross as tears tracked their way into his beard.

"I'm sorry." Duncan's voice was a hard, cracked whisper. "I'm so sorry."

The tears continued to fall, and after a time they brought a measure of peace where only anguish had been. "I'd have tried to be a good father," Duncan said, hoping there was some way the soul of his tiny son could hear his words. "I've hope I would have let you be who you needed to be."

Duncan opened his heart and allowed the dreams he'd pushed aside for years to surface. The image of his son learning to walk. The way he'd have taught the boy to use a child's sword, tromping through the burgage behind the smithy.

What would it have been like? Would they have argued and yelled, or laughed? Would Duncan have taught him to repair chains and make knives? Of course he would have. It was the way of the world. Trades were passed from parent to child.

Would Duncan and Neve have allowed him to foster? It would have broken his heart to allow the boy to leave — as his heart had shattered when he lost the dream of raising the boy.

And what of Neve?

Duncan tried to bring her face to mind, but it swam behind mists, refusing to come into view.

"Would you have stayed with me?" Duncan asked in his broken voice. "Or would you have left after that year and a day?"

Neve had grown annoyed with him more and more in the months before her death. Duncan had believed it was because of the pregnancy, but what if it hadn't been?

"I didn't love you enough, or well."

God knew he'd tried to be a good husband. He'd seen that Neve was well fed, and had anything she desired.

Duncan closed his eyes, unable to look at Neve's cross any longer. "I've learned things in the past days, Neve. I'm so very sorry. If I'd not been so callous I'd have left you free of me.

"Ciaran said you'd chosen me when we were both young. We didn't know what love was, Neve. Because of that, I didn't know enough to realize I didn't truly love you. I'd no idea. And because of it, I lost you."

Fifteen years. She'd only lived for fifteen years.

"There's a woman. I hardly know her but she does strange things to me. Every thought leads me to her." Duncan's voice began to pull itself back together. Still cracked, but he was able to make out the words he spoke. "I ache to hold her. She's teaching me, Neve. Teaching me of love. Showing me how it feels. It's nothing I've felt before."

Duncan reached out and steadied himself against the iron cross as he pushed to his feet.

"I'm so very sorry. You deserved much more than I could give you. I loved you. I did. But now I know what it is to be in love, I realize you didn't get the deep love you needed. I failed you."

On unsteady feet, Duncan left the graveyard.

He walked home and sat in the darkness. If he knew how, he'd wish the next day already past.

One more day before Brianna would be home from Galway and he could see her.

He needed her.

BRIANNA

ri stared at her name in the Bible, then looked up at Gran. "You always said I was named after one of our ancestors. It's this woman?"

Gran chuckled. "Tell me of your Duncan."

Bri glared. It was a private thing, not meant to be shared with strangers, even of the distantly related variety.

"It's happened?" Grace leaned forward, inching to the front of her seat. "You've seen Duncan at the swearing stone?"

Bri clamped her lips together. They were being ridiculous.

"You'd best share the rest of your story," Gran told Grace. "She's not likely to believe until you've said it all."

Grace sipped her tea and leaned back, nodding. "The story says that Duncan and his brother, Ciaran, were in the churchyard one summer night. It's not clear why, but Duncan put his hand through the swearing stone's hole."

Bri nodded. She could see that. The stone was a magnet for loose hands.

"As he spoke a vow, a woman appeared across from him. She repeated the words along with him and they were married."

It was like a practical joke. If Bri hadn't known any better, she'd think Gran had set her up. "You can't be serious."

Grace smiled and picked up a cookie. "That's the way the story goes. Brianna was from another time and place, but she traveled across centuries to be with the man she loved."

Bri closed her eyes and took a deep breath. When she opened her eyes, both the older women watched her. "You're saying she traveled through time?"

"What I'm telling you is going to be harder to believe than that," Grace said.

Why were things always harder and more complicated?

Grace smiled. "What the history of my line relies upon is the knowledge that *you* will travel back in time."

Bri stared at the woman. Grace was crazy, pure and simple. Which wouldn't be so bad if she hadn't suckered Gran into believing her.

Gran placed her old, gnarled fingers over Bri's smooth hand. "Our family's always known the reality of time travel."

"No. Gran, I love you, but you're allowing this woman's craziness to rub off on you."

The older women both laughed.

"Oh, dear one, what I wouldn't give to keep you here with me. Your fate lies in the past with your husband," Gran said. "You've seen him. Will you tell us about it?"

Bri shook her head, holding her hands in front of her chest as if she could shield herself from the request. This was one too many crazy things to happen on what was supposed to be a working trip. "I'm going for a walk. Maybe when I get back this will all have been a bad dream. Excuse me."

She was out the door and halfway down the street before her eyes uncrossed. Grace had seemed so normal, before the crazy came out to play.

Bri walked through the neighborhood, trying not to think.

If only her brain would cooperate. It was stuck on the time travel idea. It was the craziest thing in the crazy day.

Except — her name. It had been her own name in Grace's Bible. How was that possible? She'd always known she was named for one of her ancestors, but for the woman to share her last name as well? There hadn't been a single Hughes in their known line until her mother had gone and married the bastard who'd contributed to Bri's existence.

Bri had tried to change her last name after her mother died, but Gran insisted she keep Hughes. "Roots are important, dear one, even if we don't care for them. Perhaps especially then," she'd said. Bri had taken that name and turned it into something good for herself.

Now that name was in a Bible, linked to Duncan. Her husband.

While Bri wasn't exactly convinced time travel was possible, the fact that Grace knew what happened to her at the stone was making her rethink everything she thought she knew.

Half an hour later, Bri turned around and headed back to Grace's cottage. The nearer Bri got, the more she fought the strange pressure she'd felt whenever she'd seen Duncan. Bri was coming to both love and hate that electric vise. The idea that she might leave her time was scary. To think she might do it for a man she barely knew terrified her.

A tiny part of her mind insisted if she ever left her own time, it had better be for a man who kissed as well as Duncan.

Bri's face heated from the memory of his lips. She'd had her fair share of kisses in the past, but nothing came close to what she'd felt with Duncan. Her husband.

Her husband. If anyone had told her the warmth those words could fill her with, she'd have sworn they were lying.

She stopped at Grace's door. It took everything in her to raise her hand and knock.

The door opened quickly. Grace opened her mouth, but Bri beat her to it. "I'll listen. That's all I can promise."

The woman nodded briskly. "It's enough."

Grace led her into the back garden where Gran sat in a large, comfortable-looking chair on the patio, in the shade of a tree.

Bri sat in a matching chair facing Gran and turned to Grace. "What else can you tell me about Duncan and — me?"

"They're my grandparents, several generations removed, of course." She paused. Her eyes scrunched as she grinned. "It's a pleasure to meet you, Grandmother."

It was a good thing Bri was sitting down — there was nowhere for her to fall. Mentally, she'd understood Grace was claiming Duncan as her ancestor. It hadn't quite hit her that Grace claimed her as well.

"Did I not wait long enough?" Grace laughed. "I'm sorry, I know this is all new to you. I've spent my life wondering if I'd have the chance to meet you. You've seen Duncan. What's he like?"

"He's — he's Duncan," Bri said.

"She'd not have seen much," Gran said, coming to her rescue. "It was during the gloaming, and our Bri wasn't expecting anyone to be there. I've not seen her so surprised in years."

Grace watched a bird flitting in one of the trees, pretending not to smile. "Ah, but I know my stories. What of the other times you've seen him, Brianna?"

Gran tilted her head at Bri.

Bri flushed. "He's kind. Last night he brought food. Mutton and vegetables on a sort of hard bit of bread."

"You've eaten medieval food?" Gran glared. "When were you going to tell me?"

"I told you I had a date," Bri said, squirming.

"Right before you said you went to the churchyard." Gran's eyes sparkled as she made the connection. "I'm older than I thought to not see that before now."

"You say I go back to Duncan's time," Bri said. It wasn't easy to pretend she believed it possible to travel through time, but she found herself wanting to believe. "Why couldn't he come here instead?"

Grace bit her lip. "The stories don't say. Caitriona, do any of your side's stories explain that?"

"None," Gran said. "I've never considered it before. Since the stories are of things already past, there was never the need to second guess them."

Bri growled. Why was her life any less important to stay in than Duncan's?

"Perhaps your husband needed to stay where he could make a living," Gran guessed. "Men have always protected and provided for their families. If your man came here, what would he do? What kind of job would be open to a man with different skills and a very different education that what we have today?"

There were all sorts of things Bri could have said about the idea of relying on a man for everything when she was perfectly capable of providing for herself. Instead, she focused on Gran's question. "There are blacksmiths today. Maybe not as many, but there are definitely people who make a living as smiths."

"He's a blacksmith? I wonder why that was never passed down." Grace pinned Bri with a sharp look. "You could ask your children to pass along more details. Some of your descendants have been very curious about their heritage."

Children? Bri swallowed hard. "What? I don't want to have kids. I've never liked kids, even when I was one."

Grace laughed. "If my Bible is to be believed — or my existence, for that matter — you do have them."

Bri scowled.

Gran reached for her hand. "One crisis at a time, lass. Let's focus on the time travel, shall we?"

Bri swallowed again and bobbed her head. "If we pretend for a minute that this is possible, why would I leave everything I have here? My career's just taking off. I've spent years working to be recognized as a photographer and I've finally made it. Why would I ever give that up for a man I don't even know, just because the two of you say I've already done it?"

"We don't know when this happens," Grace said. "It could be tomorrow, or not for years."

"It will be soon," Gran said. "The stories all agree on when the wedding took place."

"In the past, yes, but time may be moving differently for Duncan than it is for Brianna," Grace said.

Bri shook her head. "It's moving the same. A day now is a day back then."

"The tale of the brothers tells us by the time of the attack on Tristledermot, Duncan had a wife." Gran's voice was certain.

"It could have been talking about his first wife," Bri said with a shrug.

"He was already married?" Grace reached for the arms of her chair.

"Well, yeah. She died in childbirth." Surely one of the old stories would have talked about that. "That's why Duncan didn't want to be married again."

Grace slowly leaned back. "But —"

"That's nothing to do with this story," Gran said. She raised a hand to still Grace's response. "Brianna, has your Duncan told you what the year is in his time?"

Bri's skin did the prickling thing again. "1405. Why?"

"The Leinster king attacked Tristledermot in 1405. Not only from our stories," Gran said, "but from history."

Tristledermot was going to be attacked, while Duncan lived there? Bri struggled for breath. She pushed herself to her feet and looked around for her purse. "I need to warn him. We need to go. Now."

Gran shook with laughter. "This was your favorite story. You've no need to do the warning."

Her favorite story. That meant it had a decent ending. She thought, trying to remember the words of the story she'd made Gran repeat every night. Her panic eased a little. "Duncan and Ciaran save them.

But what if—" Bri pulled a deep breath through her teeth as her heart pounded in her ears. "Gran, what if the story is wrong?"

Gran shifted, settling herself more firmly. "Would you have allowed the story to be passed down for today if it was?"

Hadn't Gran ever played Telephone as a kid? Stories can distort, or change to something completely different as they're passed from one person to another. "There's always the chance."

"You're rather concerned about this for someone who claims no feelings for the man."

Bri felt her cheeks heat. "I never said there weren't feelings."

Grace beamed. "So you do love him."

"I — I — No. I don't. I might be attracted to him, and want to kiss him again. I certainly want him to stay alive, but that doesn't mean I love him."

"I'd like to know how you expect to keep your man alive from here," said Gran.

"I'm more interested in how you kissed Duncan when the stories say you could only touch through the hole in the stone."

Bri looked at Grace, horror curling in her stomach. She'd done it again. If she didn't learn better control of her tongue she'd have to run away to the past just to get away from her slip-ups. She slowly sank back into her chair.

"A juicy kiss, was it?" Gran asked, giggling at Bri's embarrassment.

"We're not going to talk about that." Bri hoped that would be the end of it.

Gran patted her hand. "I've not had a good kiss in some time, but I remember the excitement. Tell us about it."

Bri shook her head. There was no way she was having that conversation.

Grace took pity on her. "Do you want to know the rest of what I'm to tell you?"

"Yes. Please." Grace might be her favorite person.

"There are . . . practicalities," Grace said. "Things for when you travel back to Duncan."

Bri bit her tongue. She didn't want to upset Grace, not when the woman had just kept her from a conversation she'd give almost anything to avoid. "Like what?"

"Modern clothes would not be accepted."

Bri looked down at her shorts and laughed. "Too much leg?"

Gran chuckled, while Grace just smiled. "I'd like to say it would be a good way to run the Anglo-Normans right out of Ireland, but we all know the truth to be different."

She wasn't going back in time. Probably. Then why was Bri so curious all of a sudden? "Do I have to wear something crazy? Or — oh! — do I get to have a silk gown?"

"Your husband isn't a lord, dear," Gran said. "You've seen too many movies."

"Do you know what a kirtle is?" Grace asked.

DUNCAN

n aching neck pulled Duncan from strange dreams filled with echoing laughter and light that seared the insides of his eyelids.

Slowly, he opened his eyes. His home was dark. There wasn't so much as the glow of a single coal in the hearth.

With a sigh, Duncan reached for a flint to light the candle on the table in front of him.

Duncan stretched his neck, trying to remember why he'd fallen asleep in a chair rather than moving to his bed.

The pain of the night came rushing back. This time, however, it was gentler, tempered by a night of sleeping like the dead. He hadn't loved his wife.

He shook his head. He'd loved Neve, but he'd loved her as a friend. At the time, he'd not known there was more.

Now that he'd begun to learn more of love, he refused to live without it.

Duncan lifted the strip of linen covering a few oatcakes, left from his morning meal the previous day. He took one and began to eat as

beyond the swearing stone

he moved to his window and swung the wooden shutters open wide.

Small beams of daylight had just begun to lick away the darkness of the night sky. Peace filled Duncan at the sight. The past would stay where it was, but there was hope in the new day.

Finished with the oatcake, Duncan readied himself for the day. As he went down the stairs to light the charcoal in the smithy, the town was just coming to life.

Wheels creaked as heavily-laden carts rolled by, and the first cries of greeting and welcome rent the air. Duncan grinned. He looked forward to market days. People came in from the surrounding areas, bringing with them broken tools and such that needed fixing. He'd stay busy today.

After starting the charcoal, Duncan went into the storage rooms below his living space and chose a selection of knives and tools to display for sale.

"Will you be using one of those knives on me?"

Duncan glanced over his shoulder and his good mood soured. "I've no time for you today, Ciaran. No patience, either. Leave me be."

With his arms full, Duncan pushed past Ciaran and hung his wares on nails hammered into the side of the smithy.

"I can't take back my words, but I can apologize for them," Ciaran said. "If you'd let me."

The weight from the night before tried to settle back on Duncan's shoulders. "I said to leave me be."

Ciaran leaned against the doorway. "You've every right to ask me to leave. I'd go, but Tara told me not to return before making things right with you."

Duncan sighed. He didn't want his foster brother hanging around the forge all day. "If I say I'm not angry, will that suffice?"

"I shouldn't have said what I did, and I'm sorry for my loose tongue. I was angry." Ciaran walked over and took a length of chain from Duncan's shoulder to hang on the wall.

"I understand," Duncan said. He did understand, and given a few days more he'd not hold it against Ciaran. "Must we speak of it?"

Ciaran went back into the storage room. When he came out he was carrying another chain, this one with smaller links. He added the chain to the wall beside the first, then smiled at Duncan. "Not if you'd rather not."

"Good."

Another cart passed the smithy. "The road was crowded with people coming to market. Do you want help today?"

All Duncan wanted was to be left alone. "Do you never have work to do at your own forge?"

Ciaran chuckled. "Aye, there's work waiting. Too much." He sobered and closed the distance between them. "Word has gone out that MacMurrough is gathering his forces. There are swords to sharpen and knives to sell. It's another reason for me to stay. I'd not have my weapons used against you. Against your neighbors, aye, but I'd not have my blades slice through you."

"It won't come to that."

"It could." Ciaran's stubborn voice refused to leave the matter be.

Duncan paused, his hand still on the fire tongs he'd been straightening. "You know in the past we've paid the Leinster king to leave us be. We can do it again."

Ciaran shook his head. "There's more to it this time. I've heard MacMurrough wants the invaders to pay for the use of roads throughout Leinster."

Duncan shook his head and stepped inside the smithy. He began to pump the bellows, increasing the heat of the burning charcoal. "You say he wants money. I say we can give it to him. He gets what he wants, and the town is left alone."

Ciaran muttered a string of curses.

Duncan caught a grin. He wasn't ready to let go of his anger toward Ciaran, but he could imagine the look Ciaran's wife would assume if she'd been there. If Tara knew the filth that came from her husband's mouth, she'd not let it near her.

beyond the swearing stone

"We'll meet whatever comes," Duncan said.

From outside the smithy, a voice hollered. The first of his market day customers. Ciaran, still mumbling to himself, took the man's chain inside to mend while Duncan spoke with the customer.

A steady stream of customers kept Duncan busy through the morning, and he found himself grateful for Ciaran's help. Perhaps it was time he agreed to take an apprentice.

His mind jumped to Brianna. An apprentice could wait. He had a wife to woo.

When the bell tolled Sext, Duncan set down his tools and joined Ciaran in the smithy's burgage. "I'm going for food. Will you come, or should I bring something back for you?"

"I'll join you." Ciaran set aside the scythe he was sharpening.

Together they walked around the corner to the market square. Winding their way through the vendors with their crowds of customers, Duncan led the way, following the scent of cooking meat.

Ciaran mumbled something about a toy for the baby and headed to a cart surrounded by children. They jostled each other, each trying to see what toys were on display.

Duncan shrugged and began to wander the market as he ate. He moved from one vendor to the next, unsure what he was looking for.

He walked the square twice and nothing jumped out at him. Duncan was oddly disappointed by that. He wanted something, he just lacked the knowledge of what it might be.

A woman passed by, several bundles of fabric in her arms.

Brianna. Duncan realized he'd been searching for something his wife would like. He grinned. Now he knew what he was after, it would be easy to come up with something.

Twice more through the square, and Duncan was coming to realize that shopping for a woman he was just beginning to know was more difficult than he'd imagined.

He was running out of time. Duncan needed to get back to work — he had orders to fill.

With no other option left to him, he went to the fabric seller. He had to push his way through a cluster of women to reach the soft piles. They shot curious looks his way, and Duncan just managed to bite back the curse at seeing the woman in the center of the group was Brogan's wife.

"Just the man we were talking about," Alana said. "I was telling the women how you said our husbands were no longer welcome at the smithy."

Duncan sighed. He should have known he'd have to face the woman at some point. Would it have been too much to ask that it not be while he was shopping for a gift? "They're welcome, so long as you ladies control yourselves. I won't have you meddling in my life. I've no need of your help. If you'll excuse me."

They all spoke at once, but Duncan's back was already turned. He reached for a head kerchief. It was blue silk, the color as pale as a robin's egg. It was as soft against his skin as Brianna's lips. It would be perfect against her dark hair and eyes.

Without bothering to argue over price, he paid for the scarf. With the kerchief in hand, he turned. He nearly toppled Brogan's wife, she stood so near.

"Excuse me. I need to get back to the smithy."

She tried again to stop him, but he didn't stop. The woman needed no help in creating gossip. The women of the town were likely to all know about the kerchief before None.

Duncan sighed. Busybodies.

When he reached the smithy, he immediately went up to his living quarters. He placed the kerchief on the table and fingered the softness once more. He hoped Brianna would like it.

Just as he reached the bottom of the stairs, a man approached to pick up a tool he'd left for repair.

A constant trickle of people were in and out of the smithy. Duncan hardly noticed when Ciaran returned and disappeared upstairs. He was grateful when Ciaran joined him. Duncan was used to being busy on market days, but this was the busiest day he could remember. Which was good, if he was going to be buying silks.

He felt his face pull into a smile.

"What's got you in such a good mood?" Ciaran asked as they began to move the tools and knives back into the storage room.

Duncan's smile became a grin. "It's been a good day."

"You'll have brought in enough to pay for the pile of silk on your table." Ciaran's voice was dry, but there was mirth behind the words. "I assume it's for your mystery woman?"

"Brianna's no mystery," Duncan said. "But aye, it's for her."

Ciaran put the last of the tools in the storage room. They latched the door and went in to clean up the smithy. "If she's not a mystery, why have you not said more of her?"

Duncan laughed, his heart warming. "I'm not ready to share her yet."

That was all. He was keeping her to himself for the time being. Duncan knew eventually he'd need to tell Ciaran more than he had, but she was too special to share just yet.

"You're in love. You can tell me of her. I won't tease you," Ciaran said. "You've no one else to talk to about her and I want to hear about the woman who has you grinning like a fool."

Duncan shook his head at his friend, but was hardly bothered by the jab. "You'll not let this go until you know something, will you?"

"Taking information back is about the only way Tara will believe you've forgiven me for yesterday."

They'd finished cleaning the smithy and preparing it for morning. As they walked into the open air, Duncan gave in. "Come upstairs and I'll tell you of her."

Ciaran grinned and turned to lead the way.

"Duncan."

Duncan turned to see Brogan walking toward them. Remembering the rudeness he'd shown the man's wife, Duncan paused. "What can I do for you?"

"My wife is telling everyone who will listen that you bought a woman's silk kerchief today."

"I figured she would," Duncan said, holding back a sigh. The only surprise was that it had taken this long for anyone to approach him over it. "It's meant for a gift."

Brogan laughed. "The women would like to know who you plan to give this silk to."

"So they sent you to get it out of me?"

"Aye. You refused to tell my wife."

Ciaran left the staircase and came over. "You can tell the ladies that Duncan was helping me shop for my family today." He clasped Duncan's shoulder. "It was only fair to make him help, since he had me working in the smithy all day."

Brogan's face fell. "Wouldn't you rather tell me you'd chosen one of the girls from town to court? It would make things much easier on me when I get home."

Duncan scratched his beard. He could let Ciaran help him out again — and after what he'd said at the feast day, the man owed him. Or he could tell Brogan he had his eye on a woman, which would make life miserable as the women ganged up on him.

"I can't help you," Duncan told Brogan. "I'm afraid you'll have to deal with your wife yourself."

The innkeeper walked off, grumbling.

"I owe you."

"You do," said Ciaran. "You can pay your debt by telling me of your Brianna."

BRIANNA

Kirtles and over-kirtles. Gowns, cloaks, and head-wear. Bri sighed. The lesson Grace had given her on medieval clothing might have been interesting, but it was overwhelming. Apparently, Bri needed to know what type of clothing was worn in town by the Anglo-Normans, and the different clothes worn by the Irish.

Thoughts of clothes had filled the drive back to Castledermot. Gran was more than happy to keep up a running commentary that made it unnecessary for Bri to be mentally present for a conversation.

By the time they arrived back at the B&B, Bri was ready for some time to herself. She helped Gran into the house and grabbed her laptop.

"Will you be alright for a while?" Bri asked. "I need to go to the library. The magazine is getting anxious and wants me to send them some of the pictures I've taken."

Hopefully they wouldn't ask for more than she had. Bri couldn't believe she didn't have more to choose from. She'd allowed herself to get too distracted.

"Aye. I'll rest a bit and work on my knitting." Gran laughed. "Then

I've a mind to work with that wee spindle you brought me. When you're done maybe you could help an old lady spin some yarn."

"Of course," Bri said. She could help — later. After she'd had space to breathe for a while.

Bri reached for the door just as it swung open. She jumped back to avoid being smacked in the face.

"Sorry about that," Ryan said. "I didn't realize you were there."

"I'm just on my way to the library." If she was lucky, everyone would leave her alone so she could actually make it there.

Ryan's face fell. "Oh. I'd hoped you might be spending the afternoon here. My father's coming into town. He'd like to see your coin in person."

Bri shivered. She didn't want anyone touching the coin. Which was completely irrational — or at least, it would appear to be. Ryan and his father wouldn't understand she'd be handing over a token of her marriage. "I'll be back in a while. I just need to do a few things for work."

Without waiting for a reply, she scooted past Ryan and out the door. She was halfway down the block before breathing easily. At the corner she turned onto Main Street. The library wasn't far, and it was nice to stretch her legs after driving all the way from Galway.

Bri paused at the library's wrought iron gate. The building was set back off the road, leaving a front garden lined with boxwoods and other shrubbery. Strips of lawn lined the drive.

The white building's lancet-arch front windows were beautiful leaded stained glass, and clearly defined the place as a repurposed church.

Bri walked up the drive and followed the short ramp to the door. She paused again, grinning, as she ran her fingers over the curls on the hinges. She would have been happy about the old world charm anyway, but wondering if Duncan created similar things made her love the detail even more.

Inside Bri found a soft, if somewhat uncomfortable, chair and set up her laptop. She itched to explore the little library, but she needed to get her work done first.

She pulled up the pictures she'd taken, scrolling through them. A picture of the round tower and another of the North Cross at St. James' Church would work. There were several from her visit to Rindoon that would be perfect, and a handful from the stops they'd made at different sites along the way back from Galway.

Her favorite picture was of the swearing stone, ringed with flowers. Her favorite, perhaps, but it was too personal to share.

As she made her final selections and put them through a round of cropping and tweaking, her excitement grew. Some of the pictures were even better than she'd hoped now she could see them on a larger screen.

She'd made it. This job was given to her as a trial, but she's nailed it with these pictures. There was no question that this trip would change her life. Even if the magazine didn't hire her full-time, these pictures would open the doors to so many freelance opportunities.

Bri had worked hard for this moment. It had taken every bit of perseverance she had. So why, when she should have felt completely fulfilled, did her victory feel hollow?

As she leaned back in her chair, noises from others in the library cut through Bri's focus. Over near the librarian, a woman crouched down to help her small daughter choose which book to look at. By the library's computers, a teenaged girl laughed and gave the boy she was with a heated look.

Every place her eyes landed, she saw connections between people. Families, friends, lovers. She'd never cared that her only connection was with Gran — unless she counted the blood connection with her father, but as she hadn't seen him in years she never did count it. But the connections around her today made her realize she'd missed out.

Bri reached into the front pocket of her shorts. The gold was warm on her fingers as she pulled out the coin. She turned it in her hand, watching the way the light caught the markings. A small trickle of power made its way up her arm. The feeling from the barrier.

It connected her to Duncan. She couldn't explain how, she just knew it was true.

She looked around the library again. Everyone there was connected. Not just to the people they were interacting with, but in some intangible way each person in this community was connected. It wasn't what she was used to. Back home, you could pass the same person every day and not even realize it.

Did she really want to go back to that? She didn't have to. She could move to a small town somewhere, where people got involved in everyone's business. Bri couldn't imagine she'd belong in a small town any more than she belonged in the city. She'd never really belonged anywhere. It had never bothered her before now.

The coin in her hand glinted. Maybe there was somewhere she belonged.

Bri shivered. She had to admit, Duncan was attractive. He probably had women falling all over him. Why, then, had he kissed her? He'd made her feel important. Beautiful. Loved.

His attentions were flattering in a way that made her love the secrecy, and the impossibility of it all. Bri was just starting to realize she was enjoying more than the feeling of being attractive.

She gasped as it hit her. Duncan made her — awkward, mousey little Bri — feel like she belonged. Bri slammed her laptop closed, ignoring the curious glances from the people around her.

She launched herself to her feet and made a beeline for the door. Outside, she stopped. She pressed her back against the wall and focused on pulling the air in and out of her lungs.

"Bri?"

Bri opened her eyes. Ryan loped toward her, his long legs eating away the distance between them. The man beside him shared his crooked nose and easy smile. She took another long breath, wishing she'd stayed inside. "Hi."

The older man held out his hand to shake Bri's. "My name is Eoin. I'm Ryan's father." He smiled.

It should have been a reassuring smile, but Bri was already on edge. "It's nice to meet you."

"Sorry to interrupt," Ryan said. "But my father can't stay in town much longer."

Eoin winked. "I'd wager she's finished with her work, son, as she's on her way out of the library."

Maybe she could escape back inside and hide out in the ladies' room. Before she could turn around, Eoin took her by the elbow and started to walk her to the street.

"Um, I just came out for a bit of fresh air. I still have a few things to do before I can call it a day." They didn't need to know she was running away from herself.

Ryan's forehead creased. "Da, we're interrupting. You can see Bri's coin next time you're in town."

Bri bit back a laugh. She'd almost forgotten the older man had wanted to see her coin. Part of her had remembered. It had to be why she'd taken an immediate dislike to the poor man.

She didn't want to share her coin. Didn't want anyone to touch it, or even see it. But they knew she had it. It would be rude to pretend she'd lost it.

"I've got a few minutes to spare," Bri said. She could have kicked herself — or Gran, for teaching her to be polite above all else.

Eoin rubbed his hands together.

Trying to push aside her reluctance, Bri reached back into her pocket.

"You can't carry around a precious heirloom in your pocket." Eoin stared at Bri, disbelief pouring off him.

Bri shrugged. "I like to keep it close."

Eoin reached for the coin. Bri barely kept herself from snatching it back from his fingers.

For several minutes, Bri clasped her hands together to keep herself from doing something Gran would scold her for. Every minute stretched longer than the last.

"Where did you say you got this?"

Bri glanced at Ryan before answering Eoin's question. "It was a gift."

Eoin harrumphed. "This is no gift. People don't give gifts like this."

Bri watched the passing cars on the street behind the men. What she wouldn't give to escape in one of them. "All I can tell you is that it was given to me."

"It's perfect, and definitely gold. The only problem is the lack of wear. A real coin from this era would be worn, even a well-preserved specimen." Eoin sounded like he was trying to convince himself. "Perhaps we could verify the age by analyzing a sliver of the gold."

Bri stopped trying to behave herself. She snatched the coin out of his hand. "I don't need it verified. It doesn't matter to me what time period anyone thinks it's from. That's not why I hold on to it."

Ryan stepped in, trying to smooth things over. "Don't you want to be able to properly insure the coin?"

"We could do preliminary verification with pictures," Eoin offered.

Bri shook her head and slipped the coin back into her pocket. "I'm not really comfortable with that."

Eoin's jaw tightened. "Don't be a fool."

If the man thought Bri was a pushover, or would be easy to convince, he had another think coming. She had nearly as much Irish blood as Eoin and Ryan.

"I should be asking you to take it to a museum," he continued.

Bri snickered. "It belongs in a museum?"

"Aye."

Eoin looked so indignant Bri laughed outright.

Ryan cleared his throat. "It's Bri's coin, Da. Her choice."

"But —" Eoin spluttered. "Who gave it to you? Where did they get it? Any new artifacts belong to the Irish museum, regardless of who finds them."

Bri shook her head. "I'm sorry. I can't tell you who gave it to me, and you wouldn't believe me if I could. If it makes you feel any better it really was a gift, not some relic I discovered at Rindoon."

Ryan smiled at her. "Sorry," he mouthed.

"I should get back inside and finish my work. I need to send an email for work." Bri nodded to Ryan.

The men didn't leave, so Bri turned and went back inside the library. Hopefully Ryan would convince his father to leave soon. The library was only open for another fifteen minutes.

Bri went back to her chair and examined her coin. So much fuss. She never should have let Ryan see it. She should have kept it in her pocket that day, or remembered to grab it when she'd gotten back to the B&B.

She sighed, watching the coin catch the light as she turned it over and over in her hand. Even if she'd wanted to, she couldn't have let Eoin take the coin for testing. It had almost become a part of her.

Gran — Grace — they'd both assured Bri she'd travel back to Duncan's time. Bri might have played along so they'd stop shoving the idea down her throat, but she didn't know if she could do it — even if it turned out time travel was possible. It would mean giving up on her dream of being a photographer. Not just any photographer, but one of the best.

The sense of rightness the coin gave her left Bri facing the question of whether she would give up her dream to live in a place, or a time, where she could feel she belonged.

Bri cursed. She was used to feeling awkward. Isolated. Why should it bother her now?

Her mind drifted back to the people she'd noticed earlier, and their connections. Her sense of rightness grew, and she knew.

She'd give up everything for the right connections. To live with a person she truly belonged with.

Bri toyed with her hair as she thought. She and Duncan needed to know each other better, but in her heart she knew it didn't matter. She wanted to belong somewhere, wanted the connection everyone around her had. If she gave up the life she had, she could have the life she dreamed of, with the man she was already starting to love.

Bri took a long, shaking breath. She'd follow through with her assignment to photograph the local medieval sites. Then, somehow, she'd find her way through time. It would be interesting to see how medieval ruins looked when they were whole.

DUNCAN

Duncan closed the front shutters with a *thunk*, hoping to lessen the noise of the town. He'd also not like his neighbors listening to Ciaran's words — the man always did raise his voice when excited.

Smoke from the candles burning on the table floated through the room and his maddening friend sat grinning at him. The floor creaked as he made his way to sit across from Ciaran.

"Do I get to meet your Brianna?" Ciaran asked. "She sounds interesting."

Duncan sighed. He'd told Ciaran much more than he'd planned. Tara must have taught the man how to extract details.

"Interesting how you can only touch her through the swearing stone." Ciaran paused. "Have you tried pushing the barrier aside?"

"Aye," Duncan said. He'd no intention of admitting the barrier allowed him to touch his own lips to Brianna's. That memory was for him alone.

Ciaran leaned halfway across the table. "When will you be seeing her again?"

"That's no business of yours." Duncan had no desire for his foster brother to join him in the churchyard. "You'll not be meeting her."

"You don't think she'd see me if I held her hand through the stone?" He laughed.

Duncan broke off a piece of his bread and threw it at Ciaran's head. "You said you'd keep yourself from teasing."

"I suppose I did." Ciaran grinned. "I'm glad you've finally found a woman who'll have you, after all these years of chasing them."

Duncan laughed.

"Sorry. I know the women have done everything they can to corner you into marriage. Still, it's nice to see you happy."

That impossible grin took over behind Duncan's beard again. His face was beginning to hurt from all the smiling. "Are you staying the night, then, or hurrying home to Tara?"

"Are you sleeping the night in your bed, or sneaking out to see Brianna?" Ciaran's challenge left Duncan wanting to wallop him.

Duncan glanced in the shadowed corners. He was unsurprised to find no one lurking in them, but he felt the need to reassure himself their conversation was private. "I hardly need sneak when it's my own wife I'd be seeing."

Ciaran grinned. "Then you are planning to see her."

"Aye. And you'll not be coming, even if you choose to stay the night. I've not seen Brianna in two days. I want her to myself."

"Not like you can get up to much with that barrier between you," Ciaran said.

"You'll stay here," Duncan said, pushing to his feet. He wasn't much taller than Ciaran, but even a small amount could be intimidating in the right circumstances. "If you don't, I'll tell Tara you wouldn't apologize properly."

Ciaran cursed. "You'd do that to me?"

"If need be." Duncan picked up the silk kerchief and tucked it into his belt. He walked to the door, keeping his eye on Ciaran. "I need time to get to know my wife. Make yourself comfortable. I'll be back by morning."

Duncan went down the stairs, whistling. There was no need to make sure Ciaran stayed behind — his threat would do the job.

A fresh layer of straw had been added to the road sometime during the day. It crunched under Duncan's feet as he walked, blending with the sounds of living that came through windows and doors.

Duncan was nearly to the tavern when Brogan came out into the street. He just managed to slide into the deeper darkness between doorways. If Brogan had been sober, he'd have noticed Duncan and stopped.

With a sigh of relief at not being waylaid, Duncan passed the tavern and made his way down the narrow street toward the churchyard.

He slipped into the peace surrounding the church. There was no hesitating this time. He went straight to the back side of the swearing stone. Anticipation filled him. He reached his hand into the hole. He was the earliest he'd yet been, but he was prepared to wait as long as needed in order to see Brianna.

Duncan's fingers immediately brushed against warmth, and Brianna came into view. Her dark hair spilled over her shoulders in soft curls, and her skin was nearly translucent in the moonlight. The bridge of her freckled nose wrinkled as she grinned at him.

His breath caught in his throat. She seemed more beautiful every time he saw her. "Did you wait long?"

As Brianna shook her head, her hair flipped around her face. "No. I just got here."

"I'd not noticed before how your hair curls just so." Duncan could have bashed his head into the stone in front of him. He'd not meant to voice his observation.

Brianna lifted a curl and gave it a look more appropriate to discovering she'd stepped in a cow patty. "It's the humidity. No matter what I try, I can't keep the curl out."

"Don't try." He sounded like a fool. He cleared his throat. "Did you enjoy Galway?"

She snorted. Duncan hid a grin — he'd never heard a woman make such a sound.

"Galway was not what I expected. Things with my relatives weren't exactly normal." Brianna looked like she had more to say, but she pulled her lip between her teeth instead.

Duncan forced his eyes away from Brianna's mouth. It was as difficult as shaping cold iron. "Will you tell me of them?"

Brianna laughed. It was a short laugh, more like a huff. "The woman's name is Grace. She has a couple of very sweet daughters." She paused. "Gran wanted to see their family Bible."

Duncan furrowed his brow. "She owns a Bible? Was one of her relatives a priest?"

"Anyone can own a Bible in my time. Books are printed by a machine now." Brianna paused again and a crease formed between her eyes. "Give it another fifty or seventy-five years and people in your time will be able to buy them."

Duncan shook his head. He couldn't understand what she meant, but he didn't care. He just wanted to look at her, and to hear her voice. "Then why would your Grandmother need to see it?"

Brianna shifted her weight. "Their family Bible — as well as ours — has a genealogy in it." She tilted her head at his confusion. "A record that shows the names of parents and children, going back in time. Ours goes back to the last part of the fourteenth century. Back to your time."

They had record of people who lived now? "Do you remember the names? Perhaps I know them."

"I don't really want to talk about that right now," Brianna said, shaking her head again. She leaned over, reaching for something. "I brought you something. The food you brought the other night was delicious. It made me think you might want to try some of the foods we eat now."

She was so excited to share with him. Duncan couldn't bring himself to tell her he'd eaten just before coming to see her.

"I stopped by the café earlier and got several different things and cut them into smaller pieces so I could pass them to you. We call this a hamburger." Brianna pushed something through the hole to him, squashing it a bit so it would fit.

Duncan raised it up to look at it. Some kind of cooked meat in the middle, with soft bread above and below. There was something green that looked similar to cabbage, as well as other things he didn't recognize. Unsure what to expect, he took a bite.

He blinked in surprise. There were so many flavors. Duncan smiled at Brianna. Her eyes were glued to his, watching for something. He swallowed. "It's delicious. The flavors are very strong."

Brianna laughed. "If that's too strong maybe I shouldn't have you try the curry."

"Perhaps a small taste." Duncan was curious about the food, but more importantly, he'd do nothing to disappoint Brianna. She wanted him to taste the foods she'd brought, so taste them he would.

He put a small amount of the food she passed through into his mouth. His eyes began to burn, and he gasped in cooler air, trying to stop the fire in his mouth.

When he could see again, Brianna's lips were pinched together and her eyes were full of laughter. She lifted an odd-looking cup with a stick poking out of it. "Would you like a drink? It will help cool your mouth down." She pointed to the stick. "I think we can get the straw through the hole and still have the other end reach the drink. Just suck on it."

Not sure he wanted to try it, but willing to do anything for the woman, Duncan leaned down and did as she said. A cold liquid filled his mouth. Little bubbles popped and fizzed on his tongue. He managed to keep his spluttering to himself. Mostly.

"I have a dessert for you to try, if you want. It's called apple crisp, and it's very sweet."

He looked up at Brianna standing above him. His heart stretched as he fell a little more in love with her. "I'll try anything for you."

Even in the moonlight Duncan could see the color rise to her face. She made a noise in her throat and passed a flimsy white spoon through the hole. He ate the mouthful off the end. It was very sweet. The most unusual thing was the combination of heat and cold on his tongue.

"How do you make food so cold?"

Brianna smiled again, her whole face lighting up at his pleasure. "That cold food is called ice cream. Do you like it?"

Duncan could only nod. The foods she'd brought had so much flavor. She couldn't possibly have enjoyed the mutton he'd given her. But she'd acted as if she enjoyed it, and he couldn't see her being untruthful.

Brianna's tongue brushed over her lower lip. It took all of Duncan's strength to keep himself from leaning in to kiss her again.

"The other night, you asked —" Brianna paused, ducking her head. "You asked me if I wanted this. If I wanted to be your wife."

Duncan's heart nearly stopped. He studied her face, but no hint of what she felt could be seen. "Aye. I did ask."

"See, the thing is, I never wanted to get married. Never wanted a family." Brianna reached up to brush hair off her forehead. "I was confused."

She didn't want him. Duncan tried to nod. He'd finally learned to care again, and Brianna didn't want him. He looked away. "I'm sorry. I'd not meant to pressure you."

Brianna tugged on his hand where their fingers joined through the stone until he raised his eyes to hers. "You didn't pressure me. All sorts of other things were pressuring me, but not you. I've had time to think about what I want, and what I feel."

Duncan straightened, waiting for Brianna to say the words that would crush him.

"I want it." Brianna's smile started small, but quickly grew to fill her face. "I want to be married to you. I want you to kiss me silly, and I want to be your everything."

Duncan stared. He couldn't believe her words. If he did, and she changed her mind — it would kill him.

Brianna bounced a little, waiting. When he still couldn't find words, her face fell. "I'm sorry," she whispered. "I thought you wanted this."

"I do," Duncan finally managed to say. He wanted it, wanted everything with her, but he suddenly found himself scared to reach out and claim it.

He watched as Brianna's smile returned. She was so beautiful it hurt.

"I do, Brianna. I want you as my wife." His voice was stronger. He was finding the ground again. He felt his beard twitch as he began to smile with her.

No longer able to control himself, Duncan reached for his wife. Her soft lips met his. The kiss started gently, just a hint at what he felt for her.

He lifted his free hand, wrapping it in Brianna's hair, tilting her head as he deepened the kiss. Her lips parted, and he kissed her more, claiming her with everything he was. She belonged to him.

Duncan pulled back a fraction, trying to catch his breath. Brianna followed him, and she was claiming him. He felt her warmth as she kissed his face, raining kisses on his eyes, and his cheeks, and in his beard before returning to his lips.

"Brianna." Duncan moaned her name into her mouth. He dropped his hand from her hair and wrapped his arm around her waist, pulling her closer, pressing her into his chest.

It wasn't enough. He needed more of her. More than her lips, more than the feel of her in his arms. More than her chest crushed against his above the stone.

Brianna's hand was in his hair, then stroking his beard. He'd never felt anything like it. The soft tugging undid him. He needed her.

With no thought beyond lifting her into his arms, Duncan let go of Brianna's hand.

The soft, pliable woman he'd held against him was gone.

Duncan allowed his arm to fall to his side. Slowly, he reached again for the hole in the stone.

Brianna came back into view. She held a hand over her heart and her large eyes were wide. "What happened?"

"I wanted to hold you properly." A need he felt still.

His wife — the woman who left him breathless — shook her head. "No. I meant — we were able to touch."

Duncan caught his breath as her words hit him. He thought of her soft hair tangled in his hand, and the tug of her fingers in his beard. The touch of her chest rising and falling against his own. "How?"

There was no denying it, no trying to convince himself he'd imagined it. He could still feel where she'd fitted against him.

Brianna let out a shaking breath. Duncan reached out his hand. The smooth softness of her cheek met his calloused palm.

He stared at his wife in wonder. "The barrier's weakening."

Brianna leaned into his palm and placed her hand over his. He brushed his thumb over her skin. "It will get weaker," he said. He was certain of it. "When it does, I'll find a way through to you."

BRIANNA

Bri watched her husband, not sure if he meant what she thought he did. "You want to come here?"

Duncan's eyebrows lowered and squashed together. "I would be with you wherever you are."

"Whenever I am?"

"If need be," Duncan said. His beard twitched, like he was trying not to smile.

She reached up, running her fingers over his beard. Brianna had never dated a guy with a beard before. It was softer than she'd expected.

Duncan's hand left her cheek. He reached for her hand and pulled it away from his face. "If you continue doing that, I may have to kiss you again."

Bri grinned. She wouldn't mind another kiss. Duncan's kisses were more consuming than every other kiss she'd had, combined. She broke her hand free and went back to stroking his beard.

Duncan groaned and pulled her to him. Not to kiss her, unfortunately. He wrapped his arm around her shoulders and pulled her in to rest her head against his chest. "Do you not want me to join you?"

Bri burrowed deeper against him, pressing a kiss against his neck. Through his cloak, Bri felt Duncan's heart speed up. She grinned. It was good to know she could get to him. He certainly undid her. "I want to be with you," she said. "But why do you want to come here? What about your smithy? Your life is there."

"And yours is in my future." Duncan traced his fingertips down her bare arm. She shivered against him. "You're cold."

"Only a little," She said. "Not enough to leave. I should have worn something warmer."

Duncan's eyes drifted down her body. When they reached her shorts, he flinched away from her. "What are you wearing?"

"They're called shorts."

Duncan cursed under his breath, muttering things Bri couldn't understand. "You'll be the death of me, if you don't die of a chill first. Legs bare as the day you were born."

Bri tried not to laugh. When Duncan couldn't move his eyes from her legs, she gave up. "They're very common."

He reached down, his hand moving slowly as he brushed her thigh with the back of his hand. Duncan cut off a moan as he snatched his hand away.

Bri bit her lip against her own moan. She wanted him to caress her leg again.

"Maybe we should think about me coming to you?" Bri hated the way her voice shook. She didn't want to let Duncan know how badly he affected her.

"You want to give up everything you have to come here?" Duncan was surprised enough to pull his eyes away from her legs.

Bri thought about Grace and her daughters, and all those names recorded in their Bible. All the people who wouldn't exist if she let Duncan come to her instead of the other way around. "I'm meant to be the one to travel through time."

Duncan frowned, pushing her away so they could see each other more clearly. "How do you know this?"

Bri hesitated. Could she tell him? Should she? Grace hadn't told her to keep the information to herself. She wanted Duncan to know. Wanted to share the burden, and the awe, with him.

Duncan growled.

"The relative I went to see in Glasgow. You wanted to know the name of her ancestors in your time." Bri put her hand up to stop Duncan's argument. "I'm not avoiding the question. Just give me a minute to answer. Can you do that?"

"Aye." Duncan looked frustrated, and Bri almost felt bad. But she was answering his question.

"The first names recorded were Duncan O'Leary and Brianna Hughes. Us."

Duncan's fingers convulsed in her hand.

"Duncan."

He didn't move.

"Duncan? Say something." Bri sighed. She mentally kicked herself. She'd had a hard time believing it and she'd had the proof in front of her. Of course it would be harder for Duncan to believe.

"The woman — is our granddaughter?"

Bri could have laughed at the shock in his voice. "With a whole lot of greats thrown in. There's hundreds of names, Duncan. Hundreds of people who won't be born if you came here instead of having me come to you."

"You want to have children?" Duncan's voice was filled with a hollow yearning, but something in his face closed off.

Wanting to snap him out of whatever fears held him, she leaned against him. Holding each other was awkward with the stone between them, but not as awkward as kissing with their hands stuck in the hole.

"I didn't. But since meeting you I can almost see it."

"I can't lose you," Duncan said. His breath was coming faster, his voice becoming more desperate. "I won't. If that means I never touch you, that we never have a family, I can live with that. So long as you're with me. I thought — I thought we could do it. I love you, Brianna. I never thought I would. Never expected to know how this felt. If you died because I couldn't control myself, because I put a babe in your belly, I'd die with you. It was hard enough losing Neve, and I never loved her like this. But now — you tell me our line survives after so many hundreds of years. It means we have children. It means I have to live with the knowledge that you could die because of me."

Bri stared at him. Horror pushed its way up from her toes and filled her. He thought he'd killed Neve, and was afraid he'd kill her, too. Panic filled his face. It became a palpable thing, filling the air around them.

Breaking a hand free of his, she reached up and gently grabbed his face. She led him down to her, stretching up to kiss him, first on one cheek, then the other. She pulled back. "Look at me. I mean it. Look at me, Duncan. It's not your fault Neve died. Yes, childbirth can be dangerous. It always has been."

"I won't put you through that."

"What are you going to do, then? Never touch me? I don't want that kind of a marriage." Bri leaned toward him and kissed him hard. "You don't want it, either, or you wouldn't kiss me the way you do."

Duncan pushed his hand into her hair again, tilting her head back. His lips met hers. His desperation made his kiss rough, demanding.

Bri gave him all she could. Every ounce of her belief in him, of her understanding, of her love.

When he finally pulled away, there were tears on his face. "I'm sorry, Brianna."

She pulled his head back down and kissed away each of his tears. "We'll work things out. We don't need to have a baby right away."

"Perhaps that's what the barrier is for." Duncan's eyes crinkled in a sad smile.

Supernatural birth control. Bri giggled, her tension easing away. "I guess we're getting a little ahead of ourselves." She stopped laughing and looked up at her husband. "I know you're worried. I can't promise that nothing bad will happen. Bad things happen every day. But I can tell you that things are good long enough for us to have several children."

Duncan paled. "You'll go through that more than once?"

"I'll go through it as many times as I need to."

They were quiet for a while. Bri didn't want to talk, she wanted to be lost in Duncan's embrace for the rest of the night.

It couldn't happen. It was too uncomfortable trying to snuggle with the stupid stone between them.

"Come home to me, then," Duncan finally said, "when the barrier goes. I'd not prevent hundreds of births to chase you into the future."

Bri nodded against his shoulder.

"When do you suppose it will go?" Duncan asked. "I'd take you with me tonight if I could."

"I don't know. Hopefully not before my clothes are ready. I don't think the town is ready for my shorts."

Duncan laughed. "I'd be forced to hide you in my cloak."

Bri liked the idea more than she should.

"What clothes are you after?" he asked.

"Grace taught me about the clothes I'll need." She paused, hoping she wasn't about to send Duncan into panic again. "Apparently we give our kids instructions to pass from generation to generation until they get to me. Grace and her daughters are sewing me some appropriate clothes."

Duncan ran his hand through her hair and cleared his throat. "I have something for you."

Bri pulled away enough to look into his eyes. "You do?"

He nodded, and cleared his throat again. "Married women cover their hair," he said, sighing.

"It's dumb," Bri said. Grace had explained she'd need to wear a headpiece.

Duncan raised an eyebrow. "Keeping the beauty of your hair for your husband's enjoyment is 'dumb'?"

A tingling warmth filled Bri's stomach. "You think my hair is pretty?"

A playful growl came from Duncan's throat, and he kissed her nose. "Your hair is beautiful. It's soft and shines with health. I love your freckles, and your eyes." He let his eyes trail down Bri's body, lingering in places. "And your bare legs drive me mad."

Heat filled Bri. She leaned in for a kiss.

"No, *a rúnsearc*."

Bri had no idea what he'd called her, but her heart melted at the endearment.

"Not now," Duncan continued. "I've a gift for you."

A gift? He'd been thinking of her while she was away? "You don't need to give me anything."

"Today was market day," he said. "This made me think of you."

Duncan reached under his cloak and pulled something out from under his belt. He held out a fistful of fabric. "If you want it." His voice had gone husky.

Bri buried her fingers in the soft, cool pile. She lifted a corner and the cloth unfurled. "Is this silk?"

"Aye."

Gran's voice came back to Bri, telling her she wouldn't be wearing silks because her husband wasn't a lord. "This must have cost a fortune."

"The price wasn't so dear as to keep me from buying it for you. It's a hair kerchief," Duncan said. He lifted the silk from her fingers and draped it over her head. He grinned. "To keep other men from wanting to touch your hair. That want is for me alone."

Bri smiled. "It's beautiful."

He glanced away. "'Tis but a kerchief."

Silly man. He didn't need to be embarrassed about giving her something so beautiful. "Thank you."

Duncan ducked his head in a nod.

This time when Bri went to kiss him, he let her.

Much too soon, Duncan pulled away. "You should sleep."

Bri frowned. "I'd rather stay here with you."

He kissed her hair. "As would I. Morning is nearly here, and neither of us will be able to do the things we need to if we've had no rest."

Bri frowned. She could sleep late, if Gran let her. She hadn't considered that their nights together might be making Duncan's life harder. "Don't work with fire today," Bri said. "It's too dangerous when you're tired."

Duncan laughed at her. "It's charcoal I work with. I'll take extra care, as you're worried."

"What will you be doing?"

"I've nails to make. The work's not as exciting as some days."

Bri hadn't thought about nails having to be made by a person. She wondered how many other things would surprise her when she moved to Tristledermot.

She looked at Duncan, standing in the dark, watching her with love in his eyes. "I don't want to leave you," she said.

Duncan rested his forehead against hers. "I'd steal you away if I could. We'll be together soon."

Bri nodded. She had to believe him.

With one more kiss, Duncan let go of her hand and faded away.

Pulling the kerchief from her head, Bri dropped to the grass. She realized with a start that she'd forgotten to ask if the town had been attacked.

Surely Duncan would have mentioned raging Irishmen if the attack had taken place. Still, she'd need to remember to mention it. She hated the idea of him facing the invasion.

Bri left the churchyard and made her way back to the B&B. As she climbed into bed she could still feel the arms of her husband around her.

DUNCAN

Duncan climbed the stairs and let himself into his home. It was brighter than it should have been.

Ciaran sat in front of the fire. "Had a good night, did you?" His voice was hushed. They tried to keep their voices low so their words wouldn't echo through the street for everyone in town to hear.

"Aye." Duncan grinned. He found Ciaran's words from the Lughnasa celebration no longer hurt. He would have children of his own to raise one day.

Ciaran's voice dropped lower. "You kissed her."

Duncan cursed. He'd been sure his threat would keep Ciaran away. "You followed me."

"You were gone a long time. I came to check on you," Ciaran said. "I thought you might have fallen asleep waiting for Brianna."

Duncan shook his head. He knew better than to believe the tale. "I told you to stay here."

"And you said you could touch your wife only through that stone."

Duncan felt like shouting. Instead, he whispered. "How long did you watch?"

He must have looked the fool, caressing the air.

"Long enough." Ciaran paused, shifting in the glow from the fire. "Your Brianna is beautiful, as you said."

"Of course she is," Duncan said. Then Ciaran's words hit him. "You saw her?"

Ciaran nodded. "Aye, but only for the time you were kissing her. Afterwards, she disappeared. I knew she'd not left, as I could hear your voice. Even you don't talk to yourself."

Duncan slammed his fist against the table. "Do you not remember I said I wasn't ready for you to see her?"

"I'm sorry. I'd not meant to intrude." Ciaran sighed.

Dropping onto a chair, Duncan looked at his friend. They'd become brothers when Duncan and Neve had married, but they'd been closer than brothers for many years before that. He'd no wish to fight with Ciaran any longer. It took too much effort. "You thought she was beautiful?"

Ciaran choked out a quiet laugh. "Aye. She's smaller than I expected, and half her length of hair is missing, but she suits you. How did you manage to kiss her?"

Duncan raised and dropped a shoulder. "The barrier is thinner than it was."

Ciaran stared into the jumping flames as if he couldn't stand the sight of him. "Will you leave to be with her?"

"I would have. I offered to, but she wants to come here." It was Duncan's turn to look away. He couldn't tell even Ciaran that his children needed to be born in this time. He couldn't talk about having children. If he tried, he'd panic. He'd not allow himself to panic. Brianna wasn't there to calm him. "Go. Sleep. Morning is nearly here."

Duncan moved to the bed. There was no need to lie down. He'd get no sleep, not with Brianna's scent still clinging to him. She smelled of flowers and something he couldn't describe. Something delectably feminine.

As he held still, hoping Ciaran would think him asleep, Duncan let his eyes wander through the room. It was large, but the clutter he'd brought in from the forge closed the walls in around him. It wasn't as clean as it should be, and there was nothing a woman would find welcoming.

He'd need to spend time with a scrub brush before Brianna could be comfortable here.

As Duncan made plans to improve his home over the smithy's storage room, his eyes became heavy. He must have drifted into sleep.

The next thing he knew, the streets were filled with noise. Children shouted as they chased each other, and voices called greetings or nattered at gossip. The sound of pounding metal came from the smithy.

Duncan forced his eyes open. The room around him was dim. The fire had burned itself out and the shutters were closed. He groaned and shut his eyes. He'd been having a good dream, filled with kisses and warm touches.

His eyes flew open and he sat up, rubbing his hands over his face. Brianna. He'd been dreaming of his wife.

As his eyes fell on a tattered hole in the blanket, Duncan remembered he'd been trying to decide how to make his home a place Brianna could be happy.

The door swung open, and Ciaran stepped inside. "You're awake. Good. The bell will be ringing for Sext before long. I've taken care of some things in the smithy for you, but I'll be needing to leave soon. I've been away from Tara long enough."

"What did you do in the smithy?" There was something Duncan was supposed to work on today, he just couldn't remember what.

"Someone brought in tools to be mended. I took care of those and made nails. Didn't you say you'd need to do that today?"

Nails. Of course. "Aye. They're needed for the Parliament Building."

"There should be enough down there now," Ciaran said. He swung the shutters open. The gloomy light of a rainy day lit the room enough to see. "What more can I do for you before I leave?"

"I've not seen you so anxious to leave in a long time," Duncan said. "Did something happen?"

Ciaran shook his head and moved closer. "Seeing you with your Brianna last night reminded me how I miss my own wife. I want to get back to her."

That was a desire Duncan understood all too well. "Let me find something to feed you before you leave, and perhaps you can tell me what to do to this room — beyond a good scrubbing — to make it livable for a woman."

"You'd have a better idea than I of what your Brianna would like," Ciaran said. He glanced around the room. "Scrubbing the corners is a good place to start. You keep your table clean, and the floor's usually swept."

Duncan shook his head. He shouldn't have asked.

"I've not known you to take care over details like this," Ciaran said. "Why are you worrying now?"

"Tara's the only woman to have set foot here in years," Duncan said. His insides squirmed. He lowered his voice. "Brianna plans to leave her own life to come here. I wouldn't have her disappointed in what I can give her."

"What is it about your woman that tells you she'll be disappointed? Neve was always happy here with you."

Duncan rose from the bed. He walked past Ciaran without looking at him. "Neve didn't want to admit to the anger she held for me near the end."

"Tara is hard to be with when a babe stretches her belly," Ciaran mumbled.

Startled, Duncan looked back. Irish men kept their business with their wives to themselves.

"She doesn't sleep, and she aches in awkward places. It makes her temper short." He looked up, his eyes full of some emotion Duncan couldn't place. "I'd guess Neve felt something similar."

Duncan had no idea what Neve had felt. She'd not talked to him of it, and he'd not bothered to ask. He nodded anyway.

"It could be hard for your Brianna to get used to things here, but she'll manage. You'll help her."

Duncan hoped she would. He was afraid she'd be giving up too much. To be able to travel to Galway in part of a morning — surely there were other things he'd consider impossible that were commonplace enough for her to not even think on.

"I'll buy you lunch at the tavern before you go," Duncan said. He didn't have anything to offer here but a bit of bog cheese.

Ciaran shook his head. "I'll stop at the baker's and get a bun to eat on my way. I've put the smithy back to rights. Rest today. You've gone too many nights without sleep. I'll come for another market day in a few weeks."

He left, leaving Duncan standing alone in the middle of the room.

With a sigh, he cleaned up for the day. He needed to deliver the nails. While he was out, he'd find food to last a day or two. Nothing that set his mouth on fire. The spices Brianna had fed him still coated his mouth.

Duncan walked down the stairs, laughing to himself. His wife likely chose the food that made him cry just to torment him.

At the bottom of the stairs he nearly ran into Brogan. Duncan held back his sigh. The man was there every time he turned around anymore.

"You're too cheerful for someone who's not found a woman," Brogan said, crossing his arms over his chest. "You're sure you haven't chosen someone to court?"

Duncan knew better than to answer such a question. "What are you after, Brogan?"

"Could you help me unload a delivery?" he asked. "I know it's a bother, but I could use the help."

The man would be using him as a servant if Duncan didn't put a stop to it. It was one thing to help a friend and neighbor, quite another to be expected to do a job every few days. "I can't today, Brogan. I've a delivery of my own to make and it won't wait."

"My wife says you're welcome to join us at table in return." Brogan's smile was desperate. "Please."

Duncan almost bent to Brogan's plea. Then he remembered Brogan's wife was the one trying to convince the village women he was in need of a wife. "I'm sorry. If I don't make my delivery, men will sit idle when they're meant to be working. You can give your wife my thanks for the invitation."

"Are you certain you can't come?"

"Aye." Duncan clapped Brogan on the shoulder. "I've a list of things I need to do for myself today."

Duncan almost felt guilty as his friend walked away. He could have spared the time. It was a matter of survival that he'd refused.

In the smithy, he gathered the nails Ciaran had made. He transferred the heavy load to a small cart and wheeled it into the road. The Parliament Building was but a short distance away, by the market square.

The ground in the square was trampled, and the slow rain brought out the smell of the straw. He made his way to the building and left his load with the man in charge of the project.

After a quick stop in the tavern for food, he made his way home. In the burgage, he filled a bucket from the rain barrel and hauled it up the stairs.

He poured water into a pot and stirred the fire to life.

While he waited for the water to heat, Duncan began to sort through his belongings. Chipped stoneware went into a pile on the table, the good pieces got stacked at the other end to wait for a clean shelf.

Slowly, he worked his way through everything on the shelves. Half the things he owned were broken in one way or another.

Duncan could have fixed some of it, but he shoved it all in the trash pile.

By the time he'd finished that, the water was steaming. He pulled it from the hearth and set more water to heat.

When the bell rang for Vespers, Duncan stretched his muscles. They were used to different work than this and promised to be sore. He'd cleared away every crumb and cobweb. The stubborn dirt in the corners had been coaxed from the floorboards. His home hadn't been so clean in a long time.

After clearing away the broken and unwanted items, he gave the table another scrubbing.

Duncan sat on the edge of the bed and looked around the room. It may not be up to the standards of the future, but it was the best he could do for now.

On the next market day, he'd buy replacements for a few things. Cooking pots, and a new blanket or two.

And perhaps he'd start leaving his mud-covered shoes by the door instead of allowing dirt to spread through his home to cut down on scrubbing.

Duncan pushed himself to his feet. If he didn't, he might fall asleep and miss seeing Brianna.

Any time he could have with her was worth being tired. Especially if the barrier continued to thin.

BRIANNA

Gran sat with her eyes closed, soaking in . . . something. Bri had never understood the fuss people made over church services. There was an odd sort of peace in this one, though. She could almost enjoy it.

As the organ pipes came to life the congregation rose around them. Bri pushed to her feet, anxious to blend in. It was pointless. She and Gran were like sore thumbs. It would be hard not to stand out just by being a visitor. There were only a couple dozen people at the service — hardly the kind of crowd you could hide in. Their voices joined the sound of the organ as the notes of an unfamiliar hymn filled the building. Gran's voice joined them. Clearly the hymn wasn't unknown to her. Maybe if Bri had joined Gran for church more often these past years she'd be comfortable joining in.

It was worth the singing just to get off the hard pew for a few minutes.

Instead of pretending to know the words, Bri took the chance to gaze around the church again. The plastered walls and rich wood ceiling. The arched alcoves lining the walls. The buttery wall at the end, brightened by daylight coming in through windows near the front. Would any parts of the building be the same as what Duncan would see?

He was so long ago. It was possible everything was different. The thought made her a little sad.

Bri sat when Gran tugged on her arm, and remained lost in thought until the service came to a close.

Gran nudged her. "I'd like to look around before we go. The church only opens for services, so we won't have many chances to explore the building."

Bri stepped into the aisle to let Gran out. Her heels sank into the softness of the red carpet.

Gran headed for the front of the chapel. Bri trailed after, looking for any connection to Duncan's time.

At the front of the church, the stained glass windows glowed with sunlight. She wasn't sure it would be appropriate to go up to look more closely. She glanced back to the church doorway where the rector was greeting the congregation on their way out. When he glanced her way, Bri decided not to chance it. She didn't want to cause a scene. Instead, she made her way to the door.

She paused to answer the smiling rector's welcoming questions before stepping into the fresh air. She stopped by the reconstructed archway to examine the stonework while she waited for Gran. It wasn't long before Gran's voice drifted outside ahead of her. Bri chuckled to herself. Gran's voice was rarely anything less than loud.

"You've not seen anything, then?" Gran was asking. She came into view, holding the arm of another older woman. "I'd heard unexplained things were wont to happen in your churchyard."

Bri's stomach sank. What was she up to?

The lady's reply was too quiet to make out. Bri moved to intercept them. Whatever the conversation was about, it seemed prudent to stop it.

"Don't worry yourself," Gran said. "Small miracles happen every day."

Bri reached out and brushed Gran's shoulder. "I'm sorry to interrupt, Gran, but we should be going."

Hopefully that would work.

After a few more minutes of Gran chattering about odd things that may or may not have happened around the church, Bri managed to pull her away.

"Why were you asking those questions?" Bri whispered. "I don't want people to start hanging out here looking for strange things. They'll just find me."

"She'll not bother you and your Duncan any. I'd hoped she might know of other people who've had something similar happen to them," Gran said.

Bri sighed. "Let's go back to Ryan's. We can play with our drop spindles for the afternoon."

Gran's eyes sparkled. "We'll need more wool soon."

Of course they would. Gran kept spinning yarn every time Bri went off to take pictures. "I'll buy more roving the next time I can." Bri paused as her mind started to form a plan. "Maybe I'll buy a lot of it. It would be a way for me to make a living in the fifteenth century."

She'd need to get natural fibers instead of dyed. Only natural dyes had been used back then. Bri grinned, liking the idea more the longer she considered it. It would be good to have a way to contribute.

If she ever managed to spin a length of yarn without it breaking.

Gran patted Bri's hand. "A spot of practice may be in order before making the decision."

Bri rolled her eyes.

At the B&B, Bri gathered their spindles and the roving and joined Gran in the front room.

Trying to remember what the woman at the shop had told her, Bri prepared the roving and hooked it to her spindle. Her first attempt wasn't ideal — the wool kept sticking to her sweater. She took off her cardigan and the next attempt went a little better, although she was beginning to think she should have changed out of her dress. She'd been taught to start the spindle spinning by running it along her thigh. Not the easiest thing to do in a dress that kept your legs from moving too far apart. If Ryan hadn't been in the room she'd have been tempted to hike up her skirt to make it easier.

Instead, she tried the slightly harder way of flicking the spindle to make it spin. It wasn't going very well. Bri almost gave up, but she'd be spinning in a dress if she decided to take the skill back with her.

"You're getting better," Gran said.

Bri looked at her small length of yarn, then at Gran's much longer length. "How are you making this look so easy?"

"Practice, my dear."

Bri growled.

"Watch. See how the twist travels up the fibers?" Gran asked. "Let it. You're putting too much spin to it. You're making it harder than it needs to be."

After watching Gran for a few minutes, Bri tried again. "Huh. You're right, this is easier."

"Of course it is. Did you think I was telling you stories?"

Bri ignored the question and kept going, winding each length of spun yarn onto the spindle and moving on to the next bit. "I think I've got it."

"It isn't difficult." Gran took a deep breath and pushed herself out of her chair. "These old bones have been sitting too long. I think I'll go for a wee walk to stretch my legs."

"Do you want me to come?" Bri asked, looking up from her spinning.

Ryan set down his book. "We can all go. I'll get the umbrellas. It looks like the rain is trying to start."

Gran, ever polite, smiled. "That would be lovely."

Bri just shook her head as she slid her feet back into her dress shoes.

"You're wearing those?" Gran asked.

"I'll be fine, Gran. I know how to walk in heels. Besides, we won't be going far."

Gran cackled and patted Bri's face. "I'm just trying to keep you in one piece for Duncan."

"Who's Duncan?" Ryan asked, coming up behind them with the umbrellas. His eyebrows were drawn together.

Bri glared at Gran. She didn't want to talk about Duncan with Ryan. There was hardly anything she could say without getting into the whole time difference thing.

"They're in a long distance relationship," Gran said.

A burble of laughter escaped from Bri. "Rather long distance."

Ryan gave her a half-smile. "Long distance romances aren't easy."

Was that hurt in Ryan's eyes? It couldn't be. She'd done nothing to encourage him, or to make him think she was available. Then again, she hadn't told him otherwise, and Gran had tried to push them together before she'd learned about Duncan. Bri reached for an umbrella. "Let's go." And please, please find something else to talk about, she silently begged.

The smell of rain filled the air, but only a few large drops splattered the ground. Bri took her place beside Gran, ready to offer an arm if the older woman wanted something to lean on.

As they headed toward Main Street, Ryan pointed out different things he found interesting. Bri tried to pay attention, but she just couldn't bring herself to care about the neighborhood stories. She was too busy wondering what the town had been like in the past.

Just as they reached Main Street, the clouds opened and rain pounded down around them.

"We should go back," Bri said. She didn't want Gran to get sick. A cold could easily turn to pneumonia.

Gran grumbled, but turned back the way they'd come.

Bri moved the umbrella closer to Gran. It didn't help. The wind had picked up again, blowing the raindrops from behind them.

Hoping to keep Gran dry, Bri moved to block the wind and rain with her body.

They made their way through the storm, moving slowly. Bri picked her way through puddles, wishing she'd taken Gran's advice about her heels. She shivered against the wind and lifted her eyes from her feet just in time to see Gran's shoe slip to the side. Bri rushed forward, trying to grab hold of her.

There was a muffled thump as Gran landed on the pavement.

"Gran!" Bri dropped to her knees beside the crumpled form. The umbrella fell from her hands and rolled into the street. "Gran, are you okay?"

There was no answer.

With shaking hands, Bri brushed aside the wet, silver hair and felt for a pulse. Under Gran's head, the redness of blood began to swirl in the collecting rain.

"Gran?" Bri's voice was a whisper.

There was no answer, not even a moan.

A faint pulse fluttered under Bri's fingers. Relief swamped her. Gran was alive.

She reached for Gran's head, wanting to see how badly she was hurt. At the last second, she pulled her hands back. She'd taken a first aid class years ago, and one of the things they drilled into her head was not to move someone who'd been injured.

Bri reached out again and wrapped Gran's hand in her fingers. She glanced around for Ryan, not knowing what else to do.

Still under his umbrella, holding it to shield them as best he could, Ryan spoke rapidly into his phone. As if he felt her gaze, he met her eyes and gave her a crooked smile that did nothing to reassure her. "An ambulance will be here shortly."

An ambulance. Bri could hardly breathe. It was bad enough for an ambulance.

Bri scrambled around Gran, checking for other injuries. She couldn't see anything else, but she didn't know what she was looking for.

The ground under Gran's head was darkening as more blood flowed from the wound.

Bri tore her sweater off and folded it. Very gently, she tucked it up against Gran's head, hoping to staunch the bleeding. It was such a small thing. Was it even helping? Bri sighed. Maybe. At least she was doing something other than just sitting there.

A siren sounded in the distance, growing louder as the ambulance neared. It came around the corner and pulled to a stop beside them. Bri got to her feet, hardly daring to breathe, as the paramedics checked Gran and moved her onto a stretcher.

One of the men spoke to Ryan. Bri didn't even try to understand what they were saying. She just stared as Gran was moved into the ambulance and the door closed behind her.

"Wait," Bri said. "I need to go with her."

Ryan caught her arm. "We'll meet them at the hospital."

Bri wanted to argue. She couldn't leave Gran. What if she was needed? What if Gran called for her?

Refusing to let go of her arm, Ryan pulled her down the street toward his home as the ambulance pulled away. "Go inside and get into dry clothes."

"I'm fine. Let's just go."

"I won't take you until you're dry."

Stubborn man. There were more important things happening. Besides, her clothes would dry. She spun to glare at him. "I'm going now. I'm all she has, Ryan. I need to be there for her."

Ryan sighed, shaking his head. "At least get a bag with some dry clothes. You can change at the hospital."

Bri raced up the stairs and grabbed the first clothes she could find. She shoved them into a bag, along with her knitting and a book. If

Irish hospitals were anything like their American counterparts, she'd be waiting a while.

Downstairs, she hurried into Gran's room, looking for anything that might be helpful. Dry clothes and shoes. A comb. Gran's Bible.

Ryan met her at the front door, holding a bag of his own. "I have snacks and a flask of tea."

Bri nodded her thanks. "I'll follow you in the rental car so you don't have to wait for me."

"No. I'll not leave you to deal with things on your own. I have my book to keep me company."

Unwilling to waste any more time, Bri nodded.

She hurried back into the rain and waited for Ryan to unlock his car.

As they got closer to the hospital, the rain became heavier. Bri couldn't see anything through the downpour. She gripped the edges of her seat and waited, knowing there was nothing she could do.

The dark clouds above were a perfect mirror of her mood and the emotions roiling under her skin.

DUNCAN

uncan hurried down the stairs with a smile hiding behind his beard. He'd thought to give his wife another gift, but had been unable to find anything good enough.

His smile widened. He would wait for her to come to him. They'd go to Dublin and he'd buy her everything she could want. They could see the newest things brought from London.

His Brianna would have the best of everything with no thought for expense. Most of the coins he'd earned since Neve died had been put aside for a time of need.

He'd not find a better need than to welcome the woman he loved.

Duncan rounded the corner of his building and headed for the churchyard. It was much too early to expect Brianna, but he was anxious to be with her again. Perhaps tonight the barrier would thin enough for her to come through.

He warmed at the thought of holding her against himself with no stone blocking their embrace.

"Duncan?" Michael stepped from the bakery just before Duncan passed. He looked at the people in the street and nodded his head toward the building. "Come in, would you?"

Duncan glanced at the sky. There was no hurry, but he was reluctant to put off his waiting.

Michael gestured again and scooted out of the doorway. Unsure what else to do, Duncan followed him into the darkened room.

"You're out later than usual tonight," Michael said, trying to keep his voice low.

"As are you." Duncan's smile faded. They were likely the two men who rose the earliest in order to heat their fires for business each day.

Michael coughed and shuffled his feet. "There's been talk."

Duncan leaned toward Michael to catch the words.

"The women — including my wife, which is how I've heard anything — are trying to discover who you're courting."

"Will the meddling fools not leave off?" Duncan put on a show of being more frustrated than he was, and chose his words carefully. "There's not a woman in this town who could hold my interest."

More shuffling noises came from the floor at Michael's feet. "They've begun talking with the other women. The unwed women."

That made no sense. They'd learned in the past that even working together they couldn't convince him to wed someone of their choosing. "What are they saying?"

"They're asking," Michael corrected. "Asking every unwed woman if you've visited of an evening. They know you're out later than you're wont to be, and comment on your happiness and smiles."

Duncan laughed. "Did it not occur to them I may be happy because they finally stopped pushing girls at me? The last one was hardly old enough to wed, and they thought to pair her to me, a man over a dozen years older."

"Och, there are many older men marrying young girls."

"I won't."

Through the darkness, Duncan could hardly make out Michael's hands raised in front of his chest. "No matter. The women are convinced you're too happy. My wife says the only man with the right to such happiness is one with a woman in his bed."

He sighed. "There's not been a woman in my bed since Neve passed, nor have I stolen in to any other beds in the darkness."

Michael raised a hand to Duncan's shoulder. "Mind yourself. Every woman and girl has agreed that you'd not been to see them. You'll likely have someone following you. I'd just thought to warn you, in case you may be going somewhere you'd prefer to keep to yourself."

Duncan considered what might happen if he were to be followed to the churchyard. He'd not have cared if he looked the fool talking to himself, but Ciaran had seen Brianna. Should anyone else see her, things would not be well. "You're a true friend. I'll watch my step."

"Where do you go?" Michael asked. "I've seen you myself, returning home so far into the night as to be morning."

"I go to think, and to talk to myself." Surely the man's wife waited nearby, hoping to hear something to tell the other women. "The women of this town are safe from me. If only I was safe from them I'd be truly happy."

"That's all?"

"Aye. My thanks for the warning," Duncan said. He turned and slipped out the door. If he had luck on his side, he'd not be bothered by the women tonight.

Duncan strode through town, heading nowhere in particular. Were anyone to follow, they'd see he did no more than wander.

When the streets had emptied enough to be certain he was alone, Duncan walked through the churchyard to his place beyond the swearing stone.

A glance around showed no one near.

Taking a deep breath, Duncan placed his hand in the hole and felt around for his wife's fingers.

Not finding them, he settled in to wait.

The women of the town were getting bold again if they were asking young widows and girls if he was courting them.

He'd not wanted to tell anyone of Brianna in case the barrier never thinned. Would it be better to start the rumor that he'd met and wed a woman from another town, and that she was readying to join him? Perhaps then he'd get peace from his friends' wives, and ready them to accept an outsider.

If he knew when the barrier would break it would be an easy choice. If he told them of Brianna, and she was unable to come for several months, it would make things worse for her when she did come. All the women would be asking why she waited so long to go to her husband.

Duncan sighed. That was more thinking than he wanted to do of an evening.

He let his mind wander to the smithy, and the jobs he'd not worked on while sorting and scrubbing. He would need to work extra over the next day or two in order to make up for the time he'd stayed away.

Where was Brianna? Wasn't she here by now most nights?

He looked up at the sky, trying to judge if she'd ever been later.

Duncan sat and leaned against the swearing stone, keeping his fingers in the hole over his head so he wouldn't miss her while he stretched his legs in front of himself.

Perhaps there were people in the churchyard with her and she waited for them to leave.

A yawn snuck up on him and he forced his eyes open wider. He scrubbed at his face with his free hand.

Some time later, Duncan began to worry. They'd agreed to meet, and she'd never been so late. "Brianna, where are you?" he whispered. What could be keeping her?

He switched and put his other hand in the hole, stretching his cramped arm in front of him.

As more time passed, Duncan's worry grew. Why would Brianna choose not to come? Had he done something to upset her?

When the first hints of daybreak appeared, Duncan pushed himself to his feet.

She hadn't come.

Duncan had thought through everything he'd said and done the night before, trying to see where he'd gone wrong. He'd not found the blame. When she left, she'd been eager to be with him again.

He stumbled through town, his brain in a stupor, as if he'd spent the night in the tavern filling himself with cheap ale. There was even a sour taste to his mouth.

As he passed the bakery, Michael's head poked out a window. Duncan didn't understand what he said. After all the words of the night before, it didn't matter. Duncan ignored him and kept walking.

When he reached the smithy he stopped long enough to douse his face with water before going in to light the charcoal.

Duncan looked over the projects that needed finishing and chose one. That done, he moved to the next. One after another, they filled his day.

When he was too weary to stand, he pulled over a stool and continued to work. It took all his focus.

Sometime after the bell rang for None, he finished his row of projects. He leaned forward, resting his arms and head on his anvil.

With nothing left to work on, his mind returned to Brianna. Had she changed her mind about wanting to be with him? Did she no longer love him?

Love didn't wane so quickly, and she'd had love in her eyes when last he saw her.

A feeling of dread crept through him and he bolted upright. Had something happened to her? Had she been injured somehow, and left unable to get to the swearing stone?

Duncan couldn't face the idea. He reached for his tools. He needed to keep his mind busy with something other than worry.

Tonight. He'd see her tonight.

Reaching to the back of his supplies, Duncan pulled out a bar of copper. He didn't often work with copper, but it would keep his mind busy.

He hammered the metal into a narrow strip and began to bend it, folding it around, and over, and under itself.

Finally finished, Duncan put the smithy to rights for the next day. He washed up in the burgage, splashing water from his rain barrel over his arms and face. He returned to the smithy for his newest creation before going upstairs.

With fading daylight coming through the windows, Duncan set the thing down on his table and lit a candle to see better.

The knot was perfect, as good as any that decorated the high crosses in the churchyard. The finest chain Duncan had ever made looped through one of the open spaces, and was long to pass over Brianna's head.

When she saw his gift, his wife would know Duncan loved her. If something had shaken her from her love for him, this would help her remember.

He hung the chain from his belt, careful to keep it from tangling.

No longer caring if anyone followed, Duncan walked through the noisy streets, back to the church. He was early, and the sky was still streaked with fading light.

With his heart in his throat, Duncan reached his fingers through the swearing stone.

Nothing. No warm fingers. No dark curling hair. No bare legs.

No wife.

Duncan settled in to wait. Surely she'd not make him wait in vain.

The bell rang for Vespers, and clouds began to cover the stars. Small drops of water fell, teasing with their wetness at first. Then the water came down in torrents.

The weather was a thin echo of his emotions.

In time it became clear Brianna would not come.

Duncan walked away, leaving the churchyard older and more stooped than when he'd entered.

Noise from the tavern spilled down the road. A drink might help him into the darkness of forgetfulness.

The air inside the tavern was warm and sticky with moisture from the rain. Duncan pushed his way through the other men, past the girls who did everything they could to keep the customers happy.

He spoke with the barman and soon had a cask of mead on his shoulder.

Getting back outside to the cold rain was difficult. Men kept pushing their way inside, and one of the prostitutes kept stepping in his path, trying to get his attention as he pushed his way to the door.

Finally home, Duncan sat in front of the fire to dry. He opened the cask. The smell of mead filled the room. Dipping his wooden cup into the mead, he finally smiled.

Usually he would sip the mead to warm himself from the inside. Tonight, Duncan poured it down his throat. Then another cupful, and another. He didn't bother keeping track of how much he'd had.

Carefully, Duncan pulled the chain from his belt and draped it over the edge of the cask. The firelight warmed the color of the copper, making it glow in the low light.

He could almost see Brianna wearing his knot.

Brianna.

Duncan's heart ached for her. Why had she not come? He could go no longer without seeing her. Without holding her in his arms.

He stumbled to the bed. The winking firelight played over the knot, taunting him.

He could last another day. He must.

He'd fill his time making Brianna another gift. And if she wasn't there again, he'd make another every day until he was with her.

It was all Duncan could do. The only way to keep her with him.

The only way to believe she remained his.

19

BRIANNA

ri stared at the raindrops making their way down the window near Gran's bed. The staff at Naas General Hospital had been kind and attentive, but Bri was ready to bust Gran out of there. All they needed was the okay from the doctor.

Ryan came up behind Bri's chair and rested a hand on her shoulder. "More tea?"

Blast Ryan's never-ending flasks of tea. "No thanks," Bri said without looking at him.

He gave her shoulder a gentle squeeze before letting go. "It won't be long."

Gran harrumphed. "If that doctor doesn't give the approval soon, I'll leave without it."

That got Bri to turn around. "No you won't. We won't go until we know for sure you'll be okay."

"It was a wee bump to the head," Gran said, waving her hand in the air as if to brush Bri's concern aside.

"A small bump that needed four stitches, a CT scan, and a two day stay in the hospital." Bri growled. "Maybe you could have gone home sooner if you hadn't waited in the emergency room for nearly two hours before anyone even looked at you."

Bri had hoped hospitals in Ireland would be better than those at home, but so far it seemed just the same.

The same smells, the same food, and the same slow bureaucracy that kept patients from being seen quickly.

"All it means is that I'd not been hurt as badly as you want to believe." Gran folded her hands primly on her lap.

"You're not fooling anyone with that sweet old lady act." Bri looked away so Gran wouldn't see her tears. Until recently, Gran had been the strong one. Now her veins stood out against her translucent skin. Seeing her so frail broke Bri's heart.

She stood up and walked the two steps to the window, wrapping her arms around herself.

Ryan joined her, standing a hair too close. It didn't bother her the way it had a couple days earlier. The man had put his own life on hold to be at the hospital with them for two days and nights, disappearing only to restock his supply of tea and snacks.

She glanced over her shoulder at Gran. Two days of watching Gran deal with her concussion had opened Bri's eyes to what she was doing.

How could she possibly leave an old woman — a woman she loved dearly, the woman who raised Bri when her father wanted nothing to do with her — how could Bri leave her to face the rest of her life alone?

And she would miss Gran more than anything. More than indoor plumbing.

But how could she walk away from Duncan? Bri may not have known him long, but she loved him. She couldn't imagine her life without him. Without his kisses, or his smile, or the gentle touch of his hand on her thigh.

Bri shivered.

Ryan touched her elbow, nodding behind them. When Bri glanced over her shoulder, she saw a nurse coming toward them.

"Everything's in order." The nurse spoke softly to avoid disturbing the other patients in the ward.

The nurse spouted off a list of instructions on caring for Gran as she recovered. Once Bri signed Gran's discharge papers they were free.

Ryan brought his car up to the curb and they helped Gran get situated in the back seat. Bri took one last look at the hospital. The roof's gables poked at the sky. She hoped she'd never see them again.

Gran grumped over Bri's fussing the whole drive back to the B&B. "You've more important things to be doing with your days than babysitting an old woman. What of your photographs? More importantly, how could you stay with me when you know Duncan will be worried?"

Bri ignored Ryan's confused glance and focused on trying not to grind her teeth into dust. She'd worried about Duncan, too, but what was she supposed to do? "I wasn't going to leave you alone in a hospital in a foreign country."

Gran huffed. "A foreign country. Where do you suppose I was born, then?"

Bri took a deep breath and held it while she counted to ten, the slowly let it out. "You have a concussion. I needed to be there to watch out for you."

"That's the job of the nurses."

Gran's scolding left Bri tired and cranky. Two nights of sleeping in an uncomfortable chair didn't help any.

"We're here," Ryan said.

Bri looked up as he pulled the car to a stop. She looked over her shoulder at Gran. She loved that old lady, even when they were both sick of each other. "Let's get you inside so you can rest."

Gran allowed Ryan to help her from the car, with only a token complaint.

"Would you like to sit up with us for a while, or go straight to your room?" Ryan asked.

"I've just gotten out of bed, you'll not force me into another one just yet." Gran glowered, but it was ruined by the twinkle in her eye.

Once Gran was settled in an armchair by the front window and her eyelids began to droop, Bri escaped upstairs to her room. She needed space to breathe her own air for at least an hour.

Bri stretched out on the bed and shut her eyes. Just as she got settled there was a knock on the door. "Bri?"

Ryan's voice made Bri wince. She just wanted to sleep. Instead, she pushed herself up so she was sitting in the middle of the bed. "You can come in."

Rubbing her eyes, Bri stifled a yawn as Ryan stepped into the room. He crossed the few steps to the bed and sat beside her, his hands clasped in front of himself as he rested his elbows on his knees. "You've had a rough couple of days. How are you doing?"

"Tired."

Flipping his hair out of his eyes, Ryan turned to face Bri. "Your grandmother is considering staying in Ireland."

"What? When did she tell you that?" And why would she tell Ryan instead of telling Bri?

"At the hospital, she said she didn't think she'd make the flight home." Ryan paused for a big breath, then hurried on, the words spilling out of him. "You could stay, both of you. Here, if you'd like."

"Here? With you?" Bri asked. She kneaded her forehead. Her brain was too exhausted keep up with the conversation.

"I know you're in some kind of relationship, but long distance doesn't work. We could be good together."

Bri stared. What Ryan was suggesting was crazy. Wasn't it?

Her mind was spinning. It hadn't been long at all since she'd wondered how she could leave Gran, and here was Ryan, offering a way to stay with Gran but still live her own life. Ryan had proven he cared about both Bri and Gran, and he'd become a friend, but—

Ryan's eyes were intense.

Clearing her throat, Bri broke the quiet that had settled around them. "Duncan matters to me."

She held her breath, waiting to see what more she'd have to say.

Ryan raised a shoulder and smirked. "I had to try."

Bri opened her mouth but couldn't find words.

"Come downstairs." Ryan stood and reached for Bri's hand. "Your grandmother wanted you to talk to some new guests that have arrived."

She kept her hands in her lap. "I'll be down in a minute."

Ryan nodded and let himself out, closing the door quietly.

Bri flopped back against the pillows with a groan and buried her face in her palms. Being friends with a guy shouldn't be so hard.

She climbed off the bed and stopped to run a comb through her hair. On her way downstairs she pasted on a smile. Gran would expect nothing less. When she saw who was sitting in the front room with Gran, her forced smile became a real one. "Grace, it's good to see you."

Grace stood up to give Bri an awkward hug. "You remember my girls, Katie and Hannah?"

Bri glanced around, then poked her head into the hall. She could hear Ryan puttering in the kitchen. Satisfied they wouldn't be overheard, she moved to sit in the chair beside Gran. "What are you doing here? The clothes can't be ready so soon."

"They are." Hannah was dancing in her seat. "It's our summer holiday, so we had time."

Bri felt the floor drop out from under her. The barrier had already thinned. Would having things as prepared as she could make them somehow brush it away? "I thought it would take weeks."

"We've been waiting for this chance our whole lives," Grace said. "We've practiced different patterns over the past few years and learned the best ways to make the kirtles."

A shiver crept up Bri's spine.

"There are a few last minute adjustments to make, but they'll only take a day or two."

Katie jumped in. "We're going to stay here with you while we make them."

"I don't know what to say." Bri stumbled over the words. "I know you've put in a lot of work, and I appreciate it, but — I can't go. I can't leave."

Maybe someday, when Gran wasn't here anymore. Bri's heart ached at the idea of a world without Gran in it.

"What are you saying?" Grace asked.

"Gran just got out of the hospital," Bri said. "She needs me."

"Nonsense. I'll not be your excuse." Gran glared. "You'll not use me to keep you from the life you were meant to live."

"Gran, I'm not making excuses. You need me. I don't know how I thought I could leave you alone."

Gran reached for Bri's hand. "You were thinking with your heart, my dear, which is as it should be."

Bri laughed shortly. "My heart tells me not to abandon you. We've only ever had each other."

"I've been blessed to have you with me, dear one, but I'll not be the reason you walk away from the life fate has given you." Gran sat taller and reached for her knitting. "Give your Duncan a chance. True love is worth the sacrifice."

How could Gran not see that even though they drove each other batty, Bri wanted to be there for her? "We can talk about it later."

"What does he look like? Duncan, I mean." Katie, Grace's older daughter asked. Her face lit up. She was a romantic.

Ryan came in then, carrying a tea tray. Bri hesitated. The idea of talking about Duncan with Ryan in the room was awkward. But she couldn't ignore Katie.

"He's — um —" As Bri forced her eyes away from Ryan's to look at the bouncing teenager an idea came to her, nearly knocking her out of her seat.

Bri must have been too focused on kissing Duncan — it was the only explanation for why she hadn't considered it before now. She was a photographer. How could Bri not have thought of taking his picture? It hadn't even occurred to her when she'd explained photography to

Duncan. "If things work out right, I might be able to show you a picture of him tomorrow."

Hannah's eyes were as round as saucers. "That would work?"

"I can't promise anything, but I'll try to get a picture of him." Bri was choosing every word carefully. She tilted her head toward Ryan, and the girls nodded.

Ryan was passing around cups of tea. "I'd like to see a picture of him myself."

Bri's hand shook as she took her drink from him, nearly sloshing the tea into her lap. The corners of Ryan's eyes crinkled and he couldn't completely hide his snigger.

"I don't have one with me, but I can try to get one." If cameras could see things from the distant past. Bri smiled, pleased with herself. She'd gotten away without promising to show Ryan any picture she might get.

They made small talk while having their tea, then Ryan carried luggage upstairs for Grace and the girls. Finally, he announced he was running over to the Mad Hatter Café to pick up some dinner.

Once he left, Katie and Hannah ran upstairs, squealing and making a general ruckus. They thundered back downstairs, their arms full of fabrics. "Try these on while he's gone." Katie grinned.

"I'm still working on the embroidery," Hannah said, pointing out the beautiful patterns along the edges. "It won't take much longer, though. Let's see how they fit."

Grace shook her head at the giggles, but she was smiling. She held up a plain linen kirtle. "This one goes on first. It will give you all the support you need — women didn't wear anything under it."

Bri felt the heat of her blush creep up her neck and onto her face. She grabbed the kirtle and hurried into Gran's bedroom to change.

She slid the kirtle over her head, lacing the front closed. The kirtle was surprisingly comfortable. She caught her legs in the fabric walking to the door and sighed. She already missed the freedom of her shorts. She straightened the skirt and went out.

Grace and the girls, and even Gran, smiled. Their ooh-ing and ah-ing would have made Bri laugh if she hadn't been busy trying not to trip over herself. She could walk in four-inch heels without a problem — a skill anyone barely five feet tall would master — but so many yards of fabric around her ankles was tricky.

"We have other kirtles as well," Grace said. "We made two like the one you're wearing, and another two with lacing on the sides instead of at the front. We thought they'd come in handy when you're pregnant. You can let the laces out as needed."

When she was pregnant. Bri caught her breath. If she stayed with Gran, she wouldn't have kids. Grace, and Katie, and Hannah — none of them would exist. Her eyes swam.

She had no choice. She never had. There were too many people counting on her going back with Duncan. Bri looked at Gran and saw the same knowledge in the old woman's eyes. Gran nodded and gave her a wobbly smile.

Bri frowned. She wanted to be with Duncan more than anything, but the idea of leaving Gran broke her heart.

Maybe she could find a way to take Gran back with her. That might work.

"Here are your over-kirtles," Hannah said. She held up a pale blue linen kirtle that would match the kerchief Duncan had given Bri. "We dyed the fabric with natural dyes so you won't stand out in strong colors."

Katie picked up three other over-kirtles. "We only used linen for the blue one. These others are wool."

One was gray, another a pale pink, and the last had the different colors of creamy natural wool. "They're beautiful. I can't believe you did all this in just a few days."

"We'd already dyed the fabrics. We hoped you'd be coming in the next year or two." Grace motioned to her girls, displaying the kirtles and teasing each other. "It's an honor for all of us to be able to help you."

Hannah stepped closer to Bri and popped the blue linen kirtle over her head. Bri fought for a few seconds to find the sleeves, then let the skirt flow down over the other. She bit back her complaint that she'd have to fight even more fabric.

"You can tuck this one up, like this," Hannah said, showing her how to adjust the fabric so the skirt of the plain kirtle showed.

The girls hurried Bri through trying the other kirtles.

"Ryan's here," Katie shrieked, spying Ryan through the window.

Bri raced for Gran's room and her pile of modern clothes. She could hear Katie and Hannah tearing up the stairs. A giggle escaped Bri. She could only imagine the crazy looks Ryan would have given them all.

A few minutes later, back in her shorts and blouse, Bri found everyone gathered in the dining room. Katie and Hannah were pulling boxes of food from the bags, and Ryan was trying to reach around them to set the table.

"Can I have a minute?" Grace asked.

Bri nodded, and they slipped into the hallway. "Thank you for the kirtles."

Grace beamed. "As I said before, it's an honor." Her smile fell. "I know you're worried for your gran. I wondered, if you don't mind — I'd like to take her home with us. We'd love for her to live with us, and it might make things easier on you to know people who care about you both are looking after her."

Bri gaped. "You want to adopt my Gran?"

"She shouldn't be alone." Grace's eyes sparkled and she reached out to squeeze Bri's arm. "You don't have to decide right away. Think about it. If you like the idea we'll invite her to stay."

DUNCAN

uncan stood beside the swearing stone, staring at the hole carved through it. Trying to build up the courage to move his hand, to place it in that empty circle.

Brianna wouldn't be there. He couldn't believe it to be possible. If he believed there was a chance to see her, and her hand didn't grasp his, he'd not make it out of the churchyard.

Two nights and three days without his wife had broken him. Duncan needed her with him, in his own time.

Most of all, he needed Brianna in his arms.

Duncan looked at the knot earrings he'd made, cradled in his hand. He'd spent half the day working to make them perfect for Brianna, once he'd finally wakened from his mead-induced slumber.

He curled his fingers, grasping the knots tightly. Using them to fuel a bravery he didn't feel, Duncan shoved his hand into the stone's hole.

Energy played against the skin of his fingers, like sparks from a flint. The feel of it ran up his arm until the power of possibility coated every bit of him.

Brianna's hand didn't meet his.

As he watched, the church before him shimmered. It was as if he looked through the smoke of a roaring fire, and on the other side of the barrier, the church changed.

The tower behind the church stretched, the conical roof squaring. The church's walls no longer reached the portal, which now stood as hardly more than an arch.

Other shapes he'd not seen before appeared. Plants, and grave markers.

And there, just crossing to go through the portal, was Brianna.

Duncan's breath caught and his fingers slipped from the stone. She didn't disappear. He watched as she neared, the way she moved burning into him. The gentle sway of her hips. The way she hopped over something in her path.

As she turned toward the stone, Brianna's eyes met his. She drifted to a stop and stared.

Duncan waited for her to come to him. Her hair blew to the side in the fingers of a breeze. A breeze he felt on his own skin.

Then she was running to him.

Duncan stepped to the side of the stone and opened his arms for her. She flung her arms around his neck and he wrapped her tightly against his chest.

His world righted itself and he became a man again instead of the shadow he'd been. Duncan whispered her name into her hair and held her more tightly. He'd not let her go again.

"I'm sorry. I'm so sorry I wasn't here."

Pulling away just enough, he pressed his mouth to hers, capturing her lips with his, demanding her attention.

She kissed him back, more demanding still.

Duncan held Brianna to him, breathing her into his soul. He'd never have his fill of her. He unwound one arm from her waist to tangle his fingers in her flying hair. "Come, *a rúnsearc*. Come home with me."

Brianna pulled away from him.

Unwilling to let her go completely, he grasped her hand, holding it to his chest. To his heart, beating hard and fast for her alone.

"I can't, not tonight," Brianna said.

Duncan's breath stopped. Before the despair could reclaim him, she was talking again.

"For the past two nights I've been at the hospital with my grandmother. She slipped and fell, and was injured." Brianna continued to talk, telling him the awful things she'd been through since he'd seen her.

Duncan waited, listening, scared of the words he knew she'd say. Waiting for her to say she had to stay with her grandmother, even knowing Brianna belonged to him as much as he belonged to her.

"So I can't come," Brianna said.

Duncan let her hand fall from his chest where he'd held it captive.

"Not tonight." Brianna paused, looking at her fallen hand as if she didn't understand he needed to distance himself if she no longer wanted to be his. "I think I'll have things worked out so I could come after tomorrow."

Duncan's stared at her. He'd not heard her right, he couldn't have. She'd just said she couldn't come. "What are you saying?"

"Do you remember me telling you about Grace?"

Duncan nodded, wondering if his drunkenness of the night before still held him. It was the only explanation for the way his head spun.

"Gran is going to go stay with her. Grace and her daughters are going to care for Gran so I don't have to worry about her."

He ran a hand over his face, rubbing his temples. "Speak plainly so I understand," he begged.

"If the barrier will let me through, I can come with you tomorrow. There are just a few more things I need to do to be ready." Brianna smiled up at him. She tucked her hands behind her back as if waiting for a scolding.

"You're coming?"

She nodded. "Tomorrow night."

Duncan reached for her again, a rumble in his chest quiet compared to the wind rustling the leaves around them.

"Wait." Brianna pulled back. "We need to stay on our own sides of where the barrier goes, just in case it won't let us back through."

His growl deepened. "I want you in my arms, wife."

Brianna grinned. She tipped her head back and went up on her toes, her hands on his shoulders. "And I want you in mine. We just need to be careful about it."

He didn't want to be careful. He wanted his wife close enough to be twined with him. He sighed. To keep Brianna happy, Duncan nodded.

She reached her lips up to his, pulling him to her, as she pressed against him.

Duncan wrapped his arms around Brianna again, crushing her to him as he kissed her harder. He released her lips and buried his face in her neck. The scent of her overwhelmed him — she smelled of rain, and flowers, and woman. A quiet mewl of pleasure came from the woman. Duncan smiled against her skin.

He pulled away enough to whisper in Brianna's ear. "I've a gift for you."

Duncan stepped back, putting some distance between them. His control was a fragile thing. Without that distance it would break and he would carry her home with no thought for her grandmother.

Brianna was blinking. She pressed her fingers against her lips as if she could still feel him there. As she shook her head, the breeze tossed her hair into her face. She brushed it aside. "You what?"

Duncan lifted his fist for her, opening it to show the earrings he still held.

Brianna lifted the earrings from his palm, staring at them. She raised her eyes to his. "They're beautiful."

Duncan sighed. She liked them. "I worried for you when you weren't here. Even when I worked I couldn't keep my mind from you, so I chose to work on things for you."

Her eyes widened. "You made these?"

"Aye."

Brianna caressed the knots with her fingertip. "Thank you. For the earrings, and for not giving up on me. I wasn't sure you'd be here tonight."

He didn't want to think on how close he'd come to staying away. "May I?" He took the earrings back. Holding the hair from her ear, he slid the thin hook through the hole in one earlobe, then did the same with the other.

Brianna reached up and touched the knots as they tapped against her neck.

Unable to stop himself, Duncan leaned in and brushed his lips in the same place the knot had kissed her skin. "There's more."

"Hmm?" Brianna's fingers were gliding up his arms again.

Duncan cleared his throat. "I've another gift."

Brianna's fingers fell from his elbows as he reached to where he'd tucked the necklace into his belt. He lifted it over her head, carefully keeping it from catching in her hair. The knot, larger than the earrings, fell to rest in the valley between her breasts.

"It has no end. If you trace the pattern, you end where you began." Duncan reached out to follow the intricate knot with a finger. "The night we were wed, I believed I was here for an ending. I was wrong. 'Twas no ending, but a bend in my path. My beginning with you. I want you with me for every bend and turn as we circle through our pattern."

With a shaking breath, Brianna reached up and covered his hand with her own. She pressed it to her chest. Her heart beat against his fingertips. She smiled. "Every single bend."

Her words hung in the air between them, a vow brought to life.

Brianna backed away from Duncan and reached for the ground where she'd dropped her things when she'd flown at him. "Will you let me try something?"

"Aye." Duncan would let her do anything.

She lifted something. "This is my camera. I don't know if I'll be able to do this with the difference in years, but I'd like to try taking your picture."

Duncan stared. "That wee thing can make these pictures you told me about?" He didn't believe it. He couldn't.

Brianna laughed, then showed him the different parts of the camera. She explained how it worked before lifting it to cover her face. She pressed the wee window to her eye. Using her free hand, she turned the round thing she claimed would make the image clear.

"Smile," she said.

Duncan tried. Several times. "How am I to smile at you when your face is hidden from me?"

Brianna peeked over the top of the contraption. "Is this better?" She gazed at him with her wide eyes. Her eyes dropped to his lips before drifting back to his gaze.

It filled him with warmth. He smiled, waiting for her to step toward him. Expecting her lips to join with his.

Click.

"That wasn't so hard, was it?" Brianna's lips curled in a wicked smile.

Duncan laughed. If he were a warlord instead of a blacksmith, he'd find a woman like her to interrogate his captives. They'd willingly give her every secret they held.

"Do you want to see?"

Brianna came to him. On the back side of her camera, she showed him an image. "That's you."

Duncan stared at her as she looked at the image. Her eyes were soft, and she smiled. What had he done to deserve this woman?

He indulged her as she took more of her pictures. She ordered him about, telling him how to stand and where to look. Duncan could have said no, but it made her so happy.

After a time, Brianna tucked the camera back in her bundle.

They sat on the ground beside each other, staying in their own times. As the night wore on, they spoke of many things. The conversation moved from topic to topic as they learned more of each other.

A day. Duncan sighed and pulled his wife in close to his side. He could last one day more.

When the night thinned and daylight threatened, Duncan rose and offered a hand to Brianna. He helped her to her feet and gave her one more kiss.

He watched as she walked back through the churchyard, under the arch of the portal. She looked back over her shoulder and smiled, then left the churchyard.

Duncan waited for the world around him to shift back to the things he knew. As he walked back through the town, everything looked different to him. How would it look to Brianna?

A hiss came from the bakery window. Duncan looked over to see Michael waving at him. Curious, Duncan went to the window. Heat from the fires seeped into the cool morning air.

Michael made a show of readying a loaf and passing it out to him. "The women," he whispered. "They're up to something."

"Of course they are. They're women."

"This is different," Michael said, shaking his head. "My wife was muttering with Brogan's wife after the bell rang for Compline. She told me naught that had been said. She was afraid I'd pass it on to you, as if we gossiped as much as they do."

Duncan looked heavenward. "Save us from meddling women."

"Amen." Michael peered more closely at him. "Mind yourself. They're up to something and it's to do with you."

Duncan nodded and kept on his way. He'd not think too hard on what they were doing. In a day, he'd be introducing Brianna to the women. Then they'd leave him in peace.

21

BRIANNA

Bri let herself into the B&B and made her way upstairs without getting caught. It wasn't exactly a walk of shame — she'd done nothing to be ashamed of — but she was glad she didn't have to explain herself.

She changed into her plaid pajama pants and a T-shirt, and pulled her wind-tangled hair into a ponytail. Bri looked in the mirror at the necklace and earrings Duncan had given her. She grinned at her reflection. Her husband was perfect.

Anxious to see her pictures on a larger screen, Bri plopped onto the bed with her camera in one hand and her laptop in the other.

It only took a minute to transfer the pictures to her computer. She clicked the icon to bring up her editing software and settled in.

Noises in the house began to drift through the walls. Hannah and Katie were giggling, the sound filling the hallway with joy.

Bri jumped off the bed and flung the door open.

Ryan stood there, his hand raised to knock. His eyes drifted over her pajamas and one side of his mouth raised in a half-smile. He cleared his throat. "I was coming to see if you were up. Breakfast will be ready in a few minutes."

She waited for him to disappear down the stairs before turning to the girls, still laughing in the hallway. She motioned them into her room and closed the door.

"Ryan was acting weird," Hannah said.

"Never mind him," Bri said. "I took pictures of Duncan last night. Do you still want to see?"

The girls spoke over each other. Bri couldn't make out any of their words, but the general answer seemed to be yes.

Bri turned her laptop so the girls could look at the picture that filled her screen. It showed Duncan, from the waist up. His lips were slightly parted, as if he was waiting for a kiss.

Katie reached out and touched the screen. She sighed. "I wish there were still boys like him."

"What does it feel like to kiss him with that beard?" Hannah asked.

Katie swatted her. "None of our business."

Hannah shrugged. "I just wondered if it was prickly."

Bri laughed. "No, it's soft."

There was a tap on the door, and Bri looked over. Grace stepped into the room. When she saw the girls huddled around the computer she smiled. "Is that what I think it is?"

Hannah and Katie spoke at the same time again. Bri didn't say anything. Grace had to be used to it, and adding another voice would only make words harder to understand.

Grace made her way over and peered over shoulders. "He's very handsome. I can see why you're attracted to him."

"It's so romantic." Katie fell back on the bed, her arms outstretched. "Love so strong that centuries can't be in the way."

"We're wanted downstairs for breakfast, Miss Romance," Grace said, pulling Katie back to her feet. "Bri, if you don't mind, I'd love a print of that picture, and one of you as well."

"Of course."

"You may want to change before coming downstairs."

Bri looked down. She'd forgotten she was in her pajamas. "Will you tell Gran I'll be down soon?"

Grace nodded and ushered her daughters out of the room.

As Bri dressed in jeans and a light sweater, she folded her clothes and sorted them into piles. Things to pack up for Grace and the girls, and things to take with her to her new life with Duncan.

A thrill passed through her. She was moving in with her husband.

There was a light tap at the door. Bri sighed. She couldn't get ten minutes to herself. "I'm coming."

"Bri, can I talk to you?" Ryan's voice came through the door.

She pulled the door open, standing so Ryan couldn't see the piles she'd been sorting on the bed. "I said I was on my way down." Bri squeezed past him and into the hallway.

"I didn't put him up to it, I swear," Ryan said. He raked a hand through his hair.

That didn't bode well. Bri narrowed her eyes. "Put who up to what?"

"My father. He just arrived with a friend of his who specializes in ancient coins."

Bri filled the hall with her curses. Whispered curses, to avoid one of Gran's lectures. "Why won't he leave me alone about it?"

"If there's one thing that holds Da's attention, it's a secret." Ryan put his hand on her back and led her to the stairs. "And he says you're keeping one."

Hysterical laughter bubbled up and caught in Bri's throat. Of course she was keeping a secret. Several of them.

Bri stomped down the stairs and into the dining room. Everyone else had started eating, but Gran had saved a spot between herself and Grace.

Bri kissed Gran good morning while pointedly ignoring the man and woman sitting across the table from her. She felt their stares as an annoying itch, like she'd rolled through an anthill and covered herself in the critters.

She kept her eyes down as she spread rhubarb hibiscus jam on her toast. The room was too quiet. Bri glanced up. Everyone was staring at her, even the girls. She sighed.

"It's nice to see you again, Bri." Eoin leaned back in his chair, his arms crossed over his chest. "This is my colleague, Dr. Walsh."

Bri nodded to the woman. She was older than Bri expected — probably retired — but not as old as Gran. Her hair was cropped close to her scalp, a no-nonsense style that wouldn't take much effort. Her skin had a leathery, weather-worn look.

The silence thickened, broken only by the ticking of a clock and the trilling call of a bird outside the window. Hannah shifted uneasily on the other side of Grace.

"Eoin mentioned he'd seen an ancient Irish coin you have in your possession," Dr. Walsh began. She gave Bri a grandmotherly smile and her face came alive with excitement. "I'm hoping you'll agree to show it to me as well. I've spent my life studying such things."

Bri swallowed her bite of toast. It scratched against her too-dry throat. "Thanks for the interest, but I'm going to just keep it to myself."

"Young lady," Eoin said, leaning across the table and shaking a finger at her. "Pieces like that coin can tell us much about our history. A coin in such good condition is a rare find. As all artifact finds legally belong to the museum, we'd like to determine if the coin is genuine."

"Da," Ryan said. "She's my guest."

Bri felt a rush of gratitude and offered him a tiny smile.

Gran's hand twitched against the edge of her plate. "I assure you, you'll not get my girl to share her coin with you by pressing her with guilt."

Bri laughed. Bless Gran for breaking the tension. "I've had lots of practice at resisting guilt. Gran is an expert at using it to get her way."

Eoin frowned.

"I only want to see the coin," Dr. Walsh said, her hands stretched out as she tried to placate them. "I'm not here to take it from you. If the coin is as pristine as Eoin claims it could tell us much more than you realize. Surely you can understand the excitement of a find like this."

"I'm sure it could tell you more than you realize," Bri said. "It was minted near here in the early fifteenth century. And yes, it's in great condition considering its age. You still won't be examining it. I've explained several times that it isn't a new find. It was a gift from my husband."

Ryan startled, knocking over the glass of juice he'd been reaching for. He ignored the spreading mess and stared at her.

Bri saw the hurt and surprise in his eyes. She bit her lip. She should've told Ryan yesterday when they'd talked — should have told him privately — but right now she had to focus on protecting the token of her marriage.

"It's a family heirloom, if you will." Or it would become one. She'd make sure of it. Bri grabbed the rest of her toast and stood. "If you'll excuse me, I have things to do."

"Now see here," Eoin said, pushing to his feet.

Ryan moved to put himself between Eoin and Bri. "Da. Leave it. She is a guest and it's time you treat her like one."

Bri moved forward and reached for Ryan's arm. She waited until he looked at her. "I'm sorry," she whispered.

Ryan cocked his head, the lock of hair falling back into his eyes. He offered her a tight smile.

Bri smiled as pleasantly as she could at Eoin. "I'm not going to keep fighting about this. I already gave you my answer. It was no."

As she left the room, she could hear Gran light into them. Bri chuckled. Gran would give them more than they bargained for if they let her get started. Not that they didn't deserve it for wanting to take her coin away.

"Bri, do you want help?" Hannah asked, running to catch up to her. She lowered her voice. "I don't like those people."

beyond the swearing stone

"Sure. I'm sorting through my things." Bri glanced behind her to be sure they were alone. "I need to figure out how to pack what I'm taking with me."

In the bedroom, with the door closed, Hannah turned to Bri. "I was confused downstairs. What coin were they talking about?"

Bri smiled. She loved that the girl wasn't afraid to ask questions. Reaching into her pocket, she pulled out the coin and handed it to Hannah. "Duncan gave it to me that first day at the swearing stone — when he married me. It was the only thing that kept me from believing I hadn't gone completely out of my mind."

Hannah's eyes grew. "You're letting me touch it?"

"Of course. You're family." Funny. Even thinking of Ryan and Eoin, or Dr. Walsh, touching the coin made it hard to breathe. Sharing it with Hannah just felt natural.

Bri walked over to the bed and looked at the piles she'd made. "I guess there's really not much I can take with me."

"I should bring in your kirtles." Hannah handed the coin back and slipped out of the room.

Bri looked at her favorite clothes and sighed. She really didn't want to leave them behind. "I'd better not trip over those skirts."

Bri cast a final, wishful glance at her flannel pajama pants. She'd miss those even more than her favorite shorts.

Hannah came back in, her arms full of Bri's new clothes. Bri held each item up against her, then set aside a plain linen kirtle and the gray wool over-kirtle Hannah had embroidered. She'd wear that when she went to the churchyard. She carefully folded the other kirtles and placed them in a bag with the kerchief Duncan had given her. The bag wasn't appropriate to the time she would be in, but it would be dark and she could always burn it.

"Thanks, Hannah. I don't know what I'd do without your help."

The girl beamed.

"Will you hand me that spindle? I'll add it here, then I want to run and buy more roving to take."

Hannah stared at the spindle. "Everyone in our family's history, boys and girls, have learned to spin and knit. Do you think you're the reason why?"

Bri shifted uncomfortably. "I couldn't be. I'm not even any good at spinning."

Hannah shrugged the comment off like only a teenager can. "Can I come shopping with you?"

"Sure." Bri was finally getting used to Hannah's rapid topic changes. "We can all go. I'm going to finish up here first, though."

She moved to the things she wasn't taking with her. "I'll pack all this stuff in my suitcase. Your mom said she'd take it home so it wasn't left here at the B&B. If there's anything you guys want, you can have it."

Bri loaded in her clothes and toiletries. Her books went at the bottom, and she buried her laptop in the middle of the clothes to protect it.

The hardest part was packing away her Nikon. For just a minute, Bri wished things were different. Not that she didn't want to be with Duncan, but it would be nice if he lived in a time period that would allow her to keep the camera. It was a part of her. She tucked her old friend into its case, nestling it into the protective foam. The sound of the zipper closing it in was her final goodbye to the profession she'd worked so hard to earn.

Finally done, Bri and Hannah went back downstairs. Bri kept an eye out for Eoin and Dr. Walsh, but they'd disappeared. Thank goodness.

"Bri invited us to go with her to buy wool," Hannah said.

Grace looked up. "That works with the plans your grandmother and I were just making."

"What plans?"

"We're driving to Dublin," Gran said. Her voice was quiet enough that Bri might have imagined the strain lacing the edges of her words.

"You need to return the rental car. Once you disappear we don't want it hanging around causing questions."

Bri dropped into a chair. "I hadn't thought about that."

Gran smiled bravely.

They made a day of going to Dublin. They did a little shopping — Bri didn't buy anything — and had lunch. On their way back to Castledermot they took a small detour to the wool shop Bri had found.

There, she did her shopping. She left with a much lighter bank account, several pounds of un-dyed roving, and a set of paddle brushes for carding wool if she could buy it in Tristledermot.

"I hope I can fit all this in my bag," Bri said. "I'm not sure I'll be able to carry it otherwise."

"We'll stop at the churchyard and hide it in the bushes. That way you'll not have to carry it." Gran nodded from the front seat of the car. "You can do the same thing once you're there. Leave things behind and take several trips so you're not mistaken for a pack mule."

The rest of the drive was quiet, everyone lost in their own thoughts.

Bri's excitement at going home to Duncan was tempered by the knowledge she was leaving everything, especially Gran and her new-found family, behind.

When they stopped at the church, the girls helped Bri hide her things. She wasn't worried about anyone walking off with them. It would only be a couple of hours before she was back.

22

BRIANNA

Bri stood at the bedroom window, waiting for the sun to set — and hiding from Ryan, Eoin, and Dr. Walsh.

Grace's car had been loaded with everyone's bags, including Bri's. After making a show of saying goodbye, Grace had driven away, leaving Bri behind.

She checked the level of the sun again. It was nearly time. Bri grabbed her purse and tiptoed down the stairs. Hopefully she'd make it down the hall and out the door without getting caught.

As she slipped through the dim hallway, she could hear Ryan talking behind a nearly-closed door. She paused, unsure if she should tell him she was going out. Would he worry more if he knew she'd stepped out and didn't come back, or if she just disappeared with no word?

Then she heard Eoin's voice as he responded to whatever Ryan had said. That made the decision for her. She held her breath and tiptoed past the door.

The barrier had better still be open for her. There was no way she was spending the night in a house with Eoin constantly popping out at her. She opened the door and slid through.

Bri stepped into the avenue leading to the church and smiled up at the canopy of leaves. They were quiet above her, with no hint of a breeze. The sound of car doors closing ahead of her pulled her attention from the stillness and Brianna hurried toward the churchyard.

Grace pulled out the bag filled with her kirtles and head kerchiefs, as well as a picture of Gran and one of Duncan she'd printed to keep with her. If anyone saw them and pressed her, she'd claim they were just really good paintings.

"There's no one in the churchyard at the moment," Grace said. She passed Bri the clothing she'd kept out to wear. "If you go duck behind the church, no one will see you change. We'll stop anyone who might come."

"Thanks," Bri said. Once behind the church, Bri glanced around before pulling off her modern clothes. She shivered — not because she was cold, it was a warm evening — but she'd never undressed outside in the open like this. She shrugged. There was no other option. She couldn't very well go back to medieval times wearing shorts.

She pulled the kirtle over her head and drew the laces tight. Adding her over-kirtle, she looped the skirt up like she'd been shown.

Bri looked down at herself. She almost felt like a different person in the dress.

She wasn't sure she liked the feeling.

Pulled her coin from the pocket of the shorts, she tucked it safely in her bodice and carried her clothes back to the car where her family waited. Bri shoved them into the trunk.

Saying goodbye to Gran at the B&B had been hard, even though she'd known it was for a short time. Now, having to say goodbye forever, Bri's eyes stung with unshed tears.

Gran slid her arm through Bri's. "We'll come with you as far as the swearing stone."

Bri nodded. As they neared the stone, the tingle of power she always felt there went crazy, pounding through every part of her. Tonight, the barrier would allow her through.

Gran let go of Bri's arm and joined Grace and the girls. Bri smiled. She'd meet her future with a wall of family at her back.

She reached her hand through the hole.

The air in front of her shimmered. The silhouette of trees shifted, and farther back, a wall came into view.

Bri smiled. Just stepping up to the stone was Duncan.

He looked back at her, his eyes wide as he saw what she wore. "You look like you belong on this side of the barrier." He paused and a wicked glint appeared in his eyes. "Your bare legs were more to my liking."

Heat crept up Bri's neck. "Shorts aren't appropriate in your time."

Duncan's face fell, but he laughed.

Bri glanced over her shoulder. "This is our family."

Duncan looked past her. "Where?"

"Just behind me. This is Gran, and here's Grace and her girls, Katie and Hannah." She pointed each of them out to him.

"I can't see them."

"Gran, can you see Duncan?" Bri asked.

"Aye, and hear him as well."

Duncan's eyes widened enough Bri wondered if they'd fall from their sockets.

Gran's voice took on a harder edge. "You tell that man to care for you well. I'll not have you traipsing through time only to learn things aren't as you expected."

Duncan nodded. "Aye, Grandmother. Brianna is everything to me. I'll not let her want."

"That's fine, then." Gran reached for Bri and pulled her away from Duncan and into a hug. "Don't worry for me, dear one. You're meant to do this."

Gran's voice, thick with emotion, brought the tears to Bri's eyes. "I don't want to leave you."

"Grace and the girls will take fine care of me. Go on, now. You've a life of your own to live."

Bri held on a little tighter. "I love you, Gran."

"Of course you do. And don't I love you? But your time here is done. Go now. The girls have pushed your things to the other side of the stone. You're ready."

Bri sniffled. "I don't think I can do this," she whispered in Gran's ear.

"Nonsense." Gran pulled away from Bri and reached a hand out to rest on her cheek. "You're stronger than that. Go, and take our love with you."

When Bri didn't move, Gran took her by the arm and led her the two steps to the stone. "Young man," Gran said. "Take her hand. She's ready for you, but mind her heart. It'll ache a while."

As Duncan's hand wrapped around Bri's, Gran gave a gentle push and Bri stumbled through the barrier. She turned for a final look at Gran but there was no one there.

They'd gone.

Bri's tears fell a little faster.

Duncan pulled her to his chest. His warmth seeped through her kirtle, and she was wrapped in the gentle pressure of his arms. "Cry, love. It will heal you."

So Bri stood in the circle of his arms and let her tears flow freely.

When her tears slowed she tucked that broken part of her heart as deep as it would go. Gran was right. Bri had to move forward. She looked up at the man who loved her. The man whose eyes were so sad for her. She smiled. It was a bit wobbly, but it was a start.

Duncan leaned down and kissed the tears from her face. "Are you ready to go home, or should we stay here a while longer?"

Bri took a deep breath. "Let's go home."

Duncan leaned down to pick up Bri's bag of clothes. He peeked into one of the paper bags of wool. He looked up at Bri, his face full of laughter. "We've sheep aplenty here, wife."

A giggle escaped Bri. She clapped her hand to her mouth, not sure how she could giggle while she was still sad about leaving Gran.

Duncan handed Bri one of the bags of roving. "We'll try to go through town quietly. There are plenty of people awake, but mostly they'll be in their homes."

Bri nodded. She didn't want to meet anyone just yet. Not until she'd washed her face, at least.

Duncan balanced her things in one arm and reached for her with his free hand. Bri wrapped her fingers in his and let him lead her from the churchyard.

It was good Duncan was looking out for her. Bri was so busy trying to see everything she hardly paid attention to where she put her feet. She wrinkled her nose. Odors mingled together — cooked meats, and sewage, and smoke. Well, she'd get used to it.

The streets were narrower than she expected, and the upper floors pushed out, hanging over the road. The windows across from each other were close enough it would be easy to toss something across. Light from fires and candles spilled from open windows and glinted through cracks in shutters.

Sounds filled the street, drifting from homes and a tavern. The noise was trapped in the narrow space between buildings. A baby cried somewhere, and voices rose in a heated argument. It wasn't the quiet country town she'd expected.

As they came to an intersection of three streets, Bri realized the layout of the roads were the same as she was already used to. It was eerie how similar and different things were at the same time.

beyond the swearing stone

Duncan led her around the corner and pointed to a narrow building. There was a small staircase that led up the side.

Bri hiked up the skirt of her kirtle. Tripping her way up the stairs was not the first impression she wanted to make.

At the top, Duncan used his foot to nudge open the door. After leading her inside, he pushed the door closed.

Bri looked around, wanting to get an idea of what she was in for. The front windows were shuttered, but a light breeze floated through the uncovered back windows.

There was a stone fireplace along the wall next to the door, with a nicked table in front of it. Shelves filled the space under the shuttered windows. Pots, knives, and the clutter of life gathered together in a homey way. On the far wall, near the open back windows, there was a bed with a drape above and curtains around the sides. Several chests were pushed up under the back windows.

Duncan set Bri's things on the table and moved to the fireplace. As he stirred the embers to life the pleasant light warmed the room. He straightened, watching Bri closely. "We can change things however you'd like. I want you to be comfortable."

Bri smiled. She'd been so busy exploring the room with her eyes she hadn't realized Duncan was waiting for her reaction. "We can take things slowly," she said. As she looked around again, a flutter of nervousness came to life and she clutched the skirt of her kirtle to keep her hands from shaking. "I don't know how to do things I probably should. I've never cooked over a fire. I've never even made a fire."

Duncan crossed the short distance between them and pulled her into a hug. "I know things are different. We'll make it work."

Bri nodded against his chest, breathing in his scent to try to calm herself. "Okay. Okay, then."

She could do this. She had to.

Duncan shifted. "I've two trunks readied for you." He pointed to the back wall and told her which would be hers.

Bri jumped at the chance for something to do. She grabbed her bag of clothes and started piling them into the trunk nearest the bed, trying to settle them so they wouldn't crease.

The pictures of Gran and Duncan, she tucked into the lid so she could see them whenever she opened the trunk. Bri brushed her fingers over them. She probably shouldn't have brought them. They were too out of place in this century.

She was going to keep them anyway. She needed some kind of connection to Gran.

Bri pushed to her feet and opened the other trunk. It was in a corner, tucked away under a series of open shelves. Bri put her roving, spindle, and knitting needles in there. The knitting needles were out of place, too — carbon fiber wouldn't be easy to explain if anyone looked at them closely — but they were another connection to Gran.

"Once the sun is up I'll show you around town," Duncan said from his place beside the table. "We've a burgage in back with a garden, and rain barrels, and a privy." He cleared his throat.

"I'm excited to see it."

They stood across the room from each other, the distance filled with awkwardness. Bri was increasingly aware of the large bed in the corner, and the husband who seemed determined to keep his distance from her.

Bri reached up and touched the knot necklace Duncan had made for her. The twists and turns under her fingers helped to soothe her. She felt herself settle.

Duncan sank into a chair at the table.

Bri frowned. He was supposed to be kissing her. He'd never hesitated before. She would just have to take matters into her own hands.

"I guess I should get ready for bed," Bri said. Without looking at Duncan, she reached down and unlaced her over-kirtle. Then she lifted it over her head and set it carefully on top of her clothes trunk.

"I'll give you privacy," Duncan said, his voice tight. He was out the door before Bri could tell him to stay.

Bri watched the door for a minute to see if he'd come back in. When it didn't open, she sat on the edge of the bed. There had to be a way to get past the discomfort that had settled between them since they'd gotten home.

Home. Bri looked around. Yes, she could see this as her home. She was going to be very happy here.

DUNCAN

Duncan leaned against the wall outside and breathed deeply of the cooler air of night.

He'd not thought of how it would be with a woman in his home, of the way it would change everything. He'd not dared think of taking her to his bed. If he'd thought of it and she'd not come through the time barrier, it would be one more way of losing her.

Yet Brianna was here. There was but a door between them. Duncan forced another deep breath. He'd had to put himself on the other side of the door.

That door was the only thing keeping him from ravishing the woman.

If there was one thing Duncan had learned in his life with Neve, it was that being ravished was not an entirely pleasant experience for a woman. They allowed it only because it was expected of a wife.

Brianna was grieving the loss of her grandmother. He'd not ravish her, no matter his desire. Duncan refused to cause her more tears tonight.

Duncan lowered himself to sit on the top step and settled in to wait. Finally, certain Brianna would be sleeping, he quietly opened the door and entered.

He couldn't keep his eyes from drifting to the bed.

"There you are." Brianna sat on the edge of the bed. She held a coin in the well of her palm, as if she'd been staring at it. The front of her kirtle was open to her waist, and her hair fell around her face in waves.

Duncan glanced heavenward, silently asking what he'd done to deserve such torment.

"I like it here," Brianna said, gesturing with one hand to show she meant their home. "It's cozy."

The woman couldn't be serious. It was a single room with none of the comforts she must have had in the home she'd just left.

She reached her hand out to set her coin on top of the wooden trunk beside the bed, then turned her gaze to meet his. "I like it most of all because you're here."

Duncan groaned and shut his eyes. If he'd no way to see her, he'd not be able to find her, to take her in his arms. He had to control himself. Brianna deserved as much.

"Open your eyes." Brianna's voice was soft.

"I can't." If he did, he'd want her more even than he already did.

"Open them," she insisted.

The quiet padding of bare feet against wood came toward him. Duncan opened his eyes. Brianna stood two paces away, her eyes demanding.

"What do you want from me?" The whispered words tripped over his tongue in his haste.

She stared at him. He couldn't look away. His strength was nearly gone.

Brianna shrugged her shoulders, one at a time. The linen kirtle slipped and fell to pool around her feet. The only thing left on her was his necklace.

Firelight painted Brianna's skin as she reached for him. "Come to bed."

"I can't." Duncan's voice was hardly more than a rasp. "I'll not hurt you tonight."

She laughed.

He stared. How could she laugh?

"Of course you won't hurt me," she said. "I trust you to never hurt me."

Duncan stared at her outstretched hand. "Then why are you asking this of me?"

Brianna crossed the two steps between them. "Because I want you. I can see in your eyes that you want me, too."

She reached down and took his hand. Never taking her eyes from his, she set his hand on her hip.

She was warm, her skin smooth. So smooth.

Duncan felt Brianna's hand cover his, guiding it over her waist and up her side.

He couldn't breathe.

"I want this, husband," Brianna said, pressing his hand more firmly to her skin. "Take me to bed."

Duncan could think no more. He'd no memory of why he shouldn't claim her, why he'd tried to control his desire.

He scooped his bride into his arms and carried her across the room.

The pale light of morning came through the open window beside the bed. Duncan smiled as he watched his wife sleep. Unable to control himself, he leaned in to kiss Brianna's shoulder.

She stirred, turning toward him and burrowing into his chest. Duncan felt her smile against him. "Good morning."

"And a good morning to you, wife." He wrapped his arms around her.

Brianna's hand drifted around his waist, pulling his hips tight against her.

Duncan sighed, then pulled away. Throughout the night, she'd shown his worries to be pointless. She'd not endured his ravishing, she'd reveled in it. Then she'd ravished him. "We should eat."

She squirmed against him, and he felt her trail of kisses climb his chest.

"I've an entire town to show you, wife." Duncan cleared his throat. If they stayed where they were any longer, he'd not let her up all day.

Brianna pulled away from him and sat up, throwing the covers off. Duncan watched as she stretched her hands over her head.

His heart sped. Showing Brianna around Tristledermot could wait. He grabbed her by the waist and pulled her into his lap.

Her giggles shook him. Duncan grinned.

"Stop, Duncan. We need to eat. And I need to use the privy." Brianna climbed off him and moved to her clothing trunk.

Duncan tucked his arms behind his head and watched her dress. She pulled on her kirtle and laced it. Then a wool kirtle. When she reached for the hem of the skirt and lifted it, Duncan found himself sitting up. She tucked it up at her waist and his heart dropped.

He'd no idea watching a woman dress could be intoxicating. His wife was dressed, and walking away from him. Duncan grinned. He'd no plan to let her stay dressed the full length of the day.

He stepped from the bed and pulled on his own clothing. He followed Brianna to the other side of the room where she bustled around, opening the front shutters.

She smiled at him.

Duncan's breath caught. She was beautiful with her hair rumpled from sleep and her eyes bleary from a night of love. It hit him anew how lucky he was that she was his, and that she was here with him.

He stepped behind her and wrapped his arms around her. She leaned back into him. She felt so small, so fragile.

A flutter of fear threatened to overcome him. He couldn't lose her. If he'd managed to put a babe in her belly last night —

No. Duncan refused to think on that. Brianna had seen proof they had several children. Several. Were she to be carrying his child so soon, there was no need to worry.

"I've blackberries and figs, and oatcakes," he offered. "If you'd like something different, I can go to the bakery."

Brianna turned in his arms and kissed him. The woman had become everything to him.

"I love you," he said. He'd said it many times through the night, but every time the words felt new.

"I love you, too." Brianna gave him a smile that pounded the truth of her words into Duncan. "Fruit and oatcakes sound wonderful, but I do need to find the privy first."

Duncan smoothed her hair, holding back a sigh. Seeing her rumpled hair left him wanting to rumple her more. "You'll need to cover your hair first. You're a married woman."

"Yeah, yeah. My hair is all yours," Brianna teased.

Duncan watched as she reached up and tried to straighten her hair with her fingers. With a start, he remembered the other small gift he'd bought. "I've a comb for you, and hair pins."

Brianna blinked at him. Duncan fought the urge to duck his head.

"You thought that far ahead?" she asked.

"Aye. I'd not have you running through town with your hair unbound before you bought them for yourself." His words were not completely in jest. Duncan would leave no chance for another man to think she might be free.

Brianna gave him a confused look. "I don't know how to do my hair. What do women do here?"

Duncan paused. The only married woman's hair he'd seen until now was Neve's. He'd never paid attention to what she'd done to it.

When it was uncovered, she'd always let it down. "I've no idea. Just up somehow. Then your kerchief covers the hair."

"I guess it doesn't matter then," Brianna said. She looked at the comb and hair pins.

Duncan reached for the comb. "May I?"

Bri flushed. "Okay."

He lifted her hair in his fingers, gently pulling the comb through it. The softness nearly had him carrying her back to bed. He would have, had she not been in need of going into the burgage.

When Duncan finished with the comb he watched as Brianna took her hair in both hands, twisted it into a knot, and pinned it to the back of her head. After that, she tied the kerchief over her hair.

Duncan frowned. He enjoyed seeing her hair. Mayhap she'd remove the kerchief when they returned.

After their trip outside they sat next to each other at the table. As they ate, Duncan asked questions of Brianna's life in the future. What she ate of a morning, and how she spent her time, and how the town had changed.

When they stood, he pulled her into his arms. He'd missed the touch of her against him while they'd eaten.

Brianna giggled as she kissed him.

"Will you see the town now," Duncan tipped his head toward the bed, "or later?"

His wife grinned and leaned into him.

"Duncan?" a woman's voice called from the other side of the door. "Are you home? Michael sent me to buy a knife."

Duncan glared at the door and thought curses at the baker's wife. He sighed. There'd be no getting rid of the woman before she'd gotten what she came for. "Go down to the smithy and I'll help you choose one."

He waited for the woman to get away from the door. "I'm sorry," he said quietly.

Brianna smiled. "I can keep busy while you're gone."

The look she gave Duncan left him wondering exactly what she might mean. "You could come meet Elizabeth. She's married to the baker."

Her hands fluttered at her waist. "I don't think I'm quite ready to meet anyone."

Duncan nodded, but he began to worry. If Brianna didn't meet people and make friends — if she could find a woman to befriend who wasn't an interfering busybody — she wouldn't begin to settle. She was comfortable here, with him, but she needed women to talk with.

And he was anxious to show off his beautiful wife.

"We can see the town later today," Brianna said.

"Today," Duncan said. He kissed her again. "I'll not lock you away in here. You should see the town. Meet our neighbors."

Brianna nodded. "I know, and I do want to." She put her hand on his hip and kissed him back. "I just want to spend a little more time with you first."

Her touch was like fire. Duncan growled and lifted Brianna in his arms. "The woman can wait."

"Put me down and go do your job." Brianna laughed. "I'll still be here when you get back."

As Duncan went down the stairs outside he wondered how quickly he'd be able to sell a knife.

24

BRIANNA

ri watched as Duncan closed the door. She raised a hand to cover her grin. She hadn't expected to love him so much, so fast.

She looked over at the bed. It was tempting to climb back into it. She'd gotten very little sleep.

She stretched as tall as she could, reaching her hands toward the thatch above her head. Her whole body ached. Her grin widened. Certain parts of her ached more than others, in a way that made her wish Duncan hadn't just walked out the door.

Bri chided herself. There was plenty of time to enjoy her husband.

She walked to the trunk in the corner and pulled out her spindle and roving. She went to set it on the table, then noticed the crumbs from breakfast. Bri set her things on a chair and swept the crumbs into her hand. She looked around the room, not sure what to do with them. They were only crumbs. She shrugged and tossed them out the window into the backyard that Duncan had called a burgage.

Bri spread her roving on the table, dividing it into narrow strips. She twisted one end of the wool around the little hook in the whorl and started the spindle spinning. Remembering what Gran had said about not over-twisting the fibers, she let the twist travel up the roving. When she couldn't reach any higher, she stopped to wind the new-spun yarn around the spindle, then continued on.

When she finished her length of roving, she added another, until her spindle was full. She carefully unwound the yarn, wrapping it around a chair's back.

When all the yarn was on the chair, Bri pulled it off and twisted it into a hank. She'd still need to set the twist, but she'd need water for that.

She started over with another strip of roving. She was getting better at spinning. Her yarn was getting more even and she was gaining confidence.

As she wrapped another length of yarn around the chair back, Duncan came through the door.

His laugh caught Bri off guard.

"When you said you'd keep busy, I imagined you in bed," Duncan said. "You do look busy."

"I'm getting better," Bri said. "I'm still new to spinning, but it's fun."

Duncan glanced around the room. "You should have more space."

Bri pulled her eyebrows together as she finished winding the yarn off her spindle. "What do you mean? This hardly takes any space at all."

She followed Duncan's eyes as he looked at the roving covering the table, and more wool on the floor near her feet, then at the yarn hanging from the chair. Maybe it took a little more space than she'd thought.

"Downstairs, I've a room to store things for the smithy. I've space inside the smithy they would fit — I'll move them. Then we can set up your spinning downstairs." Duncan looked at her and paused. "If you'd like."

"I don't know." Bri thought of having to clear away her yarn for every meal. "I don't want to put you out, but it would be nice."

Duncan grinned. "I'll not be put out. 'Tis a pleasure to give you a space of your own."

Bri started twisting the yarn into a second hank. Duncan's arms snaked around her hips and he pressed his hands against her stomach. The warmth pooling beneath his fingers had nothing to do with the heat of his hands.

She leaned back into his embrace, turning her head to look up at his face. Happiness filled her. "I like this."

A sound rumbled in Duncan's chest. "Aye. I like it as well."

Duncan's head lowered and he kissed the crook of her neck. Bri moved her head to the side so he could fit better.

"Duncan," called a voice from outside.

"Don't they ever leave you alone?" Bri asked. She was glad her husband was well-liked, but she wouldn't mind having him to herself for a few minutes.

"I'm busy, Brogan," Duncan called. He went back to brushing his lips over her neck.

Bri melted against him.

"I need your help," the voice came again, and this time the door swung open.

A man not much older that Duncan stood in the doorway. His eyes widened as he took in the scene. "You said there was no woman," the man said, his voice quiet.

No woman? Bri's joy at being with Duncan drained away. She tried to step away from him, but he held her more tightly.

"No," Duncan answered. "I told you there wasn't a woman in this town who interested me. Brianna wasn't in Tristledermot at the time."

Bri wanted to laugh, but she couldn't let go of the stinging words.

After a minute, the man chuckled. "So you did."

Duncan nodded. "You should go. I've the need of some time with my wife."

"Your wife?" The man leaned against the doorway. His face crinkled into some emotion Bri couldn't place. "You need to come to the inn."

Bri cleared her throat. If Duncan wanted to stay here with her, she'd make it happen. Even if her emotions were a bit . . . conflicted. "He said no."

Duncan sighed. "Brianna, this is Brogan. He's an innkeeper, and has lousy timing when asking for help. Brogan, my wife."

"Brianna?" Brogan asked. She nodded. "Would you come meet my wife?"

Duncan's arms tightened a fraction more. "I'm afraid we're busy."

The man frowned. "Duncan, you should both come. The women have decided you've put off marriage long enough. They're planning a wedding for you."

"What?" Duncan yelled.

Bri flinched at the shout so close to her ear.

Duncan lowered his voice to a growl. "You were to make them behave."

Brogan shrugged. "I was coming to ask for your help. If you'd overheard them making plans, you could end it before the poor lass they've chosen gets hurt."

This group of women were not only planning to marry Duncan off, but they'd chosen the bride? Her annoyance with Duncan flared into anger toward the ladies she'd never met. She tossed her yarn onto the table. "I'm going. Those women don't know what trouble they've gotten themselves into. Trying to marry off my husband."

Duncan held her still.

"Let go of me." She didn't speak loudly, but she knew Duncan could hear the daggers in her voice. And if he couldn't hear it, he'd at least feel her shaking against him.

"We'll both go," Duncan said. He spun her around to look at him. "Don't spoil your chance to have these women as friends. I'll be the one to stand up to them."

Surely there were other women she could befriend. Brogan's wife didn't sound like the kind of person she wanted to call a friend, anyway. "I'm not making any promises."

Bri stepped out of Duncan's arms and followed Brogan through the door. Duncan followed close behind. Bri would happily have attacked the women on her own, but it was nice to know he was there if she needed him.

As they walked, Duncan pointed out anything he thought she should know. They were walking toward Dublin gate. This building is the carpenter. That one sells cloth.

Bri knew which building was the inn. Even if it hadn't been larger than the buildings around it, the sound of women's voices spilled into the street.

"I'm coming in," Brogan said. "This is a sight I'd not miss for anything."

The innkeeper entered the common room first. Brianna tried to go next, but Duncan pushed her behind him. "I need to do this," he muttered.

Bri considered pushing ahead anyway, but she stopped herself. This was his world. He knew these people, and where she'd be happy to go in with her temper flared Bri had a feeling her husband would try to smooth things over. She gritted her teeth. She might not like it, but she was going to have to let Duncan do things his way. Still, she'd be ready to jump in if the ladies tried anything ridiculous.

She stepped back and let him go first but moved in right behind him.

Inside was a large room with tables scattered around. Benches had been pulled together in the center of the room so a dozen women could put their heads together. A large fireplace took up an entire wall, spilling light into the room.

At the sound of their entrance, heads swiveled toward the door.

"Duncan." There was a shuffle as things were whisked out of sight. The woman in the center of it all was painfully thin, with elbows as sharp as her eyes. She frowned as she looked daggers at Brogan, then turned back to Duncan. "What are you doing here?"

"I heard rumors."

Bri shivered. She'd never heard the dark, threatening edge in Duncan's voice. If he'd been talking to Bri, she would have cringed.

She shouldn't have underestimated him.

"Did you not think I'd hear you were planning a wedding?" He paused. "For me?"

The woman straightened. "You've wasted too many years. There are single women in this town, and it's your duty to take one of them."

"So you thought planning a ceremony would cause less trouble than all the other times you've tried to force a woman into my arms?"

Bri bit her lip and twined her fingers together to hold herself in check. This was the woman Duncan had referred to when he'd told her about people meddling in his life. The woman was trying to convince Duncan he had no say in his own life.

Bri wanted to pull the woman's hair out.

"Erin said you were in her bed last night." The woman glared at a girl who couldn't be more than sixteen. "Didn't you, Erin?"

The girl mumbled something unintelligible and shrank in on herself, her large eyes frightened.

"We all know that's untrue," Duncan said. "I've heard how you're going around to all the girls and widows, putting thoughts in their heads and words in their mouths. You'll not pin that on Erin just because she's too shy to stand up for herself."

The poor girl wilted a bit more.

The other woman, the meddler, rose to her feet. "If she says it, people will believe her."

"I wasn't there," Duncan said.

Brianna couldn't stand it any longer. This woman had no right speaking to Duncan like he wasn't worth listening to. "It's true. Duncan was at home, in his own bed."

A dozen pairs of eyes turned to Brianna. They didn't look friendly. Only the girl, Erin, looked hopeful.

A whisper went around the room. "Who are you?" someone finally asked.

"My name is Brianna," she said. She looked the meddler right in the eyes. "He was with me."

Duncan's hand settled on her shoulder. "Brianna is my wife."

The room quieted. Tears of relief tracked down Erin's face as the rest of the room erupted in noise.

Brianna ignored the women demanding to know when that had happened, and why they hadn't been told. She walked over to Erin and passed her a handkerchief. Then she crouched down beside the girl. "Do you want to get out of here?"

Erin's eyes widened. She glanced around. No one was paying any attention to her. She nodded.

"Come on, then." Bri stood up and took the girl's hand. "Let's go."

When they reached Duncan, he pressed his hand to her back and nudged her out the door. Then his voice filled the room. Bri wished she could stay and hear what he was saying. She was sure it was going to be impressive.

Instead, she wrapped an arm around Erin and led her through the crowd that was forming outside the inn.

Halfway down the road, she began to worry she might not recognize her home when she reached it.

Just as they came to the three-way intersection, the sound of running feet came up behind them. Bri tried to push to the side of the road to let the person by.

Arms caught Bri, and Duncan's voice whispered something comforting in Gaeilge into her ear as he held her. When he pulled away, he looked grim. "Let's go home. Erin, will you come?"

Bri still held onto the girl. "Come. We can talk while things up the road calm down."

Upstairs, closed away in her new home, Bri looked at Duncan. "I thought I wasn't supposed to ruin any chances at friendship."

Duncan grunted.

Bri wanted to push him, to ask what he had said to the room full of women. His scowl said she'd be better off doing anything else.

"Thank you," Erin whispered. She swallowed. "I didn't know what to do. They — the women — convinced my aunt to say I had to marry him."

"You live with your aunt?"

Erin nodded. "She doesn't want me there. She said I'd get married or live in the street."

Bri glanced at Duncan. His fists were tight. "We'll figure something out," she said.

They had to. She couldn't force this girl to go back to a relative who was ready to dump her on the street. Bri glanced around the room. They didn't have the space for the girl to stay with them.

Another knock shook the door.

Duncan cursed and swung it open. "Who are you?"

Erin leaned over to peek at whoever was outside the door. Before she could pull the girl back — there were a lot of people Bri wanted to keep away from her — Erin squealed.

"William?" The girl darted around both Bri and Duncan and into the arms of the soldier Bri could finally see.

After a lot of whispers, and several confused glances between Bri and Duncan, Erin turned and smiled at them.

"I'm taking her home with me," the soldier said. "We'll marry today."

Bri wanted to say no. She wanted to protect this sweet girl. Erin's grin held her back — the girl was clearly in love. "Your aunt won't cause problems?"

Erin shook her head. "She'll have what she wants. She'll be rid of me."

beyond the swearing stone

"Thank you for protecting her," the soldier said. "If there's ever anything I can do for you, I'm at Carlowgate most days."

They were gone before Bri could say anything else.

DUNCAN

uncan pushed the door closed and turned to Brianna.

She looked at him, worry creases by her eyes. "Do you think Erin's okay? Should we have let her go?"

"Did you mean to keep her here against her will?" Duncan pulled Brianna to him. He didn't admit he was concerned as well. It would only increase her worry. "The lad's a soldier. He's able to care for her."

Brianna didn't look convinced.

"I'm sorry. I'd thought to introduce you to the town more slowly than that." Now his wife would be used as gossip. Duncan shook his head. The women would have gossiped of her anyway, but he'd hoped it would be favorable.

"So take me out to see the town." Brianna reached down and took his hand. "I'm not scared of a few women."

Duncan held back a smile. He sighed mightily and tipped his head back to look heavenward. "Did I not deserve a quiet, meek wife?"

Brianna slapped his arm.

Duncan lowered his eyes back to Brianna and loosed his grin. "You've not a meek bone in you, and I'm glad for it. You're as fearsome as any Irish warrior. We'll go out soon. Once people have had time to get back to their own business."

With luck they'd also forget his outburst.

"What do you want to do while we wait?" Brianna glanced at the bed.

"You've something in mind?" he asked, trying to keep a straight face. His wife was changing his mind on beliefs he'd always held to be true. She'd not been timid about getting him to her bed, she worried over a girl she'd hardly met, and she didn't join with the busybodies simply because they were of the same sex.

Brianna pulled a face, and Duncan laughed.

"As soon as I try anything, there will be another knock at the door," she said.

Duncan frowned. "On a normal day I'd be in the smithy and they'd find me there."

"Do you need to work? I could keep busy while you do."

"No. I'd not leave you alone today." He fought the urge to say he'd keep her near him always. This was a woman who'd have need of space to be herself. "We could go see the town, if you stay right with me so I can stop anyone who would corner you."

Brianna straightened her hair kerchief. "Okay. I think I'm ready."

Duncan went down the stairs first, watching for anyone he needed to keep away from his wife. His urge to protect her grew as she reached the bottom of the stairs.

There were a few curious glances at Duncan's hand on her back, but mostly people were going about their own lives. Duncan turned them away from Brogan's inn. "Down this way is Carlowgate, if you've the need to check on Erin and her soldier."

"William guards the gate?"

Duncan nodded. "Aye."

An odd look crossed her face. "What does he guard it from? And the walls, what are they meant to keep out?" She paused, her eyes finding his. "Are we in danger of attack?"

Duncan thought of Ciaran's warning. He'd no desire to worry Brianna, but she should be prepared. "The Leinstermen have been known to attack from time to time."

Brianna stilled. "There's fighting? Do you fight?"

He shook his head. "MacMurrough, the Leinster King, can be paid to leave us be."

"And if he comes anyway, would you fight?"

Why was she asking this? Brianna was beginning to sound like Ciaran. Duncan felt his brow tighten. He placed his palm to her cheek. "If it comes to a fight, I'll do whatever I must to keep you safe."

Even if it meant spiriting her away in the dark of night and leaving the town to its fate.

Brianna nodded with a smile. "Ok."

Satisfied he'd put her worry to rest, Duncan turned his attention back to the town. He pointed to his left. "Just there is the Parliament Building, and behind us is the market square. Tomorrow the square will be filled with vendors who've come to town for the day. I'll take some time away from the smithy and we can find anything you need."

As they continued down the road, Duncan pointed out different shops his wife might need. When the butcher stepped out to meet Brianna, Duncan tried to hold her back. Brianna had mentioned the shops in her time where they got meats — she'd been shielded from the messiness of butchering. When she didn't flinch at the blood splattered across the butcher's front, Duncan's concern eased.

Other people approached, eager to meet Brianna. Duncan smiled as he told shopkeepers to give his wife anything she asked for. He'd see she had a purse of her own to hang at her hip, but until then Duncan would let her want for nothing.

The open appreciation in looks from a man or two had him wishing he'd a sword to hand, but he managed not to punch them.

As they made their way through the town, faces peered from windows, but they were mostly left in peace.

"Are you hungry?" Duncan asked. They'd been walking and talking for some time. The church bell had already marked the middle of the day.

"A little," Brianna said. She raised an eyebrow and gave him a sly smile. "Or a lot, depending on what you're asking about."

Duncan tried to look stern. "I'd thought we could buy some bread and cheese."

She shrugged a shoulder. "Bread is always good."

Duncan's mind went back to the way Brianna had shrugged the kirtle from her shoulders the night before. Bread could wait. Unless she'd stay in bed longer if she'd been fed. "Michael will have a few loaves set aside."

As they neared the baker's window they were met with the sound of Michael arguing with his wife. Duncan sighed. It would be better to wait and avoid putting Brianna in a position to see Elizabeth again, but he was in a hurry to get Brianna home where he could keep her to himself.

"Michael," Duncan called, knocking on the open window shutter.

The baker turned to the window and smiled. "Duncan. And this must be Brianna. Welcome to Tristledermot."

Before Duncan could stop her, she stepped forward to greet Michael. Not that he couldn't trust her with the man, but trusting Elizabeth was a different matter.

"Thank you," Brianna said. "I'm just learning my way around, and Duncan said I should meet you. I'm sure I'll see you frequently — there's nothing quite like the smell of fresh-baked bread."

Michael grinned, then looked to Duncan. "She'll do."

Elizabeth came forward slowly.

Duncan placed his hand at Brianna's waist, ready to whisk her away if Elizabeth didn't behave.

"If Duncan had spoken of you," Elizabeth said, twisting her hands, "we'd not have interfered."

Brianna tensed against Duncan's hand. "Where I come from, men are allowed to run their own lives, whether or not they choose to share the details with their neighbors."

"We're leaving," Duncan said, angling to place himself between the women. He'd not let Elizabeth ruin his first full day with his wife.

As he tried to lead Brianna away, her hand settled on his chest. Duncan stilled, glancing down at her tiny hand. Then he gazed into her face.

Brianna's eyebrow was raised. She smiled and stepped away from him.

Duncan sighed. He might understand her need to handle Elizabeth herself, but he needn't like it.

He watched as Brianna closed the distance between herself and the other woman. She moved with a sureness he'd not yet seen from her — or any woman. Even Brogan's wife, who ran the town gossip mill, moved as if she either expected to be sent away, or didn't belong in a place. Brianna walked in a way that made every other woman appear cowed.

Unable to focus on his wife's words, he watched instead the way Elizabeth reacted to her. Whatever Brianna had said, both Michael and Elizabeth were smiling.

Soon, Elizabeth placed a fresh loaf in Brianna's hands. Duncan reached for his coin purse.

"No. It's a gift," Elizabeth said, waving away his coins. "An apology to you both."

Brianna nodded her thanks and started down the road. Duncan trailed after her. "How did you do that?"

"Do what?"

"Make that woman like you." Duncan shook his head. She'd no idea the miracle she'd made. "I've never seen Elizabeth be so . . . kind."

Brianna laughed. "I just treated her with respect."

Duncan watched Brianna continue to walk. People she'd met raised their hands in greeting and offered smiles as she passed. He hurried to catch up to his wife.

As they climbed the steps to their home, Duncan smiled. Whatever knowledge and sureness the future had given his Brianna, she'd brought it here.

She was changing the town.

BRIANNA

he spindle twirled and the twist climbed up the silky wool to Bri's fingers. She stopped the spinning and wound the last bit of yarn onto the spindle.

Lengths of yarn hung from the ceiling of Bri's workroom. Small weighted hooks Duncan had made hung from each length to help set the twist as the wool dried. They were taking a long time to dry, even with a fire in the hearth. It had been raining for two days and the moisture in the air clung to everything.

Bri sighed as she gazed out at the rain. For a week, she'd spun and plied. She'd experimented with natural dyes and created some lovely yarns — and a few ugly, muddy colors.

And, while tending the dye pots, she'd entertained plenty of her neighbors. Duncan was pleased she was making friends — only Bri couldn't think of them as friends. She had nothing in common with the women. How could she build friendships on nothing more than a common location?

She hadn't expected the women to be superstitious, even if she should have seen it coming after growing up in Gran's home. Bri sighed a second time. It wasn't her place to educate the town with information that wouldn't be available for centuries, even if it would make their lives better.

They wouldn't believe her if she did tell them. Even Duncan didn't truly understand why she insisted on boiling their culinary and drinking water, and she'd explained to him the dangers of tainted water.

Bri dropped onto a wooden stool and looked around. Lifting the copper knot Duncan had made for her, she ran her fingers over the bumps and twists. She hadn't come here to change things, or improve the past, or to make any difference at all. She hadn't come to make friends. Even if she'd like them.

The only reason she'd come was Duncan. She'd refused to take off the necklace in the week she'd spent trying to build herself a life in this new place and time. Bri even wore it to bed. She needed the reminder that the turns and twists in her life were meant to be there.

The necklace was her lucky charm.

With a short laugh and a shake of the head, Bri rose. The rain was getting to her, making her moody. She was going to be fine. Just as soon as the sun showed its face.

She set about rotating the yarn, giving different batches a turn near the fire. If they'd dried properly by morning she might try to sell them at the market. The women in town weren't impressed with her work, but maybe those coming for market day would be more interested.

And if they weren't, she'd have plenty of yarn to keep herself knitting through autumn, and likely all winter as well. Or she could sell knitted shawls and garments, or teach her neighbors to knit. She hadn't seen any knits in her new time period. None. Bri shook her head. Maybe the skill just hadn't made its way to Ireland yet.

Picking up a small log, she placed it in the fire burning in the open fireplace. She adjusted things with the poker the way Duncan had taught her. Bri was learning just how much she didn't know about living without the modern conveniences she'd always taken for granted. The first thing she'd had to learn was how to build and tend a proper fire. She was probably still doing it wrong, but at least she could get a flame going without matches or lighter fluid. No one she'd known before could do that.

Bri straightened and leaned the poker against the wall just as the door opened. She glanced over her shoulder as Duncan closed the door behind him. She couldn't hold back her grin. "You're done already?"

Duncan chuckled and wiped his feet on the rug she'd insisted on using to cover the stone floor inside the door. "Not yet." He crossed the space between them, eyeing the fire.

Bri flushed. She must have done it wrong. Again.

"I'll not be done for a while yet," Duncan said, his eyes drifting to her face. "Half the town has come in needing work. Small things, as their main concern is learning what kind of a woman I've wed. If I'm to get through their repairs and orders this season, I'll not get a moment's rest."

Bri took a deep breath and hoped her disappointment didn't show. "Then shouldn't you still be in the forge?"

"Aye, but first I've the need to kiss my wife."

Duncan's arms slid around Bri's waist. Anticipation curled deep in her belly. She reached up and twisted her hands in his hair. Raindrops scattered, cool against her skin.

Duncan tipped his head down and stared into her eyes like he was trying to read her soul.

Bri forgot how to breathe. As if her lips were pulled by a magnet, Bri rolled up onto her toes. Duncan still hovered an inch above her.

Slowly, his strong arms holding her as if she was made of spun glass, Duncan lifted Bri. Her toes left the floor as he pulled her up against him.

Slowly, so slowly Bri thought he'd never get there, Duncan closed the distance. His lips brushed over hers. Bri's insides melted at the breath of touch. Her toes curled. She stretched her neck and kissed the corner of his mouth, his whiskers soft against her lips.

Duncan growled. He turned his head, capturing her lips with his as he held her more tightly.

Bri smiled against his kiss. She played with the hair at the nape of his neck, curling it around her fingers as she drew him down a fraction more.

Bri had no idea how Duncan managed it, but she found herself swept up and cradled in his arms. He moved to a chair and sat down. The chair creaked as he settled her on his lap.

Duncan's hand trailing down her side, the gentle pressure of his lips as they pulled at her own, the contented rumble in his chest — they built the fire inside her. His love softened and shaped her with the same beautiful skill he used to guide and form metal into the shapes he wanted.

A knock at the door cut through Bri's befuddled mind. Duncan pulled away, his breath stuttering.

"They'll go away," Bri murmured, trying to reclaim his lips.

Duncan shook his head and lifted her enough to slide out from beneath her, then placed her on the chair. Alone. He leaned over and tucked a stray lock of hair back under the headpiece fashion insisted she wear. "I've work to do, and you've friends to make. Build a full life for yourself here. Don't limit yourself to these walls."

"But—"

"Wheest, wife." Duncan kissed the top of her head. "I'll not make you a prisoner to my love."

He moved to the door and Bri slumped back with a huff. How could he think she wanted a life beyond him?

Duncan smiled over his shoulder and opened the door. He said something to whoever was interrupting, then stepped around them and out the door into the drizzling rain.

When her husband's broad shoulders were out of the way and she could see who was visiting, Bri grinned. Finally, a friendly face. "Erin, come in. I've been hoping to see you. Were you able to work things out with your aunt? I know you don't need to go back there to live, but keeping things friendly never hurts."

Erin's smile waned and Bri kicked herself. If the woman was trying to force the girl into an unwanted marriage, things weren't likely to have improved. Bri gestured to the bench across from her.

"She'll not see or speak with me," Erin said. She settled herself on the bench and set her basket on the floor beside her feet. Her finger idly traced the carved leaves embellishing the bench as she spoke. "It's for the best. Facing her — it's not something I'd choose."

Bri wanted to comfort her, but couldn't think of any words that wouldn't sound trite. "Oh."

Erin's face brightened. "Thank you for rescuing me from those ladies. They mean well," she added hastily, "despite not always considering those their plots revolve around."

Bri pursed her lips to keep from saying anything she'd regret. After a minute, she sighed. "I'm sure you're right."

Conversation moved on, and Bri settled in for a comfortable visit as the rain outside continued to drizzle.

After a while, Erin reached for her basket and pulled out her embroidery to work on as they talked. Bri picked up her knitting, but her eyes kept drifting to the colorful flowers and birds Erin seemed to create from nothing.

"How do you do that?" Bri flushed as her demanding voice echoed in her ears. "The embroidery. How can you make those beautiful pictures without a pattern or anything?"

Erin gave her full attention to Bri, where before she'd kept half an eye on the project in her hands. "Do you not do needlework?"

Bri shook her head. "Where I come from not many people embroider. No one I knew did, anyway."

Erin scooted over and patted the bench next to her. "Come. I'll teach you."

Bri hesitated, then shook herself. She'd never learn how if she didn't try. More importantly, now that she finally had someone she was comfortable talking to she didn't want to ruin the friendship before she had a chance to see if it could last.

She crossed over to sit beside Erin, who promptly handed Bri a piece of cloth, a needle, and some threads.

"What color silk would you like to start?" Erin asked.

Bri chose a pretty shade of blue and poked it through the eye of the needle. She knew how to do that much from weaving in the ends of her knitting projects.

Erin picked up a new cloth and showed Bri how to start stitching without tying a knot in the end. Erin must have known some kind of secret - Bri's fingers fumbled and instead of the needle doing what it was supposed to, it slipped off the silk thread and fell to the floor. Bri glared at it.

Erin laughed. She leaned down to rescue it and handed it to Bri. "Try again. Hold the needle more gently. There's no need to stab at the cloth, the needle should glide through it."

Several miserable attempts later, Erin took the needle and started the thread for her. "If you can work magic with those sticks —" she gestured to Bri's knitting needles "— a simple needle should be no trouble."

But it was trouble. Hours later all Bri had learned was that embroidery was hard. Hard and not for her. She looked at her uneven stitches. The thing she'd created was supposed to be a flower. "It's a tangled mess."

"First attempts are never quite right." Erin's lips pursed as she tried to hold in her mirth. Her eyes twinkled. "Keep the basket of silk. You'll get better, and it will be easier, with practice."

Bri looked at her thumb and fingers. Indented lines marked where she'd held her needle too tightly, and blisters were already starting to form. She really didn't want to practice any more. She bit back a sigh and forced her manners to the front. "Thank you, Erin, I'm sure you're right. Every skill takes practice. You're a remarkably patient teacher to put up with me."

Erin beamed. "Most of us women begin learning skills like this when we're small. My own mother put a needle in my hand so long ago I don't remember not being able. She'd say that idle hands belonged to the devil. There's always work to be doing, but if I've a chance to sit a while I still keep my hands from going to the devil."

Bri froze as memories of Gran came at her from every angle. She blinked back the sudden tears. "My gran always said idle hands were the devil's workshop. It's why she taught me to knit."

Erin reached over and squeezed her hand. On a whim, Bri reached out and gave the girl a hug. Erin stiffened, then softened into the embrace.

"Thank you for coming to see me, Erin. I didn't realize how much I needed a friend."

DUNCAN

With the shutters closed the only light came from the embers glowing in the hearth. Duncan looked around the room. Something had woken him, yet nothing was amiss.

Rolling onto his side, he tucked Brianna closer to his chest and breathed in the scent of her.

A light tapping came from the door. "Duncan."

Ciaran? The voice was too quiet to be sure.

The door rattled but didn't open. Duncan had taken to latching it closed to pretend he and his wife had privacy. Sounds still carried, but no one could get inside unless Duncan or Brianna chose to open the door.

The tapping started again.

Duncan slipped away from Brianna. Holding a blanket around his waist, he padded to the door and released the latch.

The door swung open and Ciaran hurtled through it. "You said you were no longer angry with me."

Duncan blinked away the last of his sleep, but his mind stubbornly held to its confusion. "I'm not."

"You left me no way in without knocking." Ciaran's brows were drawn together and his shoulders hunched.

Duncan muffled a laugh and moved to stoke the fire. "I was keeping others out."

Ciaran opened his mouth, but Duncan cut him off with a raised hand. Noiselessly, he gestured to the bed. Ciaran gazed into the dim corner just as Brianna shifted under the covers.

"Go down to the smithy," Duncan said. "I'll dress and join you."

Duncan ignored Ciaran's gaping mouth and moved to dress.

"Duncan?" Brianna's voice was sleepy, her eyes but half open.

"All's well, *a rúnsearc*," Duncan said, keeping his voice low. He pushed a lock of hair from her face and kissed her forehead. "I'll be in the smithy for a time."

Brianna looked past Duncan to where the door was closing behind Ciaran. "Who's here?"

"His name is Ciaran," Duncan said. "He—"

The covers fell from Brianna as she sat up quickly. "That was Ciaran? Why didn't you wake me?"

Duncan stared. He allowed a smile to twitch his beard. "I'd save this view for myself, wife."

Brianna's hair was a riot of waves falling around her. The only thing she wore beyond the cloak of hair was her necklace. The knot sat in the hollow between her breasts, glowing warmly in the firelight.

She was beautiful, and he'd not share the sight even with Ciaran. Especially with Ciaran.

She shook her head, moving to the edge of the bed. "Never mind that. I should meet him."

Duncan took her shoulders and pressed her back into the bed. "Stay here. Sleep. There's time for all that come morning."

As Brianna began to argue, Duncan pressed his lips to hers. In the days she'd been with him, he'd learned kissing was the best means of quieting her stubborn arguments.

When he pulled away Brianna was breathing heavily. Duncan

pulled on his leggings and doublet and hurried out the door.

The rarely used lamps inside the smithy had been lit. The light spilling from the doorway filled the narrow street.

Ciaran barely waited for Duncan to close the door on the night mist before speaking. "After all these years you've welcomed a woman to your bed."

His foster brother's face was darkened, the glint in his eyes brighter than the lamplight. Duncan paused inside the doorway. His mind still on Brianna's kiss, Ciaran's anger made no sense.

"Neve's long dead, but your woman from the churchyard — your *wife* — I imagine she would have something to say if she learned her new husband was dallying with another woman."

Duncan dropped onto a stool near the wall. "You — What?" He started to laugh. "I'd forgotten you didn't know." He glanced around the smithy at the blades covering the walls and scattered on every surface. He should have left them in the room he'd given Brianna — out of reach of Ciaran's able hands.

Ciaran's eyes were pinched to slits. "You thought I knew you'd taken a mistress? Or is she but a whore?"

Duncan found himself on his feet with a sword in hand. He looked down the blade at Ciaran. "Call my wife a whore again and, foster brother or not, I'll challenge you."

The blood left Ciaran's face. "Your wife. That woman, the one in your bed, is your wife? She's the woman from the churchyard? How is she here? You said she lived in the future."

Duncan allowed the tip of the sword to lower nearly to the floor, but kept his hold on the hilt lest Ciaran's anger flare again. "She did."

Ciaran waited.

"Something about the swearing stone allowed her to come here. She's been with me over a sennight."

Ciaran slumped against the anvil in front of him.

"I should have sent word," Duncan said. It wasn't that he'd chosen to keep Brianna to himself for a time, nor had he thought to hold back the information to express anger toward Ciaran. He'd been so focused on helping Brianna find her place in town he'd not so much as considered sending word. He'd been too busy.

As Duncan eyed his foster brother, waiting for an outburst, he saw Ciaran's shoulders begin to shake. Then Ciaran was laughing.

"What's funny?" Duncan asked.

"I'm not the one you should worry over," Ciaran said. He looked at Duncan and laughed again. "Tara is."

Duncan groaned. Tara would take it as a personal slight. He'd learned years ago to stay in that woman's good graces. She put her husband's temper to shame.

"She's been learning of the barbaric tortures your mother's people use as punishments." Ciaran doubled over in laughter.

Duncan nearly groaned again, but the fiery eyes of his own Irish lass came to mind. He grinned. "My Brianna is a warrior to rival Tara. If they were to cross each other I'm certain my wife would be in no danger."

Ciaran's laughter stilled. "Then we'd best not let them find reason to be angered with each other."

Duncan tossed the sword aside, heedless of damaging it. The blade was unbalanced and dull — it would be melted down to create something new, when time was less precious.

There was a sound behind him and Duncan turned just as the door swung open. Brianna paused in the doorway. Duncan's heart warmed at the sight of her. He reached for her, tucking her into his side. "Brianna, this is Ciaran."

Brianna turned her smile and sparkling eyes to Ciaran. Duncan tried to quench the embers of jealousy that flared in his chest.

"Ciaran." Brianna tilted her head as she looked at him. Her smile drooped. "You're not what I expected."

Ciaran shot an amused look at Duncan. "What did you tell her of me?"

Duncan raised a shoulder and shook his head. "I've no idea." He paused, watching a flush dance over Brianna's cheeks. "Coming from the future as she does, she knows things she'll not share. Do you know something of Ciaran, wife?"

The way Brianna glanced up at him from the corner of her eye made Duncan squirm. He couldn't decide if he was uncomfortable with it or just wanted to carry her back to his bed.

"I know a lot of things about you and your brother."

Duncan frowned. "My brother?"

"We're not brothers," Ciaran said. "We fostered together. Foster brothers aren't always close, but sometimes we're closer than if we shared parents."

Brianna looked up at Duncan with her brows drawn close. "But — you're supposed to be brothers. All the stories. . . ."

"We're brothers in the ways that matter," Duncan said. He lifted his hand to smooth her brow. "What stories traveled through six centuries to find you?"

Brianna's flush deepened and her hand fluttered at her waist. "I — I'll tell you. Someday."

Duncan frowned, wishing his wife trusted him with her many secrets of things to come.

"Not good tales, then," Ciaran said, turning Brianna's head with his words.

"They're some of my favorite stories, actually," Brianna said. Her smile widened and she stepped forward, pulling away from Duncan. He ached at the distance, small as it was. "I can tell you one thing now, if you want."

"Erm." Ciaran turned his eyes to Duncan. "Do I want to know what she knows?"

Duncan laughed at Ciaran's discomfort. He folded his arms over his chest and leaned back against the door. "It's your choice, but you should know my wife doesn't care to harm others. If she's offering information it's likely something she considers good."

Ciaran nodded. "Tell me, then."

Brianna reached out to rest her hand on Ciaran's arm. "Your children all live full lives and have families of their own."

Tears sprung to Ciaran's eyes. "All of them?"

Duncan's heart eased. Many faced the loss of children. Giving them the assurance Ciaran wouldn't know such a loss was a true gift.

"Your line continues all the way to my time," Brianna continued. "Hundreds of years and you still have living grandchildren."

Ciaran swayed. "Such a long line?"

"The shock takes getting used to," Duncan said.

"You — you have family in her time, too?"

Duncan nodded. "They came to the swearing stone to see her cross through time."

Brianna smiled at him. "They did more than that."

He thought of the clothing they'd made for Brianna, and the way they helped convince her to accept her fate with him. "They did."

"You're distracting me." She turned back to Ciaran, squeezing his arm in her hand. "You have around twenty descendants in my time. Not so many as you used to have — but you've met one of them."

Ciaran's frown matched Duncan's. Duncan pieced through Brianna's words. He felt his eyes widen. He burst away from the door, watching Ciaran's face for an understanding.

He saw a wariness instead. "You can't be saying what I think you are."

Brianna grinned at both of them. "You're my grandfather, Ciaran. Many times over, of course, but — you are my roots."

Ciaran stared at Brianna. His lips might have been sealed for all the sound he made.

"You could have told me," Duncan said. All the time they'd had, and she'd said naught.

Brianna shook her head. "I wasn't sure I'd say anything at all. I don't know what it will do — even something as simple as sharing information could change history." She paused and frowned. "Of course, I'm learning history is very selective in what it remembers. Everything, all the family stories, said the two of you are brothers."

"We are," Ciaran said, breaking his silence. "We've not the same blood in our veins, but we're brothers in all else."

Duncan sighed. "We're foster brothers — but we're more than that. Ciaran had a sister."

Brianna nodded slowly. "He's Neve's brother, isn't he?"

Duncan nodded. He waited for — something. Tears, or anger, or hurt. It didn't come.

"You could have told me sooner." She offered him a smile.

"She's taking it well," Ciaran said.

Duncan's chest swelled. Brianna had shown no worry he'd compare her to Neve. She accepted his past as part of what made him who he was. "I told you my Brianna is special."

Brianna snorted. "You two finish whatever I interrupted. It's late enough Michael might have some bread out of the oven. I'll see you back upstairs when you're through."

Duncan grabbed her around the waist as she tried to pass. "Your hair —" He tried to tuck an escaping wave back under the kerchief.

Brianna sighed, pulling away. "Covering my hair all the time is annoying, you know." She let the kerchief fall to her shoulders. Her hair tumbled in waves about her.

Duncan glanced at Ciaran. "Wife —"

"Don't start." Brianna's voice held a firm warning. "Ciaran won't care, and you've seen my hair before." She muttered something about insufferable men under her breath.

Ciaran laughed. "Try binding your hair up first."

Brianna rolled her eyes as she coiled her hair around her head. "Thanks, Grandpa."

Duncan laughed at the shock on Ciaran's face. Brianna covered her hair and left in a swirl of skirts.

"Let's go upstairs and you can think of how to tell Tara you met your granddaughter." Duncan left the smithy, knowing Ciaran would follow. The man was always hungry. He would cross a battlefield if word came there was food to be found on the other side.

Upstairs, Duncan built up the fire. Brianna had added wood, but she was still learning to tend the flames. Duncan shook his head. He couldn't imagine a world where fires weren't a necessity for cooking, and heat, and light.

When the fire crackled merrily, he turned. Ciaran sat at the table, eying the oatcakes and blackberries Brianna had set out for them. Duncan pushed them closer to his brother.

"One market day helping me wasn't enough?" Duncan asked. "Not that I'm ungrateful for your help, but does Tara not tire of you running off?"

"I'm not here to help with the smithy," Ciaran said, his smile dropping away. His fingers worried the edge of his oatcake, spreading crumbs across the table. "I brought word of MacMurrough."

Duncan curled his fingers into fists.

"Your government hasn't paid him the eighty marks. He's ready to push them. His plan includes attacks on Wexford and Carlow — but he's coming to Tristledermot. His men are preparing now."

"It's happening, then."

Duncan jumped at Brianna's voice. She stood in the open doorway, a fresh loaf of bread in her hands. The creamy white of her over-kirtle all but glowed. She could have been an angel but for the lightning in her eyes and the strength of her fingers curled around the loaf she held.

Duncan scratched at his beard. "What's this *it* you know something of?"

Brianna moved inside, closing the door behind her. She set the bread on the table. Its scent drifted around them, the comfort and coziness it brought at odds with the tension in the air. "MacMurrough's attack." Brianna's voice was low and certain. She looked to Ciaran. "He's coming now?"

Ciaran nodded.

A slow, terrifying smile crossed Brianna's face as she pierced

beyond the swearing stone

Duncan with her expectant gaze. "Your town is coming under attack. What are you going to do about it?"

Duncan crossed the space between them in two steps, pulling his wife into his arms. "I'll get you out. You didn't travel this far to die on the end of a sword — or to be conquered or carried off by an Irish warrior."

He swallowed a lump at the knowledge of the ways battle-crazed warriors conquered the women in their paths. He'd keep his wife well away from such possibilities.

Brianna's back stiffened under his hands. She lifted her chin to meet his eyes with her powerful gaze. "I'm not leaving."

"You are," Duncan said. Her stubbornness would get her killed. His heart twisted at the thought. He stepped away from her and began gathering her things. "We'll go with Ciaran. Tara will have extra clothing you can wear."

He felt something on his arm and looked down to see Brianna yanking at him. "You won't leave this whole town in danger because of me. I could never live with myself if you did."

Duncan barely heard her words. The haze of worry was too thick. "I'll save you, Brianna. I promised you. I promised your grandmother I'd not let harm come to you. Keeping you here would break that oath."

"No."

Duncan groaned and ran his hand over his face. Could the woman not see this was no time for stubbornness? "We're leaving. I'll see you safe."

"And what of the rest of the town?"

He looked at the trunks holding Brianna's possessions. They were too large, too heavy for a quick flight. She'd need something to wear as they traveled, but everything else could stay behind. "They know the risks that come with living here."

Brianna wrinkled her nose and stared at him, as if she'd not seen him before. "You're supposed to save them."

Duncan paused. He set Brianna's things on the bed and faced her. "I'm supposed to — You want —" It would take a miracle to save the town, and the woman wanted — expected — him to make it happen. "What would you have me do, Brianna? I'm a blacksmith, not a man of God. I've no miracles."

Ciaran cleared his throat. "The people listen to you, Duncan."

"You told me yourself offering MacMurrough our coins isn't enough this time. He can sweep through town taking it, and everything else, with him." Duncan reached for Brianna. She was the only one he could save. "There's naught I can do."

Brianna turned from him and crossed the room.

Duncan's chest constricted. "Where are you going?"

The glance she tossed over her shoulder scorched him with shame he had no reason to feel. "Downstairs. I need to think." She yanked open the door and was gone. The sound of her feet racing down the stairs softened as the door thumped closed behind her.

Duncan stared after her, trying to make sense of what had happened.

"Have you never argued with your wife?" Ciaran asked. "Never let her have the last word — or walk out."

Duncan sank onto the bed next to the things he'd been gathering for Brianna. He ran a hand over his eyes as the door below slammed closed.

"You should go to her," Ciaran said. "Don't give her time to get angrier."

28

BRIANNA

Bri closed the door and stood in the darkness of her little wool workshop. Her chest heaved with emotion.

This wasn't the way history was supposed to go.

The door opened behind her. "Brianna?" Duncan's voice was unsure. Wounded.

Bri sighed. "I'm here."

"You're angry with me."

Was she angry? Or just hurt? She couldn't see her husband in the dark. If she could, would she recognize him,? Or would she learn he wasn't the man she'd thought him to be? "You said if the town was attacked you'd do whatever you had to."

Duncan found her in the dark and pulled her against him. "I did. I promised you I'd keep you safe. The only way I know to do that is to take you away from the fighting."

Bri pulled away, gripping his elbows and lifting her face as if she could see his expression. "I don't want to go. This is our home, Duncan. How can we call the people here our neighbors while turning our backs on them? They don't even know what's coming. They'll be slaughtered."

"They have the walls, and the gates, and the garrison. The watchmen will see MacMurrough coming and they'll be ready."

"Then why are we leaving?"

Duncan's hand settled on her waist. "There is a small chance they'll break through. Can't you see I need you safe?"

Bri's breath caught. When MacMurrough came, he'd make it inside the walls. She knew he would. History insisted on it. If they left — if Bri allowed Duncan to leave, to take her away — he wouldn't do his part to turn the battle.

Had she doomed the entire town?

"You need to stay. You matter more today than ever." How could she make him see this was his moment? That he was the reason the town survived? Bri wanted to explain, to tell him the story of his heroics. Would it change his mind? Would he brush it off, saying it didn't have to happen that way?

She wanted to tell him, wanted him to know he could do this. He could save everything. She took a breath, then stopped.

She'd already told Ciaran about his family's future. Did she dare tempt time by messing with things again? Could she live with herself if she ruined everything she knew had to happen?

Bri took one step back, then another, escaping Duncan's hold. "It doesn't feel right."

"I'd take you away, wife. I'd keep you safe." There was a frantic edge to his voice that worried Bri.

"When you said you'd do whatever it took to keep me safe, I thought you meant you'd fight."

"Brianna."

"I need to think. I'm going for a walk."

"Please, wife, we must leave."

"I need some air, just for a while." Bri's fingers found the door latch and she slipped into the dim light of early morning. Duncan called after her, but Bri hurried away, trying to outpace the possibility that people would die. Soon. Because of her.

Because she didn't know how to convince Duncan he was needed.

She quickened her pace to match the racing of her mind, ignoring the startled noises from the sole man in the street as she brushed past. She thought she heard someone call her name as she ran through town, but couldn't be sure. She didn't dare stop to find out.

Bri pushed on, lifting her skirt to free her feet. She had to move more quickly.

As she reached the end of the road, Bri allowed her feet to slow. The churchyard stood before her, the round tower rising into a sky stained with the first light of morning.

She'd avoided the church since the night she'd left her own time, afraid whatever magic had brought her here would force her to return.

With unsure feet, she crossed into the churchyard.

Bri stopped, confused. She felt nothing. No tingle in the air, no pressure. No power.

She skirted past the church, larger than she remembered, and crept nearer to the swearing stone.

There was nothing.

When Bri reached the stone, she dropped to the ground. Mud squelched below her knees and a damp chill seeped through the wool of her kirtle.

The hole in front of her seemed to glare at her. Taunting. Accusing.

She was the reason Duncan wanted to leave Tristledermot. *She* was the reason he wouldn't accept his fate. *She* was the reason the town's survival was in doubt.

Bri imagined she could hear Gran's voice, telling the tale she'd jumped into. How Ciaran left his family, at great risk to himself, to get to his brother. How that brother put everything aside to warn his neighbors. How he got the women and children to safety and convinced the townsmen to join the garrison to protect the town and send the Leinstermen on their way.

None of it would happen. Duncan would whisk her away without a word to their neighbors.

People would be hurt. People would die.

There would be so much heartache.

Bri sighed. As long as she was in danger, Duncan would put her safety before that of anyone else. She loved him for his concern, but as a child she'd fallen a little bit in love with him because of his heroics on this very day. How could a man ever live up to a story?

What a ridiculous thought.

She loved *him*. Not just his story. She loved who he was, not just who her family remembered him as. She loved the caress of his callused hands, and the glint in his eye as he watched her. His humor, and his care for those around him.

Duncan might be terrified for her safety, but if his friends and neighbors were injured or killed because he'd put Bri first he would carry that guilt with him the way he'd carried his guilt over Neve's death. That kind of weight would kill him.

Bri stared at the swearing stone. The hole gaped at her in a mocking laugh.

No. She couldn't.

Through the hole she thought she saw the image of Tristledermot alight with flames.

Her stomach flipped. Was the love she held for Duncan worth more than an entire town? More than all the lives the town held?

A sob shuddered through her. She had no choice, then.

It took everything in her to raise her shaking hand to the hole in the swearing stone.

Bri couldn't think about what she was doing, or how much it would hurt her to leave. She couldn't — if she did, she'd never be able to walk away from her new life. Not even to save a town.

Forcing her mind blank, she pushed her hand through the hole.

She waited for the tingling sensation. Waited for the pressure in the air to build.

beyond the swearing stone

A light drizzle began to fall from the clouds overhead. Lightning flashed, but that electricity stayed away from the churchyard.

"Take me home," Bri whispered. "Don't keep me here. I've ruined everything."

The only response was the rain.

Bri leaned forward, resting her head on the stone. "Please."

Still, nothing happened.

"Take me away from here, you stupid rock!" Bri pounded the side of her fist into the stone.

The next thing she knew, she was on her feet, kicking and beating at the swearing stone.

Her anger and frustration slowly drained from her, as if leeched away by the rain. Her energy left her, and she sat on the ground, her back against the stone. Her eyes burned with unshed tears.

Bri sniffled. She couldn't leave. Couldn't fix the mess she'd made of history. She was stuck here, and because she couldn't escape the town was in more danger than they should be.

Bri considered. She could sit here and pout about life, or she could get up and fix things herself.

She could do this. If she couldn't convince Duncan to stay and save the town, she'd have to save it for him. Someone would listen to her, surely.

As she thought it through, she knew exactly where to start. As long as Erin's soldier was on duty at Carlowgate.

Bri made her way through Tristledermot to the western gate. The morning sounds of people readying for the day echoed through the narrow streets as Bri marched across town. She forced herself to a normal pace, when all she wanted was to run.

She neared Carlowgate and paused. She could see a small group of guards by the gate, talking amongst themselves. Bri couldn't be sure, but she thought she saw Erin's soldier, William.

The men looked up as she approached, and one broke away to meet her. "Brianna? What happened to you?"

Bri looked down. It was light enough she didn't need William's lantern to see the smears of mud on her cream kirtle. She lifted her hand to brush hair from her face and realized her kerchief had nearly fallen off.

"I'm fine." She shook her head, hoping William wouldn't press her. She looked past him at the wooden gate set like a giant, thick door into the arch in the city's stone wall. The other soldiers were moving to open it. "You need to keep the gate closed. Send word to the other gates — don't let anyone in."

William laughed. "I can't do that. I don't have the authority. Even if I did, it's market day. People will be pouring into town soon."

"You don't understand," Bri said. She clutched the front of his shirt. "The Leinstermen are going to attack. MacMurrough could be on his way right now. We need to get everyone to safety and secure the town."

"Slow down," William said. He pulled Bri a little farther away from his colleagues. He cast a glance their way and lowered his voice. "What makes you think they're planning an attack?"

Bri paused. She didn't want Ciaran to be taken in for questioning, or to be held responsible. She cursed under her breath. It would help if she understood more about how things worked in this century. "Just between us? There's a Leinsterman who came to warn us."

William gave her a funny look. "Duncan's foster brother?"

Did everyone know Duncan had that connection? "Yes. Fine. Ciaran came to warn us."

"Why did Duncan send you to me?"

Bri swallowed hard. "He didn't. I came on my own. Someone needs to do something."

William put his hand on Bri's shoulder. "Go home to your husband," he said, giving her a gentle push. "If there's really a risk, Duncan can handle it. It's nothing you need worry over."

Bri stared at the man. He was going to blow off her warning, just because she was a woman? Or was it because he didn't want to get in the middle of a marital spat? Either way, he was going to be no help. "Promise me you'll keep your eyes open for anything out of the ordinary."

"I always do. It's part of my job."

With a huff, Bri turned and walked away. That was it. The only thing she'd known to try.

She could start going up to people and telling them about the impending attack, but if William didn't believe her no one else would. She'd be labeled a crazy person.

Not that Bri cared what people thought of her, but if people started thinking she was crazy there was no chance of getting anyone in charge to take her seriously.

She walked slowly back to the center of town, trying to decide what to do. She had no idea who any of the city leaders were. If she showed up at the Parliament Building, would any of them even talk to her? Or would they say to run home like a good little wife and let her husband take care of it?

Bri fumed at the idea.

Maybe she'd be able to find someone to believe her, if she went in confidently. Weren't some of the most important Irish warriors women?

Of course, she wasn't dealing with the Irish. It was the Irish who were planning the attack.

Bri sighed. History said Duncan, not Brianna, was supposed to save the town.

She straightened her shoulders. She'd do the only thing she could: she'd tell Duncan the story fate had placed him into. She'd just have to trust that time would work itself out if she tangled it too badly.

DUNCAN

uncan stood at the bottom of the stairs trying to decide if he'd given Brianna enough time for her to understand their need to leave.

He glanced up the stairs to where Ciaran leaned out the door watching.

Resisting the urge to scratch at his beard in exasperation, he knocked as he swung the door wide.

Duncan stepped into the dark workshop, as dark as it had been earlier. "Brianna?"

His voice didn't echo in the darkness of the space he'd given Brianna as her own. If it was anyone else, the lack of lit lamps would make it clear the room was empty, but Brianna had a strange fondness for the dark. She didn't fear it, or the demons it held, as others did. She welcomed it. It calmed her.

"Brianna?" he asked again. Dread settled over him at the complete silence that met his ears. Surely she'd not stayed gone so long.

He moved to the windows, swinging the shutters wide to let in the glow from the lanterns in the roadway. He turned his back on the

beyond the swearing stone

people beginning to move about and looked into the shadowed corners.

Brianna wasn't there.

Duncan slammed the shutters closed in frustration and bolted out the door. Halfway up the steps, he met Ciaran's questioning gaze. "She's not returned."

The look Ciaran gave him said he wasn't surprised. Duncan was grateful his foster brother kept the words to himself.

"I need to find her."

"I'll come," Ciaran said.

Duncan shook his head. If Brianna didn't agree to leave willingly Ciaran needn't witness him throwing Brianna over his shoulder to carry her safely away. "You should stay here in case she returns." He turned and started back down the stairs.

"I'm coming with you," Ciaran repeated. "If I've learned one thing from having a wife, it's to not get in the way of a riled woman. Your Brianna wants this town saved. She'll not be back here until it is."

Duncan growled. He'd been certain he could get his wife to safety. He felt the need of something to pound on. He was used to taking his emotions out on the metals in the smithy. He looked to Ciaran. Could he be convinced to join him for another wrestling match? If there'd been less need to hurry, he might have asked. "Do as you will."

Ciaran fell into step beside him as Duncan thought of where to begin his search. There'd not been the time for Brianna to make many friends, and the ones she had made weren't likely to welcome visitors before the day had truly begun. Where would she go?

He turned toward the market square. It was large enough Brianna would be able to get the air she'd been in need of.

A place where she could be away from him.

Duncan muttered to himself. Ciaran raised an eyebrow at the stream of curses but held his peace.

How could Brianna be still been angry with him? He explained he only wanted to see her safe. Any woman would be glad to know she was cared for.

As they passed the bakery Michael called out to them. Duncan tried to ignore him, but —

"Did something happen to Brianna?" Michael asked. "She seemed well when she came for bread first thing, but when she passed a short time later she didn't have so much as a neighborly smile. I called after her and she ran."

Duncan's stomach dropped. He crossed the distance to the baker's window in two steps. "Where did she go?"

Michael gestured down the road. "That way." His eyes narrowed. "Would she be running from you?"

Duncan didn't answer; his feet were already pounding into the straw-covered mud of the road as he ran after Brianna. Toward the churchyard. He could think of only one reason she would go there.

The swearing stone.

He should have listened when Brianna said he was supposed to stop the Leinstermen's attack. If he'd done as his wife had wanted, she'd be with him still.

Duncan's breath hitched. Heaven help him if she'd gone back to her own time.

With a final burst of speed Duncan reached the churchyard. He looked through the gloomy light toward the swearing stone. Brianna wasn't there.

Blood pounded in his ears. His chest tightened as he tried to hold his heart in one piece, but flesh couldn't be worked and shaped as metal could.

Duncan's strength gave out, his knees buckling like iron heated overlong in the flames. The world shook around him as his shins fell to the muddy earth. He pressed his palms to his face, but his hands did nothing to block out the memory of his wife slipping out the door. Escaping the tie to his life.

The weight of Ciaran's hand settled on his shoulder. His foster brother's voice droned somewhere in the background, the words confused and broken. Because of her.

Ciaran pulled Duncan to his feet. With a steady pressure, Duncan's hands were forced from his face. He met Ciaran's worried eyes. Saw his lips moving as he spoke words that didn't reach Duncan's ears.

Duncan pulled away, stumbling as he turned. There'd be no point staying in the churchyard. No point reaching through the swearing stone. He'd not find Brianna's hand waiting for his.

Slowly, moving as if his legs might give way and land him back in the mud, Duncan made his way back along the road. He trudged past a pair of children sitting in a doorway, dangling a string for a cat and her kittens. Men and women called greetings to each other as they led their carts to the market square.

One day soon the Leinstermen would come, MacMurrough leading the charge. Would it be today? Or tomorrow, perhaps?

God, if they're coming, bring them today, Duncan prayed. *Let them end me.*

Would death hurt? It could be no worse than the pain he felt already. No matter the pain, it was well deserved.

He'd lost the miracle he'd been given, when all he'd wanted was to protect it.

The children in the doorway behind him laughed and squealed.

Duncan sighed. He deserved the fate the Leinstermen would bring, but those children didn't. His neighbors deserved the chance to live. Brianna had wanted them to have that chance.

A weight settled on him. He had to do it. If not for these people he'd chosen to live beside, he could do it for Brianna. He had nothing more to lose but himself.

Duncan found the strength to straighten. He turned again, ignoring Ciaran's questions. The children smiled up at him and held out one of the kittens as Duncan stepped near. After scratching behind the creature's ears, he smiled back. He blinked quickly. "Have you boys grown enough your mother might let you help me? I've need of some sturdy boys to run up and down the roads calling everyone to the market square."

The older of the two stood tall. "Yes, master smith. We'll do it."

Duncan nodded, and the weight bearing him down lessened a fraction. "Be quick about it." He paused. "Thank you. You're helping save this town today."

The boys grinned and took off down the road, yelling as loudly as they could.

Duncan turned to Ciaran.

"Have a change of heart?" Ciaran asked.

Duncan wanted to wipe the smirk off Ciaran's face. Instead, he nodded. "I may deserve the fate MacMurrough brings, but these others don't."

"What will you do about it?"

"I'll stand between the Leinstermen and Tristledermot if needs be. The Leinstermen can have me, but I'll not allow them anyone else." Duncan paused as the words sank in. They felt right. He'd do anything to save this town. He'd do anything to live up to the expectations of the wife he'd lost to his own pride and selfishness. Despite the ache of losing her, he smiled at Ciaran. "What say you? Are you ready for adventure? I may have need of your help convincing everyone what's coming."

"I'm always ready for adventure." Ciaran's grin drooped at one corner and his voice sobered. "When this is through you'll need to tell Tara I stayed far from the fighting. My wife agreed I could warn you, not fight alongside you."

Duncan paused. He'd nothing to lose, but Ciaran had family. It would fall to Duncan to keep his friend from the fighting. He nodded. "You'll guard the women and children."

Ciaran grimaced and muttered to himself. Duncan laughed at him and headed for the market square.

He had a town to protect.

BRIANNA

The excitement of market day was coming to life as Bri reached the center of town. Laughter filled the air, and the shouts of children bounced through the noisy street.

As she neared the smithy the road became more crowded. People poured out of doorways. Some were alone, others moved in pairs, groups, or families. They came from everywhere, filling the street. Brianna quickly found herself in the center of a human river. She was swept up in their momentum, pushed along the middle of the road. Pushed past the smithy and into a crowd trying to fit into the market square.

Through a lifetime of living in a big city Brianna had learned to use her tiny size to her advantage — slipping between groups of people to get where she needed to go. It had always worked before, but the crowds had always been moving. This crowd had ground to a stop. She pushed, nudged, and eventually shoved, all to no avail. The townspeople created a barrier surrounding her — a barrier as strong and immovable as the wall surrounding the town.

A voice rang out through the square. A voice Bri knew. She stretched onto her toes trying in vain to see Duncan.

"Neighbors. It's not the day for news such as this, but we've a problem." The chattering in the square died down as Duncan's voice drew attention. "The garrison was put here in order to protect the town, and they've done a fine job of it. I've learned we've an attack coming, one our garrison may not be large enough to turn aside."

Murmurs swept through those gathered. A woman near Bri scoffed to those around her. Bri bristled and turned to give the woman a piece of her mind. Her eyes landed on Erin.

Erin shook her head at Bri and turned to the other woman. "Wheesht. Let the man talk. Our blacksmith has a good heart."

Bri shot Erin a grateful smile. Raising the hem of her now-filthy kirtle, Bri managed to elbow her way through the distracted crowd to where her new friend stood.

"MacMurrough is coming," Duncan continued.

From her new placement, Bri could just see Duncan through the people shifting around her. He stood on a cart, raised above the rest of the townsfolk. Ciaran stood beside him.

If only she could be closer. For so much of her life she'd dreamed of this story, this very moment of history. That she couldn't see it properly now, when she could truly experience it, irked her.

Duncan scanned the crowd, as if looking for something - or someone. Bri wanted to run to him, wanted to tell everyone to listen to what he was saying, but she couldn't break the spell he was weaving. His words were all that stood between Tristledermot's survival and a town full of heartache and death.

"The Leinstermen hope to catch us unaware. They'll cut through this town like a scythe shearing grain at the harvest. Our women —" Duncan's voice broke. Bri could just make out his hand clasping Ciaran's shoulder for strength. "Our women and children will suffer unless we stand against this attack."

Bri stared, frozen in place. People moved, blocking her view. She didn't need to see — she didn't want to see. The pain in his voice stabbed into her. Speaking those words, Duncan had been defeated. Broken.

Tears threatened, and Bri gazed up at the sky to keep them from falling. A flock of birds flew overhead, crossing the town and disappearing in the distance, as if they knew what fate was coming.

Brogan's voice cut through the tension filling the marketplace. "You chose to tell us of this when you could be getting your wife to safety?" He chuckled, releasing the anxiety that had gathered. Relieved laughter rippled across the crowd.

Bri couldn't join in. She stood alone, watching her husband. His pinched, anguished face smoothed and he seemed to grow, not just taller but broader, becoming bigger than life.

"My wife is a wise woman. I'd have taken her to safety, but she insisted our place was here with you." Firmness filled Duncan. A steadiness and a rightness that couldn't be quenched. "I'm ready to fight. I'll stand between this town and the invading men, alone if needs be. My wife would have it no other way, nor would I. I will see Tristledermot safe. What say you? Will you join me?"

A wave of awe flowed through Bri. Duncan claimed he wasn't a leader. He claimed no one would listen to him.

Oh, he was wrong.

Men throughout the market square were reaching for long knives hung at their waists, or shorter knives tucked into boots. Women nudged their husbands while gathering their children closer around their skirts. The air rang with shouts as blades were thrust high in the air all around.

Could Duncan truly not see he'd been born for this? Bri caught glimpses of him as he raised his own blade overhead.

As the roar lessened, Duncan's voice rang out above the noise. "Brogan. Michael. Take men to the gates and see those who've come for market day either get safely within the walls or make haste to their own safety. Once that's done, close the gates. Ciaran, gather the women and children and barricade yourselves in the church. Any men who choose to help but are unable to fight, assist Ciaran at the church."

Men began pushing through the crowd to follow Duncan's directions. As Duncan continued to shout his plans Bri turned away. The baker's wife, Elizabeth, was beginning to herd the nearby women into a group and sending them toward the church.

Bri approached her. "Don't send them away. We can't just do nothing. We should be helping, not hiding away inside a church."

"You expect us to fight?" Elizabeth asked, hardly pausing long enough to glance at Bri. "That's not how things are done in Tristledermot, or in any civilized society."

Bri stomped after Elizabeth as she continued to push the women in the direction they'd been told to go. The straw-covered mud under her feet squelched from the force. It was oddly satisfying.

"I come from a *civilized society* where women are perfectly capable of fighting alongside men." With training, which these women, including Bri, lacked.

Bri chose to ignore that detail.

Elizabeth whirled around, a curl peeking out from under her headpiece. "Do you not trust your husband to protect you? We all want to do our part, but that part isn't fighting. We support our husbands by doing as they ask, as should you. All that's been asked of us is that we stay where the men have no need to fear for our safety. It's best for us, and for the men who fight to protect us." She turned her back to Bri and continued moving toward the church.

Bri stared after the woman. More than anything, she hated the idea of huddling inside a church, knowing there was fighting going on and having no way of knowing if her husband was injured or worse.

"There has to be something we can do to help," she called after Elizabeth.

The woman continued on.

Bri stomped her foot. Too many people were moving, jostling her this way and that. She had to do something or she'd go crazy. Ignoring the chaos around her, she made her way home.

The road outside the smithy was oddly empty, even as sounds from around the corner echoed loudly. She slipped up the stairs and inside. The shutters were still closed, leaving the light dim and peaceful.

Fear pulled at her, threatening to take over completely. If a Leinsterman jumped out of a corner she would happily have grabbed a knife and pounced on him, despite her lack of training. Just to have something to do.

Her laughter at the thought surprised her.

When all this was over she'd make Duncan teach her to use a knife — or even a sword — to protect herself. For now, she'd need to find another way to contribute.

Bri gazed around the single room of her home as she thought. She hadn't brought anything with her to help — dresses certainly wouldn't scare off an invading clan of Irishmen. A cooking pot — also no good.

She glanced at the table and saw the loaf of bread she'd bought to feed Duncan and Ciaran that morning. Or years ago, if she went by how it felt.

She grinned. There was something she could do after all, but she'd need help.

As quickly as she could, Bri made her way to the church. Women and children were still trailing into the churchyard. Ciaran stood at the entrance to the church, the giant archway that stood on its own in the time Bri had left behind.

"Ciaran." Bri pushed her way to him and grabbed the sleeve of his *leine*. "Ciaran, I need to talk to you."

Ciaran turned to her, ready to brush off some nuisance. When he saw her, his eyes widened. He grabbed her arms and lifted her off her feet as he swept her around the corner of the church.

Bri looked up at the round tower. Its conical top stabbed at the gray sky.

Ciaran gently shook her. "Where have you been? I've never seen

Duncan so upset. He teetered on madness when we saw the churchyard was empty."

Bri looked up at her many-times great-grandfather. Fury etched his brow. He opened his mouth to continue, but Bri beat him to it. She had to convince him to help her.

"You can yell at me as much as you want when this is over. For now, I need your help," she said. "Please."

Bri watched the emotions fighting for control of Ciaran's face. Eventually, he sighed. "What do you plan to do? I'll help with nothing that puts you in danger. Duncan would never forgive me if I allowed you to do something foolish."

Bri bit her lip. "Would it be foolish to send people to gather food? Everyone will be getting hungry. Not just those of us about to be locked away inside a church, but the men preparing to fight. If someone could bring food and cooking pots here we could prepare something for them to eat."

When Ciaran just stared at her, she kept going. "And some cloths and thread? If there's going to be fighting we should have bandages ready, and sanitized needles. The basket of silk threads next to my yarn would be good to have, too."

Ciaran blinked.

"Oh, and we should probably have alcohol on hand, too."

Ciaran raised his eyebrows. He finally dropped his hands from her arms. "This is your plan, to get the women drunk?"

"Of course not. The alcohol is for cleaning any wounds." Bri paused and looked into Ciaran's eyes. "Although I don't suppose a drink would be a bad thing right now. It would make the waiting easier."

Ciaran didn't reply for so long Bri worried he'd decide to go back to yelling at her.

Finally, he sighed. "Let's find someone to gather your supplies. Duncan has ordered me to stay here, away from the fighting."

"So MacMurrough and the rest of the Leinstermen won't consider you a traitor?"

Ciaran laughed. "No. So he can tell my wife my life was never in danger. Not that Tara will believe it, but Duncan's a coward about anything that ends in facing Tara's temper."

Bri rounded the corner, Ciaran on her heels. She paused at the sight of the gathering women and the noise of boisterous kids who knew they were about to be forced to sit quietly. "Why would he care what your wife thinks?"

"Tara is quite like you. Kind, headstrong, and confident she's always in the right." Ciaran smiled. "If she was of a mind to, she could scare a warrior in the full bloodlust of battle."

Bri made a mental note to never upset the woman.

DUNCAN

Men left, running to secure the town gates. Other men were helping get the women and children safely to the church. They would be protected, and where they couldn't distract the men from the job they'd set before themselves.

Duncan wished his part were through. Wished someone else could take his place. He sighed and straightened his back. He'd made a vow, not to himself alone, but to every person in the town. He would stand his ground.

Then, if he survived, he could rest. He could mourn.

If luck favored him, he'd not survive to face life without Brianna.

Duncan's lungs stretched, bellows pulling in all the air they could hold. "Men," he hollered.

All around, heads turned at the force of his voice. "Gather into groups and send one man from each group to meet at the front of the Parliament Building." He paused. "And someone fetch the garrison leader."

"No need," said a voice behind Duncan.

Duncan turned. The garrison leader stood there, his grizzled hair pulled back from his lined face. "Chambers. You're here. Good. We've things to discuss."

The older man raised an eyebrow. "Such as why you're planning to use these men as an army?"

Duncan placed his hand on the shoulder of the man's wool military coat and began leading him to the place he'd asked the other men to gather. "Your men are good at what they do. We need them, but we need more men than you've been given."

"I heard your speech. I agree we could use more soldiers, but these men lack training." Chambers stopped Duncan. "Every man who fights with us could be facing death this day."

Duncan stared straight into the man's eyes. Chambers believed he knew every possible degradation battle could provide. "They understand. Perhaps you don't. These men fight not for coin, nor for their country. They fight for their families. For their homes. You'd do well to not underestimate them."

The garrison leader paused, his eyes cutting to the side. Duncan followed his gaze and saw the chaos this leader would see. He hoped Chambers could look beyond the surface. The obvious chaos floated over determination and wills strong as iron.

After what felt an age, Chambers returned his gaze to Duncan. "How would you have my men help?"

Duncan felt his shoulders ease. The battle was far from over, but this was one fight ended before it began. "We need lookouts. The Leinstermen plan to surround us and enter through every gate. How they plan to get to the gates, I've no idea."

Chambers nodded slowly. "I've posted lookouts at every other tower in the wall. When MacMurrough's men near, we'll know. I'll send word to hold each gate at all cost. My garrison was stationed here for a reason. We'll do our duty."

Scuffling feet at the meeting point drew Duncan's attention. "The men are ready for me. I'll send groups to each gate as a support to your men."

"I hope we won't have the need, but I thank you all the same. I'll send a runner for you when we see them coming." Chambers clasped Duncan's elbow before turning to disappear in the crowd.

Duncan turned his attention to the men each group had chosen as their leader. They were good men, all. He hoped they survived.

The weight of uncertainty pressed on Duncan. He pushed it aside. There was no time for self-doubt.

The sun crept across the sky, dragging the day with it.

Word came from Ciaran that the women had prepared a meal. Duncan sent the men to the church in groups to eat and rest for a short time. He refused to rest himself, but when Michael brought him a trencher with a hearty meat stew he gratefully swallowed the meal.

The memory arose of the similar stew he'd given Brianna through the swearing stone. He allowed the memory to linger for only a moment. There was no time for wallowing in what he'd lost.

The market square had gone quiet. Men rested as they were able, with swords and knives close at hand.

Duncan looked to the older lads gathered under a shop window. The age of Ciaran's son, they were too old to be patient waiting with the women and children, yet lacked the strength to survive a true fight. They waited to be needed as runners.

Duncan caught the eye of one of the lads and motioned him over. He'd no need of runners at the moment, but the boys needed a useful assignment. "I need you lads to check in at each of the gates, and at the church. See what's needed."

The lad took the assignment back to his companions, and they took off in different directions, running with the endless energy of youth. The only word they brought back was that Ciaran wanted Duncan to stop at the church when he could. That was one thing he refused to do. Seeing the families would leave him longing for his own wife.

Just as the bell rang for None a shout echoed through the square. Duncan rose to his feet as the lad raced to him. "It's time. They've come. I'm to tell you they're in the open, coming quickly. They have torches, and arrows, and the garrison man said there could be a danger to the gates."

Duncan thanked the lad, then raised his voice to carry through the market square. "Groups assigned to the gates, make your way there now. The next group assigned to protect the women and children, go there. Each group should take a runner. The rest of the men will remain here until the runners return telling us they need more strength."

Duncan knew he needn't have reminded the men what to do. They knew the plan. They'd gone over it thrice between each ringing of the bell. He'd reminded them again not for their sakes, but for his own peace of mind. He nodded at the runners before they left. The lads returned the gesture. The moment there was fighting in any area, the lads would find him. Duncan refused to allow the other men to fight without him. He'd found himself leading his neighbors, and he'd stand alongside them. He'd choose to stand before them if he knew where he'd be needed.

The men remaining behind gathered into their groups of scores. Some joked quietly with their neighbors. Others shifted uneasily, checking the sharpness of their blades as they'd been doing for so much of the day. Duncan made his way around the square, stopping at each group with encouraging words and smiles.

Every man was ready to fight. They'd not revel in it — they were anxious to put it behind them and reunite their families.

Duncan walked back to the wagon in the center of the square where he could be easily found when he was needed.

The waiting stretched and his patience pulled thin. Shouts from the distant gates carried through town and an eerie quiet settled over the men who waited.

Finally — finally! — a runner came into view. Duncan stood still, his fist clasping, then loosening around the hilt of his long dagger. He reached for the sword leaning against the wagon beside him and strapped it to his waist.

The lad came to a stop at Duncan's elbow. Doubled over, hands on his knees, the lad struggled to catch his breath. "Tullowgate," he gasped. "They're coming in. Someone opened the gate." He looked up at Duncan, his eyes wide and unseeing.

Duncan cursed. He gestured to the group waiting to be called to Tullowgate. The leader of the group joined them.

"The men — men are falling," the lad continued. He choked on the words. "Torches. They brought torches."

Duncan motioned another man over. "There will be fires near Tullowgate. Get what water you can, and rugs to smother the flames."

Duncan looked to the lad beside him. "I'll be fighting at the gate. I'll need you here. If I'm needed elsewhere, come find me."

He walked away, joining two score men as they left for the breached gate. The shaking lad he left behind would be safe. He trusted his neighbors to see to it.

The clash of swords echoed down the road. Up ahead men were fighting in the narrow space. Torches flared against the muted light of the overcast sky.

Duncan urged the men faster. They ran, and the air surrounding them filled with the tension of men readying for battle.

A torch-bearing Leinsterman broke through the fighting. Before the reinforcements could reach him, he held his flame to the straw spread over the ground. The straw began to smoke, and a small flame burst to life.

Duncan pushed himself harder, forcing his feet to cover the final distance. He pulled his hand back before smashing the hilt of his long dagger into the Leinsterman's temple. The man staggered. Leaving him to the men at his back, Duncan wrenched the torch from the Leisterman's hand and shoved the flame into the rainwater still filling the trench at the side of the road.

Men around him stamped out burning straw. Duncan stepped on a damp, smoldering pile beside him. They'd been lucky — if the straw hadn't held moisture from the recent rain, the entire street would be aflame.

"Find the other torchbearers," Duncan yelled. "Stop them before they burn anything else."

The men shouted as they pushed into the fight ahead.

Duncan drew his sword. Pressing against the wood buildings he moved past groups of fighting to the front of the conflict. The sound of blades ringing and men's voices filled the air, and the stench of smoke and blood.

Tullowgate stood open. Garrison soldiers fought shoulder to shoulder with townsmen as the Leinstermen fought for entry.

Duncan threw himself into the fray, stabbing and parrying as he fought to stop the invaders from spreading through town.

The press around him closed in as more bodies fought to force the Leinstermen back through the gate. Duncan tossed his sword away and reached for his long dagger. The hilt slipped in his sweaty, blood-streaked hand. He held the knife more tightly and aimed himself at another foe.

His body screamed against the abuse of battle. Duncan parted his lips and snarled back. Brianna had promised the town could be saved. He'd see it happen.

As the townsmen pushed the Leinstermen out through Tullowgate, the garrison men formed a wall of soldiers to keep them out.

Pockets of fighting within the wall still clashed. Duncan joined one and grinned as he recognized Brogan beside him. One by one the invaders fell and the townsmen moved to stand with the soldiers, strengthening their wall as the gates were closed again.

Brogan smiled at Duncan. "Glad to see you join the fight."

Duncan laughed and opened his mouth to joke with his friend. He stilled as behind Brogan a Leinsterman Duncan had thought dead pushed to his knees and raised a dagger.

Brogan said something, but Duncan couldn't hear the words over the pounding in his ears. He'd not the time to warn his friend. The injured man on the ground was already moving.

Duncan dove forward, knocking Brogan aside.

The blade aimed for his friend found Duncan's side and dug in.

Duncan heard Brogan yelling. He looked at the blade buried in him. Blood welled up and spilled down his side. The Leinsterman's hand fell from the dagger as he toppled, landing in a heap.

Pain seared through Duncan, breaking through his battle-hazed mind. With the pain came his earlier thoughts of dying in the fight to avoid life without his wife.

He cursed. He'd not even managed to be killed properly.

BRIANNA

Bri stared at the other women as she rolled and re-rolled linen bandages, then as she checked her supply of henbane and poppy tinctures. How could these ladies be so calm? They stood in groups, smiling and gossiping while their husbands fought for their lives. The quiet laughter and shouts of children made the gathering feel more like a town social than a vigil.

She piled the bandages and tinctures into a large, shallow basket as a group of young boys raced past. At least they'd been outdoors where the kids could blow off steam. Ciaran had agreed they could stay in the open air unless the churchyard came under attack.

Word had come of fighting at every gate, but so far the men had held the invaders at bay.

Bri lifted her basket and went inside the church. It was dim and blessedly quiet. The chapel stretched out in front of her, longer than she expected, making it feel larger than it should. The air was cool, the stone walls and floor blocking out the warmth of the day. Bri's skin prickled from the change and a shiver trickled up her spine.

"You should be outside with your neighbors."

Bri spun, startled by Ciaran's voice behind her. "I'm not in a celebrating mood," she said.

Ciaran stepped nearer and lowered his voice. "It may appear they're celebrating, but the women worry for their husbands and sons. You're not the only woman praying her husband still lives, or will yet live when this is done."

Bri stepped away, refusing to meet his gaze. "I thought I'd set up an area for any men who are injured."

He followed her down the aisle, crowding into the space she needed for herself. It was made worse by the way Ciaran's words pounded into Bri, crowding her even more than his presence.

"Do you think many men will be injured?" she asked, her voice hushed not by reverence for the church as much as by the fear she couldn't acknowledge.

"Any who are injured will be tended by the physicians. The monks are here to help as the men come in, as well as their own families. It's not your responsibility."

Bri bristled. Of course it was her responsibility. If she hadn't pressured Duncan he wouldn't have rallied the townspeople. If he hadn't convinced the men to fight they wouldn't be in danger.

It was her fault, which made it her responsibility to care for the wounded.

Before she could reply there was a commotion in the doorway as the first of the wounded was carried in. The man's arm was sliced open. His blood flowed freely, dripping a trail along the stone floor. The pulsing muscle of his forearm could be seen as he twitched. Bri fought back a gag and tried to keep her breath steady. She hardly cared when Ciaran took her arm and led her back into the fresh air.

A woman and her daughter hurried into the church, leaving a pall of silence behind them.

Once Bri was convinced the hours-old stew would stay in her stomach, she straightened. She pushed the image of the man's arm to the back of her mind. In her worry she'd forgotten there were reasons beyond hating math that had kept her from going into medicine. Still — "I want to help. Surely they need something. Someone to carry water, or change bandages or something."

Ciaran's hand still held her arm and she had no choice but to follow him as he half-dragged her around the side of the church, then around to the far side of the round tower. No one was back there — everyone else had gathered near each other.

"Worrying does no good, and you'll be in the way inside the church gawping at the injuries. No one can be spared to care for a woman who faints or is sickened by the blood." His voice gentled and his eyes softened. "Find something else to do. Speak with your neighbors. Sleep. Anything to keep your mind off what's happening."

Ciaran left her standing alone as he went back to whatever job he'd given himself.

Bri leaned her back against the tower and let the relative peace melt the tension from her neck and shoulders.

How had Gran's stories never mentioned the awful waiting, or the constant worry? Nothing about injuries and death. They'd all lauded heroics and bravery.

There was nothing heroic or brave about the knot in her stomach.

Bri slid down the tower wall until she was sitting on the ground. She wrapped her arms around her legs, pulling them tight against her chest. She rested her forehead on her knees and focused on breathing.

The world shook. Bri started and pried her eyes open. The back of her neck was stiff and achy.

Everything shook again. "Brianna."

Bri lifted her head to see Ciaran leaning over her. His hand shook her shoulder.

"Are you awake?"

Bri mumbled something she hoped was yes. She rubbed her eyes and stretched. "Is it over?"

Ciaran raised one shoulder in a shrug. "Nearly. That's not why I'm here." He paused and held out a hand to pull Bri to her feet. "You're needed inside the church."

Bri was shaking her head before he'd finished his sentence. "I'm not going back in there. The blood almost made me sick already. Besides, you told me to stay away."

"That was before," Ciaran said. He muttered something Bri couldn't understand. "Now I say you're needed."

"Doesn't work both ways, Gramps."

Ciaran's brows lowered. "Just come. Duncan needs you."

"Duncan is back? You could have started with that," Bri said. She started to make her way to the gorgeous arched entry.

"Wait," Ciaran said. "You need to know what's happened."

Something in his voice stopped her. She glanced over her shoulder to where he stood.

Bri's stomach dropped and she wrapped her arms around her middle. Ciaran's face was twisted with quiet pity.

The world tilted. Certainty of dread settled in Bri's heart. Her knees buckled. "No. No."

Ciaran raced forward, reaching her just as she hit the ground. "He's not dead, just injured. Do you hear me, Brianna? He'll live."

The words rolled over Bri. As they began to sink in her hands shook. She was trembling all over. "He's alive?" She clutched Ciaran's arms and forced him to look into her eyes. "You're sure?"

He nodded and pulled her to her feet, so gently she didn't realize it was happening until he was guiding her to the front of the church. "He's alive — but he would much prefer otherwise. He believes you left him, that you returned to your own time."

Bri's feet wouldn't move, as if they'd grown deep roots in the grass. How had he found out she'd tried to leave? What — How could he not know she was still here? She'd hardly stayed hidden, working with the women to make food for everyone, staying in the churchyard. . . .

Oh. She'd been in the churchyard the whole time, but Duncan hadn't seen her there. He hadn't come even to eat. "He thinks I'm gone." Her whispered voice cracked on the words.

Ciaran uprooted her as he yanked her arm. "He does. You'll show him you're here. If he doesn't see you he won't let the men treat his wound. He's lost too much blood already."

Bri found her feet and began to run. She burst through the church doors and took in the scene.

Men with various injuries were scattered through the pews, surrounded by their families. Bri ignored them all as her eyes reached the front corner. Men stood in a huddle, leaning over a prone form.

Duncan.

Every time one of the monks reached to hold the bandage, or to pour water in his mouth, Duncan raised a weak hand to brush them aside.

The men raised their voices, arguing over whether they let him give up or hold him down and force the physician's ministrations on an unwilling patient.

Stupid men. All her husband needed was incentive.

Bri stomped up the aisle, her eyes directly on the clump around her husband. The sweaty, dirty men took one look at her face and stepped away. The monk and physician moved to intercept her. Bri pushed past them.

When Bri reached Duncan she tried not to look at the blood-soaked bandage at his side. There wasn't time for fainting. "Open your eyes."

Duncan moaned.

Bri gave in to her anger, allowing it to rush through her. Welcomed it as it drowned out her fear. She fought the urge to stomp her foot on the stone floor. "Open your eyes so you can look at me when you explain why you allowed someone to cut into you."

"My wife," Duncan breathed. "Not here. Not real."

From the corner of her eye, Bri saw Brogan step forward. "The blade was aimed at me. He pushed me out of the way."

Bri spared a glare for Brogan and turned back to Duncan. "Fine. If I'm not really here, it won't matter if I take your dagger." She reached out and snatched the long dagger held loosely in his fist.

Duncan's hand, caked with half-dried blood, fumbled around as if looking for it.

Bri's breath caught in her throat as Duncan's eyelashes fluttered. He cracked his eyes open. He stared at her, then his eyelids slid closed.

She pulled a face. She'd been sure once he saw her, he'd believe she was there. What would get a reaction he'd believe?

Nothing pleasant. He'd just think he was hallucinating. She needed something to make him worry — not enough to be dangerous, just enough to get his attention. An idea — an absurd, crazy idea came to her. If she was lucky, it might work.

"I'll be going now. I need to catch up to the Leinstermen quickly if I'm going to have any chance of burying this dagger in Art MacMurrough's heart."

The men behind Duncan started to protest. Bri pinned them with a death glare and they quieted, but a couple of the men moved closer to her as if they could stop her from leaving. She held her breath and counted to five.

"Here I go." She took a shaky step back. She had to make this work. Every moment he thought she wasn't real was costing him precious blood.

Duncan's eyes fluttered open.

Bri held up the dagger and smiled. She pretended not to notice the way the dagger shook in her hand. "Thanks for this. Hang on until I get back. If you die on me, I'll have to kill you." It didn't make sense, of course it didn't. Bri hoped that would help him believe she was real.

Holding her breath, she turned and started to walk away. Please let it work. Please let it work. Please let it. . .

"Wife." Duncan's voice was a rasping breath.

Bri grinned and raced back to his side. The dagger clattered to the floor as she went.

Duncan's fumbling hand reached up and touched her face. "You're here."

"I'm here." Bri leaned down and pressed her lips to his clammy forehead. "Of course I'm here."

Duncan's hand dropped from her face and fell to her arm. He wrapped weak fingers around her wrist. "You'll be staying with me."

Laughter bubbled up, spilling out of Bri's mouth. "Yes. I'll be staying. You won't get rid of me that easily."

Duncan nodded his head. His eyes drifted closed and his grip on Bri loosened.

Bri looked at Brogan. "Thank you for getting him here. Bring my basket of supplies from over by the door."

Brogan hurried to get it. He returned quickly and set the basket beside her. She reached for the poppy tincture and dribbled a small amount into Duncan's mouth. The least she could do was take the edge off his pain.

"How bad is it?" Bri asked. Her hand hovered over the blood-stained bandage. She didn't want to look.

"The physician needs to stop the bleeding. Your husband has been fighting the idea."

Duncan coughed, his body spasming against Bri's hands.

"What were you thinking? Don't be a mule. Let the man fix you for me." Bri kept her voice quiet as she berated and begged. She leaned down and rested her head against his. She dropped her voice so not even the nearest man would be able to hear. "I didn't travel through six centuries of history to have you leave me the first chance you got."

Duncan's chest shook. His eyes crinkled and his breath jerked.

He was laughing at her.

Bri could have hit him. She could have kissed him silly right there, except there were more important things in that moment.

"Aye, wife. As you will." His voice was marginally stronger. Bri let go of the breath she'd been holding.

The physician pushed his way in, moving between Bri and her husband. "This will be unpleasant. You could go outside while I work."

Bri shook her head. She moved to Duncan's other side and took hold of his hand. "I'm not going anywhere. And you can use the supplies I brought. There's alcohol in there for cleaning the wound."

The physician didn't try to convince Bri to leave. Either he knew it would be useless, or he was anxious to get Duncan's wound cared for. He pulled back the bandage.

Bri's throat closed. There was so much blood. How could a person lose that much blood and still be conscious? She forced her eyes away.

Ciaran crouched beside her. "The edges of the cut are smooth. It should heal well, now you've convinced him to have it tended."

"But — all that blood." Bri shuddered.

"He'll be weak after losing it, but there'll be no lasting damage."

Duncan's fingers pulsed in hers. Bri settled her eyes on his face.

A small sound of warning came from the physician. Duncan spasmed, his back arching off the ground. His fist clenched Bri's hand so tightly she was sure her bones would snap.

Duncan's hand went limp, he fell to the floor, and his eyes rolled back.

Bri covered her face with her free hand as she breathed deeply. When she felt brave enough, she peeked through her fingers to see what the physician had done to make Duncan lose consciousness.

Duncan's side was wet, covered in the ale, or mead, or whatever it was Ciaran had found for her when she'd asked for alcohol. The wound looked less angry with the extra blood cleaned away, but as the physician started poking at it Bri looked away.

Still holding Duncan's limp hand, Bri reached her other hand to his face. She brushed his matted hair aside and tried to focus on seeing him fully healed.

33

Duncan ignored the dull ache in his side and pulled his wife closer. She made quiet, sleepy sounds against his shoulder as she burrowed into him. The touch of her skin on his did more to heal him than all the physician's efforts.

"Good morning," Brianna mumbled.

Duncan smiled as her fingers trailed across his chest. He buried his face in her hair and kissed the top of her head. He'd have liked her lips, but he couldn't get to them without disturbing her.

Brianna stretched in his arm. Her toes pushed down his calf and over his ankle. She arched her back, her body pressing against his thigh, his hip, his side.

Duncan fought the urge to pull her on top of him. If she felt the small raised wound, just beginning to scar, she'd not continue.

His patience was rewarded when she tipped her head back and brought her lips to his.

He returned the kiss. He ached to deepen it. His body screamed for Brianna. For a fortnight he'd watched her, allowed her to care for him. For a fortnight he'd been denied anything beyond a gentle touch. He'd go mad if she insisted he needed more time to heal. The physician agreed he was healed enough to return to the smithy. Surely he could return to loving his wife.

Brianna hooked her leg over his.

Duncan's body came to life. He pulled her to himself more tightly still and wrapped his hand around her hip. Her smooth skin was as silk under his calloused hand.

He rolled them so Brianna was on her back beneath him. Her dark hair pooled beneath her head and tumbled over her shoulders.

Duncan gazed at her through the dimness of the curtained bed. "Brianna, *a rúnsearc*. My love." He touched her hair, trailing his fingers down the glossy river of her hair trailing over her breast.

He'd more he wanted to say, more his heart demanded he tell her. As he gazed at the love in her eyes the words slipped away.

Brianna's small hands slid up his chest. The gentle pressure of her fingers wrapped around the back of his neck as she drew him down to meet her waiting lips.

The same tingling power he'd felt when first he'd seen his wife started where her body met his and grew to fill their home.

Bri curled against Duncan. His warm arms held her against his chest in a lazy embrace. Tears threatened, as they had every day and night for two weeks. She'd nearly lost him.

If he'd given up, or stopped the physician from healing him, Bri had no doubt Duncan would have died of an infection or blood loss.

The scar under her fingers was the only visible sign left to her of that day. A handful of buildings had been set on fire, but they'd all been repaired while she'd made sure Duncan would heal. Everyone had gone back to their normal lives. Even Ciaran had returned to his wife and family, promising to bring Tara to meet her soon.

beyond the swearing stone

The only real change was that the garrison was being pulled out of Tristledermot. After word had gone out that the townsmen had risen to protect their homes and repel MacMurrough's attack, it was decided the garrison wasn't needed anymore. The soldiers and their wives — including Erin, — were being sent to another town.

Bri traced the raised line of Duncan's scar. Her neighbors might forget what happened, and what part Duncan had played in saving their town, but Bri wouldn't. She would remember. The tale of how Ciaran risked being named a traitor to come warn them, and of Duncan rallying the townsmen to rise up against the Leinster King and his men — Bri would make sure that story survived the centuries.

Duncan placed his hand over the top of hers, stilling her fingers against his scar. "There's no need for worry, wife. I'm well."

Bri raised onto her elbow so she could look him in the face. "I wasn't worrying. Just thinking." She didn't need to see the crease in his forehead to know he didn't believe her.

"What are you thinking, then, to keep you so quiet? I've not seen you quiet oft."

Bri laughed. "I was thinking about the tale we'll tell our children. The story of how you saved the town."

Duncan's stomach tensed against the heel of her palm.

How long would it take before he could believe he didn't need to worry about losing her in childbirth? Yes, so-called experts believed history could be changed based on a single beat of a butterfly's wings, but Bri refused to believe it would. Her future was already part of her past.

"We've no need yet to plan how the tale will be told," Duncan said. He sounded like he was trying to reassure himself.

Bri felt a pressure in her chest. Should she tell him? She didn't want to worry him, and it was still early. So early. Anything could happen.

She'd only known for two days herself.

Taking a deep breath, Bri took Duncan's hand and placed it low against her stomach. "About that," she started.

Duncan stared at the thin hand pressing his palm into Brianna's flat stomach. His chest clamped around his heart. "What are you telling me?"

"I'm pregnant." She looked up at him. The corners of her eyes creased as she smiled at him, her face filled with awe. "We're having a baby, Duncan."

No. She must be wrong. Women could be wrong about their bodies. "Mayhap one day."

Brianna's laugh filled the room. She pushed aside the bed curtain and stepped to the old plank floor. She faced him, and a breeze swept through the open back window, teasing her hair. "Look at me, Duncan. Look at my body."

Duncan looked. He saw his wife, and the softness of her curves. He'd the mind to pull her back on the bed, but she'd likely not stand for a ravishing when she'd a point to make. He rose to his knees and truly looked. "What is it you'd have me see?"

"I'm changing already." She beamed at him. "It's way too early for my stomach to show, but there are other changes."

He'd no idea what changes she meant for him to see. He studied her face. She was so certain. Could she be right? "Mayhap we should have the midwife in to check?"

"No need. I went to see her the day before yesterday." Her grin widened and she pounced onto the bed beside him. The straw mattress shook beneath them. "She said she's never had a patient who's so healthy and strong, and she doesn't have any worries."

Duncan swayed. Brianna wrapped her arms around his shoulders. "It's okay. I'm going to be okay. We're all going to be fine, I promise. All three of us."

As Duncan looked into her eyes her smile faltered and her eyes widened. Her brows drew together as the silence stretched.

The tightening of his chest loosened. He could give her this moment. "What is it you say – OK?"

Brianna nodded.

"I'll try not to worry overmuch." It was the best he could offer.

The strain left her face.

"How many children did you say we have?" he asked.

She pulled her knees into her chest and wrapped her arms around them. "I don't remember. Five or six, at least."

So many times he'd have to worry for her. So many chances for things to go wrong.

Duncan looked at his wife, curling in on herself as she waited for his acceptance. He could fill himself with the pain of losing her while knowing she'd live to raise several children.

He sighed. Worry would pull him away from his wife. It would stop him from loving her fully, the way she deserved to be loved.

Duncan pushed aside the heartache and protectiveness that swarmed him, and chose instead to love Brianna more deeply. He'd known the pain of believing her lost to him. He wanted to live the joy of truly being with his wife.

"Have you thought yet what you'd choose to name our child?" he asked.

Brianna startled from the ball she'd formed. "I hadn't gotten that far."

Duncan held back his smile. His eyes crinkled from the effort. "Our first daughter should bear the name of your grandmother."

It felt right. If the woman had not used Brianna's love to convince her to put her hand through the swearing stone that day, he'd not have his wife.

Brianna sat back and pulled her lower lip between her teeth and tipped her head to the side. "I'd love that. But — I thought you'd be more upset."

Duncan's happiness spilled out in a laugh. "No, *a rúnsearc*, I'd not be upset with what our love created."

Brianna's smile was as the rising sun, filling him with warmth and hope for the coming days.

With a playful roar Duncan scooped his wife into his arms and buried his face in her neck.

Years he'd spent, perfecting the craft of forging and shaping metals. Now he'd master the art of shaping his heart to Brianna's. She was his life. He'd not waste a moment of the time they'd been given.

Setting History Straight

While I tried to keep many aspects of this book historically accurate, there are things I changed to serve this story. Some of the changes were tiny, others were . . . not.

In this section you'll find clarification on the largest changes. If you're drawn into the past with these details and want to go down the rabbit hole with me, you can find resources and interesting tidbits on my website.

The Attack on Tristledermot

First and foremost: It's true that in 1405, Tristledermot was attacked, but I didn't do the Leinstermen justice in my portrayal. The Leinstermen were seasoned warriors and would never have been so easily defeated. The attack on Tristledermot would likely have taken place early in the day to ensure the fighting wasn't hindered by nightfall. Also, the Leinstermen would not have expected to burn buildings that were wet or damp; they would have certainly paid attention to the weather. The biggest thing, however, is that the Leinstermen won. They sacked the town. Historic records show the government sent funds to help rebuild the town after it was burned in the attack by Art MacMurrough.

Art MacMurrough

Another large change I made was in the timeline of Art MacMurrough's life. As the focus of this book wasn't the Leinster King, I needed to make his motivation for attacking the town understandable, yet simple enough to avoid bogging down the story. The glimpses I shared of him wanting the return of his wife's land, and his levies for keeping the roads open, were true. They just happened earlier.

The more I learned of MacMurrough, the more fascinated I became. He was known to be generous to monasteries and churches. He was chivalrous. He was an impressive leader. Someday I'd like to write his story. For now, I'll give you a brief glimpse into his life leading up to the attack on Tristledermot.

Art MacMurrough became a knight when he was just seven. As a teenager he began exacting levies on the roads, and fought to keep the Anglo-Normans in check as they tried to carve out more space for themselves. At twenty, Art took his deceased father's place as a leader.

When he married the daughter of the 4th Earl of Kildare, Art's position was strengthened. Unfortunately, when the Baroness of Narragh married MacMurrough the estates which should have been hers were taken from her because she'd married an enemy of the King of England. MacMurrough declared war.

Eventually, King Richard II agreed to negotiate terms of peace. MacMurrough got his wife's lands returned as part of the 1395 deal, and he swore fealty to King Richard.

The peace didn't last. Art MacMurrough took Carlow in 1397. When his warriors defeated the enemy army at the Nore river, killing the Viceroy, King Richard returned from England. MacMurrough refused to back down. Threats and dire promises were made on both sides. We can't be sure what would have happened from there had King Richard not been urgently called away, but I'd have bet on MacMurrough as the victor.

A few years after King Richard left Ireland (returning to England where he spent the short remainder of his life in prison after finding he'd been dethroned in his absence), Art MacMurrough took and kept three towns, and sacked Tristledermot. This is the attack that would have coincided with the timeline of Bri and Duncan's story.

The attack had devastating results, but it didn't end Tristledermot's trouble with the MacMurroughs. In 1415 Art's son attacked the re-built town.

Tristledermot/Castledermot

I went to great lengths to keep this town as accurate as I could. Through Dr. Sharon Greene's assistance I was able to study the oldest surviving map of the town and an archaeological excavation report, both of which gave me wonderful insight and helped me build my version of Tristledermot. I literally built myself a little town, using pictures of medieval buildings, so I could keep it all straight in my head.

The one thing my beta readers kept asking about the town is when it changed names.

About half a century after this story takes place, a castle in the area was rebuilt. It was at that time, the town became Castledermot. Unfortunately, the remains of the castle have yet to be found, and no one is quite certain where exactly it was.

For more information on Castledermot, please visit the Extras section on my website.

www.rebeccamckinnon.com

acknowledgements

No book is the effort of a single person. To thank everyone would be impossible, so I'll limit myself to just a few.

My husband and children are my biggest cheerleaders, and they don't get annoyed when I spout random facts about time long gone. I'd never be able to do this without them.

When I began my research for this book I was frustrated with how little information I could find. Finally, I reached out to the Castledermot Historical Group on FaceBook in hopes of being pointed in the right direction. What I got in return went so far beyond what I'd hoped for. Dr. Sharon Greene informed me that most of the information wasn't available online. She emailed me the most amazing resources. She answered countless questions, sent me pictures, introduced me to the oldest surviving map of Castledermot, and became a dear friend. She was so generous with her extensive knowledge. Any historical inadequacies within these pages are mine alone.

My sincerest thanks to my beta readers for their unwavering support and their love of these characters that are so dear to me.

about the author

Rebecca McKinnon enjoys playing with her imaginary friends and introducing them to others through her writing. She dreams of living in the middle of nowhere, but has been unable to find an acceptable location that wouldn't require crossing an ocean.

Beyond the Swearing Stone is Rebecca's sixth book.
For more information about her, to learn more about books, sign up for her newsletter, or contact her, please visit her website.

www.rebeccamckinnon.com

Made in the USA
San Bernardino,
CA